WEB
OF
SHAME

PATRICIA FINCKEN

To Mick with my love as always

Also by Patricia Fincken:

NEVER TO KNOW

Chapter 1

Monty's Café, situated on the Millington Industrial Estate just off the M25 motorway on the London/Kent border, as usual, was bustling with its early morning regulars. At this time of the year, not only did it give its customers refuge from the cold, blustery, end of September weather, it served them good wholesome food, in a scrupulously clean environment that people came from miles around for.

Joe Cannon, eating his ritual Tuesday morning breakfast of fried eggs, bacon, sausages, tomatoes, baked beans and fried bread, sat at his usual table listening to the intense noise of fused voices. He looked around at the faces occupying all the seats, some he recognized, some he didn't.

He noticed, not for the first time, the crisp, fresh, red chequered cloths covering the tables, which were laid with spotlessly clean cutlery, serviettes, and a small vase of good quality artificial flowers in the middle. He also glanced at the pictures of old London that decorated the walls, along with photographs of a few, less well-known, celebrities that had, at some point, graced the premises with their presence.

Turning his attention back to the occupants at his table, Alf and Trevor, two of Joe's most trusted employees, he asked. "Another cup of tea lads?"

"No thanks Joe," Alf said as they both rose to leave the table. "That order for Lottie has to be shipped by midday."

"All right, I'll be back soon to give you a hand," Joe said as he gestured to Maggie, his favourite waitress, for another mug of tea.

"You enjoy the rest of your breakfast in peace Joe," Trevor laughed. "We can manage the order, half of it is already loaded."

Joe smiled his thanks to the two men. "Breakfast is on me today."

"Thanks Joe," they replied in unison.

Joe nodded his reply as he watched the two men turn from the table, and make their way to the door, both acknowledging a few acquaintances on the way.

Joe was a good employer and, apart from paying his work force a substantial wage, he would readily roll up his sleeves and help whenever required. He listened to any problems his staff may have, and helped where he could. In turn, they did a good, hard days' work and were very loyal to him.

When Alf had lost his wife six months earlier after a short illness, Joe had helped him as much as he was able to financially, as Joe realised that Alf not only had his own bereavement to cope with, but that of his children's as well.

Joe always felt embarrassed when he heard Alf tell people that he would always be indebted to his employer, and that without his financial, and emotional support he would never have dealt with his loss as well as he had.

Maggie approached Joe with his mug of tea, and as usual she had a quick, smutty joke to tell him. He listened intently and laughed when she reached the punch line. He ordered another slice of bread and it was as Maggie left his table that Joe noticed that the café had somewhat emptied, and the noise had abated to an acceptable level. With a sigh of contentment, Joe looked forward to the next ten minutes of peace and quiet before returning to work.

It was just as he was about to finish the last of his breakfast that he heard his name being called.

"Joe! Joe Cannon! I can't believe it, after all these years."

Joe looked up from his breakfast and saw a man that he didn't recognise sitting at the table beside him.

"That is you Joe, isn't it?"

"Well yes, but I'm sorry I don't..."

"Andy. Andy Bolan," the man interrupted.

Joe studied the man, and still failed to recognise him. "Look I'm sorry mate, and I'm not being rude, but do I know you?"

"Yes, but obviously you don't remember me. Well, it was a long time ago."

"What was?" Joe was beginning to feel slightly agitated, he only had ten minutes left on his break, and this man was invading his precious time.

"School."

Joe studied the man again, and shook his head in frustration. "I'm sorry mate, but I definitely don't recall you at all."

"Come on Joe, we went to the same school. We weren't in the same class, but we were definitely in the same year. West Gate Secondary School?"

Joe nodded his head. "Yes, I went to that school, but...I'm sorry, I just don't remember you."

"Well I remember you. You used to hang around with Ted Cartwright, and you had the nickname of 'Cocky Cannon'."

"Yeah, that's right," Joe answered, becoming more interested in the conversation.

"It's good to see you again Joe," Andy said excitedly, holding his hand out for Joe to shake.

Joe shook the hand reluctantly, and ran his hands through his short, spiky blond hair as he tried in vain to place this man from his childhood.

"I see you've still got the same haircut," Andy said laughing, pointing to Joe's head, and asked. "Do you know what ever happened to Ted Cartwright?"

"Yes, we've stayed friends, and he's fine."

"That's good to hear, I always liked Ted. Do you work locally Joe?"

"Yes, here on the industrial estate."

"So I suppose you use this café regular."

"At least once a week, usually on a Tuesday."

"I'm in this area fairly often, and come in here quite a bit. I just can't believe I haven't seen you before this," Andy said excitement sounding in his voice as he squeezed Joe's shoulder. "When I think of what we used to get up to at school." Andy laughed, then lowered his head and began to scratch his scalp as in thought. "What was that kid's name that everyone took the piss out of?"

Joe thought for a while, and exclaimed, "Mickey Noble!"

"Yes that's him, Mickey Noble," Andy readily agreed. "I've got to be honest when I think of what that poor sod went through it makes me shudder. He's either a right hard nut now, or a quivering wreck," Andy laughed. "Anyway Joe, what are you up to these days?"

"I keep myself busy. I've had my own business for about fourteen years and have really built it up, but working hard like the rest."

"What's your business?"

"Cannon's Household Supplies," Joe answered proudly. "I supply shops in Kent, Essex and parts of the London area, and pleased to say I'm adding new clients all the time," Joe paused before he continued. "And I intend to get bigger."

"If I remember rightly Joe you were always the optimist," Andy laughed.

"No one does it for you. What about you?"

"Like you, not done too bad for myself. Dabble in a few things, make a few bob if things work out, and lose a few if they don't. But I've got to be honest, although I do sometimes work long hours, it's not really hard work, just a bit stressful at times."

"What kind of business are you in that's not hard work?" Joe laughed.

Andy didn't answer but just smiled. "Married Joe?"

"Yeah, thirteen years to my lovely Ruth, two children and one due in just over four months' time."

"How old are your children?"

"Tyler's twelve and Abbey's eight, going on eighteen," Joe laughed again.

"Sounds like you've got your hands full there. I'm divorced with no children, although I've got to say that's my one biggest regret, not having any children," Andy sighed.

"Yeah, I know what you mean," Joe agreed. "As much as they're a pain in the arse sometimes, I wouldn't be without them."

Andy laughed. "I've got two dogs, and they're my babies. Anyway Joe, it's been good seeing you again, but I've got to go I've an appointment in fifteen minutes." Andy rose from the table and put his jacket on. "Joe...I'd like to keep in touch now that we've met again."

"Yeah sure, that would be good," Joe replied, retrieving a business card from his jacket pocket. "Here's my card, it's got my office and mobile number on there, so ring anytime."

"Yeah will do, maybe a drink?"

"Yes, I'll be up for that."

"Great, see you soon," Andy said as he left the table.

Joe watched the back of Andy Bolan as he made his way to the counter to pay, and fervently tried to remember him. Joe had always prided himself in remembering names and faces, but this one definitely escaped him. He would ask Ted if he remembered Andy from their school days, but Joe laughed to himself as he recalled that Ted had the worse memory of any one he knew.

Turning his attention back to the last of his breakfast and mug of tea, Joe was irritated to find that both were now stone cold. Pushing his plate away he hastily rose from the table and took out some change from his pocket to leave on the table for Maggie. After paying for the food he left the café shouting his goodbyes and thanks.

The following week had been a busy one for Joe, and it wasn't until he returned to Monty's Café the following Tuesday that Andy Bolan entered his thoughts again. He scanned the interior on his entrance, and felt slightly disappointed that he wasn't there.

Joe sat at his usual table, without Alf and Trevor this week, and Maggie was immediately at his side ready to take his order.

"Morning Joe. Usual?"

"Yes please Maggie. Err...Maggie do you remember the man I was talking to last Tuesday, I just wondered if he had been in at all this week."

Maggie thought for a while before replying. "I can't say I really recall him Joe."

"He said he uses this place quite often," Joe said, doubt now setting in.

"Well if he does, I don't remember him, and you know this little Rottweiler," she said pointing to herself and laughing. "Not much gets past me."

"Very true," he laughed, and within five minutes all thoughts of Andy Bolan had left him.

Chapter 2

The following Thursday afternoon Joe sat back in his office chair, with a mug of tea, and reflected on the events of the morning. He had gained two new clients, one of which was in an area new to him. His business was doing well, and he felt satisfied in the fact that he was able to keep Ruth and the children in a comfortable lifestyle.

As Ruth had only just over three months left till her due date, Joe had begun to phone her on a regular basis during the day. It was as he was about to pick up his mobile phone to call her that his office phone rung.

"I have an Andy Bolan on the line for you," Joe's secretary said as he answered the call.

Surprised at hearing this news Joe answered. "Thanks Laura, put him through."

"Hello Andy, its Joe."

"Hi Joe," Andy said casually. "You must be doing well to have a secretary. How's it going anyway?"

"Good to hear from you Andy, and believe me a secretary is a must. Most of the calls that come through are orders, and I don't have the time to sit here all day and take them. But I'm working hard as usual. How are you?"

"Yes, fine thanks. I was wondering if you fancied a drink one night next week, can do Tuesday if that's all right with you."

"Yes, Tuesday's fine. Where?"

What about that pub on the corner of Elvin Road, do you know it?" Andy asked.

"The Pond and Swan? I use it quite often."

"Would seven-thirty suit you?"

"Suits me fine mate, see you then. Bye."

As Joe ended the call he wondered why he was getting involved with Andy. He was someone from his childhood; someone he couldn't even remember. He decided that he would meet him just the once, and it was for this reason that he also decided not to mention Andy to Ruth. He would tell her that he had a business meeting with a potential client.

Over the next few days, Joe tried to remember Andy from school, but as much as he struggled with his memory he still couldn't recall him, so it was with reluctance that Joe met Andy on the following Tuesday night.

Joe had convinced himself that he and Andy would have nothing in common, but after their first meeting he realised how wrong he had been. In fact, Joe was totally amazed how similar they were. They had the same attitude towards life; work hard and enjoy it. Both men enjoyed football, motor racing, and fishing, although they had agreed that their working lives did not leave a great deal of spare time for recreational pursuits. They had laughed when, to their surprise, they discovered that as much as they enjoyed their leisure activities they had both, unintentionally, devoted their life to making money.

Andy had told Joe that his favourite saying was a Mark Twain quote. *'Don't go around saying the world owes you a living. The world owes you nothing. It was here first'.*

Andy was an innate storyteller. If he wasn't telling a joke, he was quoting a funny story. It amazed Joe, not only how many jokes and stories that he knew, but how he remembered them all. Andy was a natural communicator, and his ability to converse with anyone fascinated Joe.

Joe and Andy became relatively good friends in a short space of time, and Joe thoroughly enjoyed Andy's company. Over the weeks Joe had told Andy about his warehouse business, the good and the bad times, but Andy had been very vague on the subject of his profession. Although he had revealed to Joe that he was part of the investment industry, Joe was still intrigued how Andy actually earned his money.

Joe was a loyal man, especially to his family and friends. He had never lied to Ruth, but for some reason he still hadn't told her about Andy, and had said that his weekly visit to the pub had been with work colleagues and friends from the industrial estate, which she readily accepted and never questioned him on the subject.

Joe soon discovered that Andy was an extremely generous man, and when he insisted on paying for every round of drinks Joe found this extremely arduous and embarrassing. Being raised in South London by working class parents, they had installed in Joe that you paid your way through life. There were times when Joe had to practically fight Andy to pay, and Andy would laugh as he often told Joe that he had more money than he knew what to do with, and because he had no children, and not much of a family, he liked to treat friends.

The Pond and Swan public house, a large old building, had been a communal point many years ago, but as with pubs of its size most of the space was now occupied by a restaurant area. The lounge bar was small in comparison, which could get quite busy at times, especially early evening. While having a drink one Tuesday after work, about two months into their friendship, Joe noticed that Andy was unusually quiet.

"It's very busy in here tonight," Joe observed as he scanned the bar from where they sat.

"I suppose so," Andy replied a little abruptly.

"You all right Andy? You don't seem yourself tonight."

"Sorry Joe just got a few things on my mind."

13

"Anything I can help you with?"

"Not really."

The two men sat in silence for a short while when Andy suddenly said, "I never talk about my work."

"I've noticed that," Joe laughed.

"It's something I've always wanted to keep separate from my personal life."

"I know what you mean, but sometimes our jobs are our lives, I know mine is. It's a catch twenty-two situation really, you need to work practically twenty-four hours a day to keep your business going to support your family, but you miss out on so much of the family life. I look at my children sometimes and know I'm missing their childhood, whilst trying to give them the best upbringing possible."

Andy, pensively, nodded his agreement, and after sitting quiet for a couple of minutes he looked at Joe as if deciding whether he should divulge his problem. As if coming to a heart-felt decision, Andy puffed up his cheeks, and blew the air out with a sigh. "Joe, do you mind if I talk to you about a problem I have with work."

"Of course you can," Joe answered surprised, as well as intrigued.

"As I've mentioned before I earn my money on investments, and believe me if you know what you're doing, it's an easy way to earn a living. I always deal in long-term, and over the years I've earned vast amounts of money. A friend of mine is part of a small investment group that deal in short-term investment only, they like to see a quick return on their money, although short-term can be a much riskier business. Well, this friend has invited me to invest some money on a new project that's coming up. Naturally, all investments have a risk factor but he's assured me this one is quite safe."

When Andy didn't elaborate any further, Joe asked bewildered. "So what's the problem?"

Andy laughed. "Would you believe money?"

"But....."

"Yes, I know what you're going to say. All this money I keep throwing around I must be loaded. Look Joe, over the last couple of years I've invested a huge amount of money and in about a week's time I'm due to invest in the biggest deal of my life." He paused slightly, collecting his thoughts before he continued. "I'll need a hundred thousand pounds if I want to go into this short-term investment, but I really want to tie my money up long-term where I get more of a return. I've got to make the most of my money. I can find half of a hundred thousand, but not the full amount. If this had come up at any other time I wouldn't have a problem, but it's such a shame because it's too good a deal to miss out on, and I feel really torn between the two deals."

"Why don't you put up fifty thousand, and let them find someone else with the other fifty."

"They only want a small number of people in the group. My friend is doing me a favour here, and believe me if I can't put the whole amount up there are plenty of people who can." He paused again and shook his head as if the decision was too much to bear. "This is such a good opportunity to miss out on and I really don't know what to do. But I do have to ask myself when does investing as a profession turn into greed?"

"Of course it's not greed, it's your job, and we all work for the same reason."

"Yes your right mate, but this is my problem and I shouldn't burden you." Andy suddenly stood up and drained the rest of the beer from his glass. "Anyway, enough of my problems, my round I think," he said as he walked away from the table.

As Joe watched Andy make his way to the bar where he ordered the drinks and started to talk to the man standing next to him, Joe sat and digested all that his friend had said. *'An easy way to earn a living'; 'earned vast amounts of money'; 'a good deal to miss out on'.*

What was the comparison between all the hours and hard work that he had devoted to his warehouse business, and the relatively small amount that Andy had committed to his job? There wasn't one. Andy obviously had been one of the lucky people who fell into a profession that not only paid well, but didn't take all the hours that God sent. Although Andy always stated he worked long hours, in comparison to Joe, it was part-time work.

Joe again watched Andy as he returned to the table with the drinks and sat down. "I could come in with you with the other half," Joe said without hesitation.

Andy stared at Joe for a couple of seconds before he began to laugh and said. "I don't think so, to commit fifty thousand pounds to a risky business you know nothing about is really fool hearted mate. I wouldn't let you do it."

"Why not? You've earned a good living out of it all your life."

"Joe, let me be honest with you. When I talk about how easy investments are and all the money I've earned that's just bravado. Believe me I've lost money in the past, lots of money."

"But you've earned heaps as well, and besides, I trust you. I've always prided myself as being a good judge of character." Joe felt excitement surge through his body so tried to calm himself before continuing. "Look Andy, although we only met a few months ago, I feel as though I know you, and I don't think you would consider investing money into this short-term proposition unless you were sure about it."

Andy considered this statement. "You're a hundred percent right Joe, but that's me, I can't let you put that much money into it. How would I feel if you lost it, and you know there's always that risk."

"Of course I know that, but look at it this way. If I come in with you that's my choice, and if it pays off, then it's done us both a favour. We all have to take a risk now and again."

"But you've got to bear in mind that your half wouldn't be in your name. As I explained earlier they want one person with a hundred thousand, not two names."

"That's all right, I'm sure we can come to some arrangement between us."

Andy sighed, and shook his head. "I don't think it's a good idea Joe, I wish I hadn't said anything now."

"Come on Andy, give me this chance, if it pays off, this could be the start of something new for me."

Andy sighed again, and deep in thought took a sip of his beer. He suddenly reached down to retrieve his briefcase which was resting against the leg of the table. Taking out some papers and passing them to Joe he said. "Look, I'll do a deal with you. Take these home and study them, but as you read these documents, always keep the word 'risk' in your head. It's too easy to get carried away when all you can see are the pound signs at the end. Think about it hard for a couple of days, sleep on it. Talk to your wife if need be. The only problem we have is that I need to give them my decision by Friday evening, no later than six o' clock."

"Thanks Andy much appreciated, I'll let you know before then." Joe took the papers, and quickly glanced at them before placing the papers in his own briefcase.

"We would need to sort out a contract between us," Andy said when he had Joe's attention back.

"That sounds all right."

"I can organise that if you want, or by all means you can."

"Maybe best if you do, as I know nothing about this business. Will we need a solicitor?"

"You can if you feel happier having one involved, but I've drawn up many contracts in the past and never had a problem."

"Andy mate. I trust you completely. You get the contract drawn up, and I'll sign!"

Andy laughed. "You're too trusting Joe, read the papers first."

"As I said before I'm a good judge of character, and that has never let me down before. I promise I'll spend tomorrow going over those papers and ring you. Is Friday afternoon all right?"

"I'll ring you," Andy said. "I've a lot on Friday so it'll be easier for me."

Joe nodded his agreement.

They spent the next half hour discussing various topics but Joe couldn't erase the investment proposal from his mind. He was sure that a door of opportunity had now been opened for him, and he was preparing to walk through it.

The following day Joe spent a couple of hours reading through the paperwork that Andy had given him, and checked the website address which he found very impressive. Joe was in no doubt that this business venture was for him. He had been grateful to Andy for giving him this opportunity, and would not let the small problem of a mere fifty thousand pounds stand in his way.

Chapter 3

Two days later, not having slept well the two previous nights, Joe sat in his office contemplating his new venture. Although he had decided to invest with Andy, he still didn't have the fifty thousand pounds, but he was not willing to lose this opportunity.

His plan was to apply for a bank loan to cover the money, and once the investment paid out he would pay off the loan, and invest the profit in another venture. He had applied for the loan yesterday with no problem, but needed a bridging loan to tie him over. He realised the high cost of a bridging loan from a bank, and had racked his brain as to where he could get the money on a short-term loan. He came to the decision to ask Ted, and hoped his friend would be accommodating.

Ted Cartwright was a tall, thin, dark-haired, mild-mannered man, and he and Joe were like brothers. Although they were complete opposites in character and appearance, they had been through nursery, primary, junior and secondary school together, and had been inseparable. They left school together, started work together, chatted up girls together, and were known by their friends, and eventually their parents, as the 'Cannon Cart boys'.

Joe had phoned Ted after lunch, and explained how he had met Andy and the opportunity placed before him. Joe had explained to Ted that he needed fifty thousand pounds by next week, but wouldn't have the money in his bank until the week after.

Ted had laughed, stating that most friends called to ask for a lift to the doctors or the airport, not to borrow fifty thousand pounds. Joe, naturally, understood his friend's concern so suggested a visit to Ted after work to explain fully.

Joe had spent the rest of the afternoon, with difficulty, trying to keep his mind on his work. He had called Ruth to explain he was visiting Ted and Heather straight from work, but did not divulge the reason why.

Ted greeted Joe with enthusiasm as he opened the front door to him, and as he led Joe into the lounge he turned towards his friend. "I've been intrigued ever since you phoned earlier, and I honestly thought you were joking at first."

"Ted, would I joke about a business deal where there's good money to be earned?" Joe answered confidently.

"Do you want tea, coffee or a beer?" Ted asked as Joe seated himself in an armchair.

"I'll have a beer please."

Ted left the lounge, and returned thirty seconds later with two bottles of beer, and handed one to Joe before going to stand by the solid oak mantelpiece which was the focus of the room. "Fifty thousand pounds is a ridiculous amount of money to ask for Joe."

"I know, but think of it as a bridging loan," suggested Joe.

"I'm not thinking of it as anything. I can't believe you're asking me. You know all my money is tied up in the house adaptations needed for Heather."

"Of course I know that Ted, and I wouldn't be asking you if I could think of another way." Joe paused slightly before he continued. "As I explained to you earlier, I've applied for a bank loan, and have practically been told I've got it, but because of the amount I want to borrow it can take a little longer, and the money may not be in my account until the week after next. If I'm in with a chance of this deal I need the money by next week, and as soon as the loan is in my account I will transfer it straight back into yours."

Ted sighed. "Joe, I have fifty-five thousand pounds in the bank, and every penny of that is needed for the adaptations to this house." He motioned around the room with his hand to emphasize his words. "A stair lift, outside ramps, wheelchair accessibility to every room, bathroom adaptations, and that's without all the little bits that need doing. The work is due to start next week, which means as soon as it's all finished the builders will want their money."

"I know Ted, and the money will be back in your account within the next two weeks, so you have nothing to worry about."

"I take it Ruth knows all about this new venture of yours."

"Well...err...no...I didn't want to worry her."

"Worry! I thought you said it was a sure thing. Why would she worry?"

"Oh, you know what I mean, the baby is due soon, and anyway I thought it would be a nice surprise for her, all that extra money."

"But surely this kind of investment should only be entered into if you have the ready cash." Ted said frustration sounding in his voice.

"Yes, maybe you're right, but I've just got a feeling about this, and can't let it go."

"I'm sorry to keep going on about this Joe, but something just doesn't ring true, and fifty thousand pounds is a lot of money," his friend said defiantly.

"I know, but I just think this is an opportunity for me to begin another aspect in my career. I know I'll be paying interest to the bank, but anything I earn will go into another investment. I trust Andy and know he will help in any way he can."

"That's another thing I wanted to talk to you about, this Andy fellow, I don't remember him from school at all."

"Ted, you have trouble remembering last week, let alone...what...twenty-eight years ago?" Joe laughed.

"You remember him then, do you?"

"Well...no...but he remembers me, he even remembered my nickname of 'Cocky Cannon'. He also remembers you, and Mickey Noble. I've every faith in him Ted and I've got to know him well over the last few months."

Ted studied his friend before he asked. "Joe, can you assure me, one hundred per cent that the money will be back in my account Friday week the latest?"

Joe jumped up from his chair and going over to his friend said excitedly. "Ted, of course I can. Would I put you in an awkward position, especially where Heather is concerned?"

"I suppose not, but it just doesn't feel right somehow," Ted sighed. He thought for a while before he continued. "All right Joe, but you had better not let me down on this one."

"Thanks mate," Joe answered, and as relief overwhelmed him he took his friend in an embrace. When Joe pulled away he asked. "How is Heather? I've not seen her since I've been here."

"Not too good today, she's having a lie down at the moment."

As much as Ted loved Joe as a friend, the main love of his life was Heather. When Ted had first met her it was love at first sight; literally. Heather had not been in good health for many months before she met Ted, but they announced their engagement and wedding date three months after meeting. Sadly, just two weeks before their wedding day, the doctors diagnosed Heather with multiple sclerosis, and had explained that further symptoms could develop and increase over time.

Now twenty-one years later, Heather was in a wheelchair and needed help with most everyday tasks.

They had considered selling their house and buying a bungalow, but because they both loved the house, especially the garden, they decided to stay there and have the property adapted for Heather's needs.

Ted was a landscape gardener, and was profoundly accomplished at his craft. Their garden was Heather's solace, and when they had discussed moving, although Ted knew he could design any garden she wanted, he had admitted that the 'feel' of their garden could not be guaranteed in another.

Neither, Ted or Heather had family that they could turn to. Both were only children, and Ted's parents had both been killed in a car crash just after he and Heather had married. Heather's parents lived in Scotland, and even though her mother told her, on the rare occasion when they spoke on the telephone, how much she loved and worried about her, no offers of help, whether financial or physical were ever forthcoming.

"Hope she feels better soon, and give her my love."

"I will do thanks."

"And Ted, I really can't thank you enough for this."

Ted just smiled at his friend.

"If this comes off, and I know it will, maybe in the future you'll come in with me."

"No thanks mate, but thanks for the offer. I'll make my money the only way I know how."

Both men now laughed, as Ted glanced at his watch and said. "I must go up and check on Heather."

"Of course," Joe replied and took this as a cue to leave. He withdrew a piece of paper from his pocket with his bank account details on for Ted. "Thanks mate, I came prepared," he laughed as he passed the piece of paper to him.

"That's fine," Ted replied. "But don't let me down on this one Joe."

"You know you can trust me Ted."

"Do I? So why do I feel so worried?"

Chapter 4

True to his word, Andy phoned Joe at his office on Friday afternoon.

"I'm in!" Joe had announced proudly, trying to contain the excitement in his voice.

"OK Joey boy, I'm not going to try to dissuade you again. I'll contact my people and tell them I'm in, and I'll get our contract drawn up and get back to you."

The following Wednesday Joe received a large envelope through the post containing two sets of a contract that Andy had drawn up. Joe had to sign and date both copies, but return one copy to Andy.

The following night the two men met at the Pond and Swan as arranged. Once they were both settled at a table with drinks in front of them, Joe handed Andy the envelope.

"All completed and signed?" asked Andy.

Joe nodded his answer.

"Do you want to go through the contract with me now before we go ahead?"

"No," Joe answered.

"Have you kept a copy?"

"Yes."

"Did you see the instructions in the envelope explaining where the money had to be deposited to and when?"

"Of course I did, and I followed the instructions explicitly," Joe answered with a slight sarcastic tone in his voice.

"All right, it's just that I won't be around for a couple of weeks, but I'll call you as soon as I'm back. We'll go for an Indian."

"I'll look forward to it," Joe said as he raised his glass in a toast. He felt elated now his business prospects were advancing in two different directions, and although he knew to keep his head out of the clouds with regard to his new investment venture, he could not help but revel in that flush of excitement.

"Joe, are you sure you haven't left yourself in dire straight financially? You should only invest with money you can afford."

"Andy!" Joe exclaimed. "Will you stop worrying, I'm a business man like you, and know what I'm doing, and what I'm letting myself in for."

Andy laughed. "All right, but you can't blame me for worrying. I've never got a novice involved like this before."

"Well I'm glad you did. Now, I'm buying the drinks tonight because I don't know about you, but I'm celebrating."

***

When the letter arrived at his office the following Monday morning, he had to read it twice. His heart was pulsating through his body, and the walls of his office seem to close in on him. His application for a loan had *'not been successful'*. He read those words over and over. Not successful? How could he not have been successful? When he had applied in person at the bank, Gerry, who had conducted the interview, had told him that he could not foresee any problem, and that the money was practically in his bank account.

He had explained to Gerry that the loan, although taken out for a two-year period, would be paid back within six to nine months.

After reading the letter for the third time, Joe immediately phoned the bank and asked to speak to Gerry, but the woman who answered the call advised him that Gerry was unavailable. Joe explained his predicament to her, and she in turn advised that it was a head office decision whether or not a customer was successful with regards to a bank loan. She suggested he called them, and gave him the required telephone number.

Lethargically Joe ended the call, and tried to gather his thoughts. He could appeal against the bank's decision, but knew that this could be a lengthy process, and it was time that he was short of; as well as money.

Ted's words had also been haunting Joe. *"I take it Ruth knows all about this new venture of yours."* If he was truthful with himself, he never had any intentions of telling her. He knew that she would have definitely been against the idea, especially borrowing fifty thousand pounds that he could ill afford.

Ted was not expecting the money back into his account until Friday, so that gave him four day's grace. The problem being, where was he now going to get fifty thousand pounds before Friday? He had to think. *'There's always a solution',* had always been Joe's philosophy, and he laughed to himself as he thought *'not always the right one, but a solution none the less'.*

Over the next few days Joe had asked a couple of reliable friends with regard to moneylenders, and they all recommended Barry McGraw. Mainly because he had no upper limit to the amount he would lend.

Joe had frequented McGraw Estate Agent on many occasions when he had bought their current house. What Joe didn't know, at that time, was that although Barry McGraw looked a respectable business man, the estate agency, although well-known and successful, was a front for a very lucrative money lending establishment.

When, three days later, Joe entered the premises of McGraw Estate Agent, surprisingly, nostalgia overwhelmed him. Nothing had changed in the four years since his last visit, and he was positive that it was the same staff members sitting behind the same desks. Barry immediately rose from his desk to greet him, and

Joe thought he saw a glint of recognition on the man's face.

"Elda Avenue," Barry said as a statement, rather than a greeting as he shook Joe's hand.

"Yes," Joe said amazed. "How did you remember that? It was over four years ago."

"Always remember a beautiful house," Barry answered proudly. "But sorry," he smiled, "not so good on names."

"Joe Cannon."

"Of course," he smiled as he remembered. "Right Mr Cannon, what can I do for you today? Selling up?"

"Please call me Joe, and it was actually other business I wanted to talk to you about."

Barry studied Joe, and said abruptly. "Come into my office."

Joe followed him into a small, cluttered, side office and sat in the offered seat in front of a desk. Barry walked around to the other side and positioned himself slowly into his chair.

"How much do you want?" Barry asked.

"Fifty thousand pounds."

Barry whistled through his teeth. "That's a lot of money Joe."

"Yes I know, but I've been told that you were the one to come to."

Barry looked cautiously at Joe across the table, and without comment to this statement he picked up the telephone on his desk. Without taking his eyes off Joe he said into the mouthpiece. "I don't want to be disturbed." He replaced the instrument softly back on its stand, pulled a pad in front of him and said, "Right, let's see what I can do for you."

Joe soon learnt that Barry's terms were not negotiable, and he insisted on an eighteen month repayment plan. After the eighteen month period Joe would have paid back the fifty thousand pounds with a good substantial amount of interest.

Joe knew that the interest on borrowing that amount of money from Barry McGraw would be extortionate compared to what he would have paid back to the bank. It just meant that his profit would be substantially smaller, or even a loss.

Later that afternoon, once Joe had returned to his office, he called Ted to tell him that his money would be back into his bank account within the next couple of days. He did not, however, tell him that the bank loan had been unsuccessful, as Joe knew he would receive a justifiable lecture if he told his friend where he had borrowed the money from.

After he had wished Heather well, and said goodbye to Ted, he felt a satisfying aura surround him, and suddenly felt like celebrating. He wondered if Ruth would be able to get a babysitter at such short notice so they could go out for a meal tonight. Just as he was about to pick up the telephone to call her, it rang.

His third child was about to make an early entrance into the world.

***

Lewis Bradley Cannon entered the world four weeks before his expected due date, which came as a complete surprise to everyone, especially his mother and father. Joe reached the hospital just minutes after Lewis had been born, where a nurse informed him that he had a healthy, six-pound one-ounce baby boy.

Joe paused slightly as he opened the door of the delivery room, and as he entered and saw Ruth cuddling their new-born baby, a feeling of contentment overwhelmed him. He had a gorgeous wife, three adorable children, a beautiful home, a successful business, the beginning of a new venture, and Christmas, his favourite time of the year, was just around the corner. His life was perfect.

Of course Joe had no way of knowing that his idyllic world was about to collapse; dramatically.

Chapter 5

A month after depositing the investment money into the account that Andy had given him instructions for, Joe became surprised and a little worried that he had not heard from Andy, so it was with relief when he eventually answered a phone call from him.

"Joe, hi mate, sorry I've not been in touch, but I've been really busy, and decided to go away for Christmas."

"That's fine Andy, just glad to hear from you. Good Christmas?"

"Yes thanks. How was yours?"

"Yes, good one thanks. The kids thoroughly enjoyed themselves, and we had a surprise visit, our new-born son decided to arrive early in time for Christmas."

"Wow. How is he?"

"He's doing well, thanks."

"Good. Listen, I was going to suggest that we meet, but something's come up and I have to go away again. There's nothing to report on the investment, but its early days yet," he added reassuringly, and continued. "I hope to be back by the end of January, so I'll ring you then."

"All right Andy, speak to you soon," Joe said as he placed the receiver back on its stand. He smiled to himself as he realised that Andy was being as secretive as ever over his movements and whereabouts.

***

It was now the second week in February, and at least five weeks since Joe had last heard from Andy. Joe's thoughts were constantly on his money problems, and although he had paid his first instalment to Barry on time, his second payment was now due, and he only had half of the money available.

What had possessed him to agree to monthly payments of three and a half thousand pounds? He realised now that he had not thought this financial venture through sensibly, and had become engrossed in the splendour and greed of it all.

He knew that to guarantee this month's instalment he would have to delay payment to some of his suppliers, and chase his own clients, especially the bad payers. He could not chance the wrath of Barry McGraw, and worried how he would manage to pay Barry every month until the investment paid out.

Joe continually recalled the meeting with Barry McGraw. Barry had reluctantly agreed to lend Joe the full amount, and had naturally dominated the proceedings. Joe had no say in the payment plan, and had known from the very onset of the meeting that he either agreed to the terms or went home empty-handed.

Joe urgently needed to contact Andy to get an up-date on the investment, but realised he had no way of getting in touch with him. It suddenly dawned on Joe that Andy had never given him a business card, and it was always Andy that did the contacting.

Joe had never questioned Andy with regards to contact between them, and had just accepted that it would be Andy who would initiate all communication. He now tried to recall what he actually knew of Andy's personal and working life. He worked in investments, divorced with no children, and had two dogs. He had mentioned a couple of hobbies, but they were exactly the same as Joe's. Not much information from a man who Joe had numerous drinks and evenings out with, and who he thought of as a relatively close friend.

Joe instantly reprimanded himself; this was not the appropriate time to doubt a man that he had recently given fifty thousand pounds to. He suddenly remembered that the contract that Andy had drawn up between them was in his safe, surely that would give some contact details. He again reprimanded himself for not thinking of this before.

Going to the safe in the corner of his office, he retrieved the contract and returned to his desk. Pulling a pad in front of him, he made a note of the telephone number, email address and postal address displayed at the top of the contract.

It suddenly dawned on him that Andy had never mentioned having an office before, and always assumed he worked from home.

He picked up his mobile phone from his desk and dialled the number. He waited as the device tried to connect, but realised it hadn't when he heard the unobtainable tone. Assuming he had dialled the digits wrong he dialled the number again, but this time on his office landline.

When the same tone came to him the second time alarm overwhelmed him. It was after the third try that he phoned the telephone company and asked them to check Andy's line, and after waiting a couple of minutes the operator confirmed that the number no longer existed.

He could only assume that Andy had changed his telephone number. He would send him an e-mail; even if he was out of the country surely he would still pick up his messages.

Pulling his keyboard in front of him, he typed a quick e-mail to Andy asking him to call. Two minutes later, to Joe's surprise, he received a message from the server stating that the e-mail could not be delivered as the 'Recipients mailbox is full or their account has been disabled'. Joe double checked the e-mail address that he had typed in, and confirmed that he had addressed it correctly. He sent another e-mail only to receive the same 'unable to deliver' message back.

Joe tried to rationalise the situation. People changed their contact details, especially e-mail addresses all the time. Joe assumed that Andy didn't tell him that he had changed his because Andy hadn't given him any in the first place. His only other option was to pay a visit to the postal address. Putting on his coat and tying a scarf around his neck to ward off the cold, he left his office telling Laura that he would be out for the rest of the day, and that he had his mobile phone on him should he be needed urgently.

Joe was not familiar with the East End of London so he set his satellite navigation system to direct him to the address. Thirty-five minutes later as he pulled up at his 'reached destination' as directed by the machine, surprise engulfed him to see a boarded-up shop displaying a 'To Let' sign.

He got out of his car, and walked up and down the street to make sure he had the right address. When satisfied he had, he returned to the shop and looking at the premises again wondered why Andy would have needed such a big office, if he needed an office at all. Maybe it was a friend's business and he used the address for correspondence. Joe now wondered if the contract was still valid as some of the information on it was no longer correct.

Making a note of the estate agents name and address displayed on the board, he set his route finder again which informed him the address was a ten minute drive away. On arrival at the estate agency Joe realised that he was unable to park directly outside, but found a parking space just a two-minute walk away.

A pretty young receptionist greeted Joe as he entered the premises. "Good afternoon sir. Can I help you?"

With his hands slightly shaking he placed a piece of paper, with the address of the boarded-up shop, on her desk and said. "I'm interested in this property and believe it was used as an office before it closed down recently."

The receptionist smiled. "Let me check sir."

As she began to search the property on her computer, Joe looked around noticing how shabby his surroundings were, and compared them to Barry's pristine premises.

"No sir, it was a launderette."

"Launderette! You must have it wrong," Joe exclaimed.

"I'm sorry sir, but it was a launderette, and the property has been empty for over a year now.

"That's impossible. I'm in business with the man who rented it previously."

Noticing Joe's disbelief, she turned the computer screen towards him to confirm all that she had said.

The receptionist watched as Joe slightly swayed on his feet, and the colour drained from his face as he scrutinized the screen. She immediately hurried around her desk and guided him to a chair, and fetched him a glass of water. As he gulped the water, he suddenly began to choke as the liquid gushed down his throat.

Feeling absolutely distraught, Joe returned the glass to the receptionist and mumbled his thanks. He staggered out of the building and made his way back to his car. With shaking hands he opened the driver's door and slumped into the seat and placing his head in his hands, he lent on the steering wheel, and swallowed the nausea rising in his throat.

After a few minutes, Joe slowly straightened his body and tried to comprehend what had happened. Andy Bolan had disappeared; the man who he had called a friend, and trusted completely. The man he had boasted to that he was a good judge of character, how Andy must have been inwardly laughing at him.

He was the victim of a scam; a hoax which would cost him thousands of pounds. How could he have been so stupid to fall for it? He had no need to ask himself that question as he knew the answer; greed. Had he become a greedy man? He had seen a quick and easy way of making money, and grasped it with both hands. He had not thought the proposal through, and went ahead without a structure or plan. He didn't even take into account the consequences of borrowing such a large amount of money from a moneylender. He slowly placed his head in his hands again and reprimanded himself. "Bloody fool! Bloody, bloody fool!"

All these years working so hard; for what? To possibly lose everything he has worked for. How he wished he had mentioned Andy to Ruth. At least if she had agreed to the investment he would have a shoulder to cry on, but he was alone, unable to divulge his stupidity to anyone; not even Ted.

Noticing a run-down pub on the corner, Joe decided that he needed a drink to calm his nerves, and try to put together a plan to rectify his foolishness. On entering the building, he walked across a threadbare carpet to the well-worn bar and ordered a pint of beer. He glanced around the pub and noticed the wallpaper hanging off the walls, the peeling paint, and the dejected looking people sitting at the tables. He took his pint from the bar, thanked the barman, and found himself a table in the corner so he could sip his pint and reflect on all that had happened; and his limited options.

The one decision he had to consider was whether he should explain everything to Ruth. Although he knew she would be furious with him, he also knew she would stand by him and help all she could. The unfortunate thing for Joe was that pride stood in his way. He had always been proud that he was the one that provided for his family. He was the one that had built the business up. He had never worried Ruth with work problems, and had no intention of starting now. He had always dealt with any situation that had come his way, and made a vow to himself that he would handle this dilemma.

He now laughed to himself as he thought of his grand ideas for expanding the business that were in the pipeline. He was grateful that Ruth wouldn't be questioning him on that subject as she knew nothing about them. He realised now that he was right to keep Ruth out of all his business affairs; for both their sakes.

Although he had mellowed with the years, he did not earn the name of 'Cocky Cannon' by letting people walk all over him. He would first sort out his financial problems, and then find the man who had tried to destroy his life, and bring him to justice.

Cannon's justice.

Chapter 6

Ruth sat in her warm, cosy lounge gazing at Lewis, fast asleep in his Moses basket. Tyler and Abbey had been in bed for about an hour, and Ruth was waiting for Joe to come home.

Her thoughts this evening had constantly been invaded by Stella, her manipulative, devious, cunning sister. Ruth had argued with Stella earlier today over a red dress, albeit, a sexy, figure hugging, beautiful red dress.

Ruth had fallen in love with the dress the instant she had seen it on a mannequin in Marie's boutique whilst on a shopping trip with Stella yesterday afternoon. Unfortunately, they didn't have Ruth's size in stock, but the shop assistant had assured Ruth that they were expecting a delivery the following week which, hopefully, would include her size.

When Stella had phoned this morning informing Ruth that she had returned to the shop and had bought the dress, Ruth had been furious with her.

"You knew I had every intention of buying it!" she had shouted down the telephone line at her sister.

"Oh, grow up Ruth, they didn't have your size, but they had mine, so I went back and bought it."

"How could you, you knew how much I wanted that dress."

"Well, we can't have everything we want in life, can we little sister," Stella had replied with satisfaction in her voice.

As young girls Ruth and Stella dreamt of being famous dancers. Although there had been harsh competition between them, they would also spend hours putting together dance routines, and staging shows for their parents, family and friends. Even though Ruth was by far the better dancer, Stella, being thirteen months older than her sister, would always take the leading role.

When Ruth left school, at the age of sixteen, her parents had paid for her to attend a private dance school, and to help with the finances, Ruth took a part-time job in a local insurance company. They gave Stella the same opportunity, but she saw no need to work.

Ruth had enjoyed her time at the insurance company, but gave notice when she won her first professional dancing role at the age of seventeen. Ruth and Stella had gone for the audition, among a hundred others, but Ruth's talent shone through and the producer of the show had no trouble deciding which girl to choose. Although another twelve girls were also selected for the dance troupe, unfortunately Stella had not been one of them.

At the time of Ruth's new-found fame, Stella had been incredibly jealous and bitter towards her sister. Ruth would often find items of her dance clothing missing, and hair and jewellery pieces ruined.

Ruth had been in the show for six months when she decided, one Friday morning, to shop for new dance shoes needed for rehearsals. When she returned home around lunchtime, her mother had informed her that Stella had taken a call from the producer saying that Ruth was no longer needed as the show had closed due to financial problems, but they would contact her if the show could be staged at a later date. Ruth had been absolutely devastated, and cried for the rest of the day.

As youngsters, the sisters argued constantly, normally over clothes that belong to Ruth that Stella had worn without permission, or Ruth's accessories that often went missing. It was during one of these arguments that Stella had admitted that there had been no such call from the producer, and the show had not been cancelled. It was Stella who had called him, and introducing herself as their mother, informed him that Ruth would have to leave the show due to ill-health. Devastation had overwhelmed Ruth that her sister could do something so cruel and callous to her.

Although Ruth did, again, land a substantial position in a new musical, her dancing career ended at the age of nineteen due to an ankle injury. The doctors had informed her parents that it would never heal properly if she continued to dance. Ruth had been heartbroken, but Stella had been in her element, and had even been heard to say that '*the dancing industry was a much better place now that her sister was no longer a part of it.*'

Ruth had never understood the ways of her sister, and often wondered why she was such a malicious person. Had she become that person, or was she born with such traits? She often thought of the saying; nature or nurture. Ruth realised that it was not nurture as their parents were the kindest people she knew.

Guilt suddenly overwhelmed Ruth. Why was she thinking of Stella and not Joe? Joe her husband of thirteen years, the man she loved more than life itself. It was a month or so back that she had noticed a change in him, but that change had become more apparent over the last week.

Arguing had always been a rarity in their life together, but now it was constant. Ruth knew that Joe was keeping something from her, and she had questioned him many times over the last month, but he had categorically denied there were any problems, and had apologised for any mood he may have been in.

Ruth tried to recall exactly when the change in Joe had begun. Had it been gradual? Had she been too busy, wrapped up in the children to notice? She had also noticed that he had lost a little weight, which on Joe's build did not suit him.

When Joe had arrived home from work last night, later than usual, Tyler and Abbey had been in their bedrooms, and Lewis, in his baby chair, was crying for attention. After Joe had hung his coat and scarf on the stand in the hallway, he had walked into the lounge and glanced over at the baby, but made no attempt to approach him. Kissing Ruth slightly on the cheek, the smell of alcohol penetrating her nostrils, he had asked where Tyler and Abbey were, and to her sorrow, she realised that his question was more of a formality, rather than one of concern or interest.

After being told they were in their bedrooms, he hurried up the stairs to his office, telling Ruth that he had work to catch up on. As he reached his office door, he had called down to Ruth demanding that *'she do something with the baby to stop him crying'*. Ruth had been furious, and as she began to climb the stairs after him not only to vent her anger at him, but to question the amount he was drinking lately, she heard his office door slam and the lock engage.

When she had questioned him this morning about his outburst, he had apologised as usual, and stated that yesterday had been a bad day, and he had just stopped off for a quick pint before coming home.

Ruth had first met Joe when she was sixteen years old, whilst working for the insurance company and thought he was the most handsome man she had ever seen. Joe had been an insurance salesman, and Ruth had always looked forward to his weekly visit when she would blatantly flirt with him.

Although flattered with Ruth's advances, Joe was six years older than her, and regarded Ruth as a young, silly girl. He preferred his women older, and considerably more mature. When she had left the insurance company to further her dancing vocation Ruth often thought of Joe, but he did eventually fade from her thoughts.

When Ruth's dancing career had come to an abrupt end, she applied for a job as a receptionist/secretary with an advertising agency, and was successful. Her employer and the owner of the agency, Adrian Scott, although a quiet, unassuming man, expected nothing less from Ruth other than conscientiousness, efficiency and loyalty; which he received willingly. It was the most exciting job Ruth could ever have wished for.

When Joe had entered Adrian Scott's reception one Friday morning and approached her desk, Ruth recognised him immediately even though she hadn't seen him for over three years. "Good morning sir, how can I help you?" she had asked when he made no sign of recognising her.

"Joe Cannon is the name, and I've an appointment to see Mr Scott at eleven-thirty."

Ruth had laughed to herself as she realised that he was still the same lovable, cocky Joe Cannon, and after checking the appointment book replied. "Take a seat Mr Cannon, and I'll tell Mr Scott you are here."

As he sat in the luxurious waiting room, Ruth had found it hard to concentrate on her work. She wasn't surprised to see that his spiky blond hair was still styled the same way and, with her heart racing, she noticed that his prominent, sparkling blue eyes shone even brighter in his handsome face. When Adrian Scott telephoned from his office asking her to send Mr Cannon in, it was with relief that she escorted Joe into the office.

When Joe emerged an hour and half later from his meeting, he stopped at the reception desk to ask Ruth her name. She immediately pointed to her name badge which proudly showed it.

"Well Ruth," he had exclaimed, "I've got another appointment for next Friday, and hopefully when I arrive, you will be gracing that desk with your beauty."

With her whole body shaking, and unable to speak, Ruth had just smiled at him as he turned and left the reception.

Once Joe had left, Adrian Scott came out of his office and said. "Mr Cannon has another appointment next Friday at eleven-thirty." Noticing Ruth's complexion he asked. "Are you all right Ruth? You look awfully flushed."

"Yes, I'm fine," she mumbled.

He continued to study her with concern on his face. "Are you sure? Shall I fetch you some water?"

"No...no...I'm fine, honest."

"All right, if you say so," he replied hesitantly, and placing Joe's paperwork on her desk in order for her to register him, he continued. "I've a funny feeling that we'll be seeing quite a lot of that gentleman. He knows where he's going in life and intends to see the journey to the end." He glanced at his watch before he continued. "If we can arrange a time for three-thirty this afternoon Ruth, we'll go through Mr Cannon's campaign."

Ruth nodded her agreement and smiled at her employer.

"Thanks Ruth, I'm going to lunch and I'll be back in an hour."

Once Adrian had left the office, Ruth looked at Joe's notes and had read that he was renting a large warehouse on the London/Kent border just off the M25 motorway. He was buying and selling all types of household goods, and had placed a large advertising contract with Adrian. He had his address as South London, and apart from that there were no more personal details. She wondered if there was a Mrs Cannon on the scene. How she desperately hoped not.

The following week when Joe had returned, he again sat in the waiting room eager to begin his meeting. After spending at least an hour with Adrian, Joe emerged from the meeting looking as pleased as anyone possible could.

"Well Ruth," he had said as he approached her desk, "Are you coming out to celebrate with me tonight?"

"Celebrate what?"

"The start of my new business venture, that's going to make me a very rich man."

"No wife to celebrate with you?"

"That Ruth is a long story, but the answer to your question is no. Well, how about it?"

"I'd love to," she replied smiling.

"All right then," he said triumphantly. "Write down your address and I'll pick you up at seven-thirty."

As she wrote her address on a note pad, she could feel his eyes boring into her, so it was with embarrassment that she gave him the piece of paper. As he was about to leave he pointed his finger at her, and mimicking a Humphrey Bogart voice said. "Put your best dress on doll, coz we're gonna paint the town red."

That evening had been the most memorable night of Ruth's life. He had taken her to an exquisite restaurant in the West End of London, and on to a show, followed by a night-cap in an exclusive nightclub in Soho.

She had never laughed so much in her life. Joe was the funniest man she had ever met. When she had disclosed that she was the same Ruth Donny who had worked at the insurance company, Joe had stared at her in amazement.

"I would never have recognised you!" he had exclaimed, and added. "You were just a pretty little girl, but wow, you've grown into a beautiful woman in those three years."

They began to date on a regular basis, and Ruth thoroughly enjoyed her time spent with Joe. They discussed his plans for the warehouse, informing her that his aim was to buy large quantities of household goods and sell them to shops and market stalls, not only in the local area, but Essex, Kent and most parts of London.

She had studied him as he spoke with enthusiasm about his new project, and realised he was a man who fully intended to carry out all his ambitions in life. She admired his good looks, his short cut blond hair and the fact that he did not look his twenty-six years. She loved everything about him, including his cocky attitude, and even the earring that graced his left ear, but most of all she loved to hear him call her 'Ruthie'; his special name for her.

It was in his bed, one Saturday afternoon, that Joe told Ruth of his five-year marriage to Karen. He had admitted that he had been absolutely devastated when she had run off to France with one of his best friends, but assured Ruth that Karen was now out of his life, and he hoped never to see her again. Ruth had snuggled in his arms, before they had made love again, and knew, even at that early stage in their relationship, that she had already fallen in love with Joe Cannon, for the second time.

Although Ruth's parents adored Joe, Stella took an immediate dislike to him. She thought he was obstinate, arrogant and uncouth, but she had no intention of talking her sister out of dating him.

They had married two years later, she was twenty-two and he was twenty-eight. Ruth had wanted to help Joe build the business, but Joe insisted she stay at the advertising agency, convinced that a husband and wife team never worked well together.

Three months after their marriage, the newly-weds discovered that Ruth was pregnant, and when, later in her pregnancy, they found out they were having twin boys, Ruth and Joe were ecstatic. Deciding to name them Bradley and Tyler the couple prepared the second bedroom in their rented flat and waited eagerly for the arrival of their sons.

Her pregnancy had gone well up until the last two months when she explained to the doctor that she could only feel one baby kicking. He immediately booked her in for an ultrasound scan just to make sure that all was satisfactory.

Unfortunately, all had not been satisfactory. One twin had died. The doctor had explained that she would have to carry both twins until the birth. Although devastated at the news, Ruth knew she had to try to carry on as much as normal for the sake of the surviving twin.

Tyler was born a healthy six pound baby, but sadness also consumed the day when Ruth and Joe had held their dead baby son, and said goodbye before the nurse had taken him to the morgue.

When Joe had suggested that Ruth gave up work to stay at home with Tyler she had been more than agreeable, and when Abbey came along four years later her life was complete.

Tyler had been eight years old and Abbey four when they had moved into their current house. She remembered vividly how proud Joe had been the day he had shown her the estate agent's leaflet. She had actually gasped as she gazed at the most beautiful house she had ever seen. She recalled that the leaflet had boasted four large bedrooms with an en-suite in the master bedroom, a downstairs toilet with a family bathroom upstairs, a kitchen/diner, a spacious lounge with patio doors that led to a contemporary family garden, and a large wrought iron gated drive that would hold at least four cars. She also remembered how excited she had been when she noticed that it had an office that would be ideal for Joe.

It had been a far cry from the small two-bedroom flat that they had privately rented, where Tyler and Abbey had to share a room. The flat had been ideal for their first home, not only because of the affordable rent, but it was near to Joe's warehouse with easy access to the M25 motorway.

Although the house was only a ten minute drive from their flat, it was a different world. It was a ten minute drive from the shabby housing estate and although they had always felt safe living on the Dalton Estate, it had deteriorated rapidly in the last few years that they had lived there.

She had not seen Joe that proud since Tyler and Abby had been born. Happy memories also came flooding back as she remembered, not only the hard work, but the good times they had as a family.

She also recalled how elated Joe and the children had been when Lewis came into the world two weeks before Christmas. Joe, at first, had treated him like a precious piece of porcelain, but sadly now didn't even acknowledge that he existed.

Tyler and Abbey were both still enthralled with their baby brother. Tyler, at the age of twelve, played with him constantly, and Abbey, at the tender age of eight, was a natural with him. Sadly, it was Joe who had lost all interest in his son. When Ruth had told him last April that she was pregnant, although surprised, he had also been thrilled. Everything was fine until at least six weeks ago when she noticed a change in him, not only his attitude towards Lewis, but everything and everyone.

The loud knock at the front door startled Ruth. She quickly rose from the sofa and walked into the hall closing the lounge door behind her to keep in the warmth. The cold air hit her as soon as she opened the front door, but that was nothing compared to the image that stood before her.

"Joe at home love?" asked the bigger of the two burley looking men that stood on her doorstep. They were both dressed identically in immaculate well cut, black, pin-striped suits.

"No...No..." stammered Ruth. "He's not home from work yet...can...can I help?"

"Just tell him Barry's boys called to have a word with him."

"Okay."

"Tell him to make sure he gives Barry a call."

"I will."

"You won't forget now will you love."

"No....No....of course not."

The two men stared menacingly at Ruth, but it was the smaller one who now spoke. "And tell that husband of yours that he knows the consequences of ignoring Barry."

It was in unison that both men immediately turned and walked away without acknowledging her any further.

As Ruth closed the door and put the safely chain on, she could hear her heart beating through her body, and hurried back to the lounge to check on the still sleeping Lewis. On instinct, she now ran up the stairs to check Tyler and Abbey but they were thankfully both fast asleep.

Returning to the lounge, she sat on the sofa and recalled the conversation. What on earth was that all about? Who were those men? More important, what did they want?

She had tried to call Joe several times that evening without success, so all she could do now was wait for him to come home. She glanced at her watch and noticed it was nearly ten minutes past nine, and again wondered, for the umpteenth time that night, where her husband was.

Joe arrived home about twenty minutes later and Ruth had immediately informed him of his visitors.

Upon hearing the news she noticed a reaction in his eyes, but couldn't decipher if it was surprise or fright.

He immediately assured her that he knew of their visit, as they had called his mobile just before he had left the warehouse. She had questioned him on how they had managed to get through to his mobile, when she had tried several times without success, but he had just shrugged his shoulders, and shook his head.

When she had asked him who the men were, he had said that they were suppliers, who he had forgotten to pay, but the account had now been settled.

Ruth knew he was lying, and confronted him as to why suppliers would come to their house in such a threatening manner. He had tried to explain that they were a small company based in East London who, obviously, had not learnt the etiquette of business, and assured her that he would never use them again.

When she had questioned him on how they had known his private address, he had pleaded with her to forget the incident, and assured her that the episode had now been resolved.

That Joe would lie to her was inconceivable, and all of a sudden Ruth lost her resolve to fight him, so it was with a heavy heart that she had turned away from the man that she thought she knew.

Chapter 7

The following day Joe had managed to delay a few payments to his suppliers, but had struggled to chase his bad payers for settlement. February's instalment to Barry was now overdue, and he still didn't have the full amount.

He had, in desperation and at every available opportunity, searched the house for spare cash. He even considered raiding the holiday jar that he knew Ruth put all her spare change into, and the children's money boxes, but he stopped short of that misdemeanour.

He did consider asking Ted for another short-term loan, but knew the builders had practically finished the adaptation work in their house so would soon require payment.

Joe was at a loss of what to do, and sat at his desk remembering his life before Andy Bolan, so it was with tears in his eyes that he took a call from Laura.

"Joe, I've got a Charley Kerry in reception for you."

Joe had not seen his old friend for at least two years, so he rubbed the tears from his eyes, and tried to sound as normal as possible. "Thanks Laura, send him through." He rose from his desk to greet him.

"Charley, what a surprise," Joe exclaimed as his friend entered the office, and they shook hands.

"Hi Joe, good to see you, thought I'd pop in as I was passing. I'm on my way to see my mum, she lives in Orpington now."

"I'm surprised your mum moved out of London."

"Yeah we all were, but case of having to I'm afraid. She needs sheltered accommodation now, and didn't like anything her council offered her, so my sister, who already lives in Orpington, got her a place near her."

"I didn't realise you had a sister Charley."

"Yeah, I don't see much of her as she's quite a bit older than me, and we don't always get on," Charley said with a touch of sadness in his voice.

"Anyway, sit down mate," Joe said. "I'll order us some coffee."

"Sorry Joe, haven't got time, it's just a flying visit to say hello. I've passed this way a couple of times and promised myself that next time I'd pop in and see how you're doing."

"Yeah, everything's fine. What about you?"

"Yes, mustn't grumble." Charley said, and asked. "How's your wife and kids?"

"All doing well thanks, got three children now."

"Congratulations. Is that why you're looking so tired?" Charley laughed.

Although taken aback by this comment, Joe decided not to retaliate. "Anyway Charley, you still working?"

"Yeah still working for old man Thompson, I've been there some years now," Charley laughed and studied his friend before he continued. "Sorry Joe, no offence meant just now, I just thought you looked a bit washed out."

"You know what it's like working all hours, and the baby crying all night," Joe lied.

Joe couldn't recall the last time he had enjoyed a decent night's sleep, and had even spent a few nights sleeping at his desk in his office at home. Food was another rarity these days; even the thought of eating made him feel ill. He also knew that it was not only his appetite that had diminished; it was his interest in his wife and children. He remembered with guilt when Ruth had told him last week that Lewis had smiled for the first time, and he had made no reaction whatsoever. His baby was now smiling and cooing, and he had seen none of it, but even more disgraceful he couldn't remember the last time he had kissed and cuddled not only Lewis, but Tyler or Abbey. He couldn't recall the last time he had watched Tyler play football, ask him the score or discussed a game with him.

He was now arguing with Ruth constantly, and when they weren't arguing they were ignoring each other. He knew he was moody, irritable and tired, but most of all he was scared.

When Ruth had told him of the visit last night he had felt physically sick. He knew that she hadn't believed him when he told her that they were calling of behalf of a supplier. Unfortunately, on the spur of the moment, he didn't have time to think of anything more plausible.

Would Barry harm him or his family because he was a month behind with a payment? Surely not.

"I understand," Charley said, bringing Joe out of his reverie. "I don't sleep too well myself these days, what with one thing and another, but I've found the answer."

"The answer to what?"

"Not sleeping," Charley answered, and proceeded to place his hand in his jacket pocket and pull out a box of tablets. "These little babies are my salvation," he announced waving the box in the air.

"What are they sleeping pills?"

"Sleeping pills, de-stressing pills, headache pills, happy pills, you name it, and they cure it!"

"Where did you get them from, your doctor?"

"No, don't bother with them quacks. A mate of mine can get any tablets you want, at a fair price of course," Charley replied, and added. "You definitely look as though you could do with something Joe."

"Well as I said, I'm not sleeping too well."

Charley threw the box for Joe to catch. "Try these, if they do you any good, I'll get you more."

Joe missed the catch, so bent down to retrieve the box from the floor. He glanced at the packet as he stood up. "Err...no, that's all right Charley."

"Try them, if they're no good you've not lost anything."

Slightly hesitating Joe replied. "All right, thanks. How much do I owe you?"

"You can have those on the house Joey boy. Just let me know if you want any more. You've got my mobile number haven't you?"

Joe reached for his mobile phone to check for Charley's number. "Does in end in 8247?"

"Yes, that's the one."

"Thanks Charley, very much appreciated."

"That's all right Joe," Charley answered as he made his way to Joe's office door. "Nice to see you again, and don't forget that those babies are just a phone call away if you need anymore," he continued as he pointed to the tablets in Joe's hand.

Once Charley had left the office, Joe read the instructions on the box, poured a glass of water, took two tablets from the packet and swallowed them.

He hoped and prayed that 'those babies' as Charley had called them would accomplish everything he had said they would.

Chapter 8

Ruth did not sleep well that night either, her thoughts constantly returned to the two threatening men who had violated her doorstep. She did not believe Joe when he had told her they were from a supplier. Who were those men, and what did they want Joe for?

As Joe normally left the house at six-thirty for work every morning, Ruth had deliberately set her alarm for six forty-five to avoid him. She must have fallen into a deep sleep at some point because it was with surprise that she woke the following morning and noticed that her bedside clock stated it was seven-thirty.

She jumped out of bed with the realisation that they had to leave for school in an hour, but also remembered, with irritation, that she had a dentist appointment booked for nine-fifteen.

She quickly roused the children and ushered Tyler into the family bathroom and Abbey into her en-suite, while she ran downstairs to organise breakfast, make the children's packed lunch, and to prepare a feed for Lewis.

On entering the kitchen the first thing she noticed was a note propped up on the toaster from Joe. It asked her to take his navy pin striped suit to the dry cleaners for him. An injurious pang hit her as she realised that their main source of communication these days were either texts or notes left in the kitchen.

While the children ate a rushed breakfast of cereals and toast, she fed Lewis, and hurried upstairs to have a shower and dress.

On her return to the kitchen she heard Tyler and Abbey in the lounge, so she shouted instructions for them to make sure that they had packed their school bags properly, when Tyler ran into the kitchen with a letter in his hand.

As her son approach, she noticed how tall he was getting. He had always been on the small side compared to other children of his age, and his blond, curtain style haircut, surrounded a face that was so like Joe's that it sometimes unnerved her.

"Sorry mum, I should have given you this last week."

"Oh Tyler!" she exclaimed as she read the letter. "It says you're booked on a school trip to the Science Museum in London today, and there's a list of things you need."

"I forgot all about it," he whined.

She quickly read the list of items needed; a pen and paper; a packed lunch; three pounds to buy a souvenir (optional), and good walking shoes. "Quick Tyler," she said with urgency sounding in her voice. "Run up to your bedroom and get a pen and pad, and change into your new trainers as they will be more comfortable." When Tyler made no effort to move she shouted, "Now Tyler, the coach leaves at nine-twenty, and if we hang around any longer you'll miss it."

When Tyler eventually ran upstairs to obey her order, she placed three pound coins in Tyler's bag, gathered Lewis in her arms, picked up the baby bag, her handbag and called instructions for Abbey to put her coat, scarf and gloves on. Hurrying from the kitchen she made her way to the hall table to pick up her car keys, but to her surprise they weren't there.

"Abbey, have you seen my keys? Abbey!"

"What keys?" asked the independent eight-year old, as she nonchalantly entered the hall; her long blond hair platted either side of her pretty porcelain skinned face.

"My car keys, you know the ones that are always on the hall table," Ruth answered as rational as was possible.

"No."

"Tyler," Ruth now shouted up the stairs. "Have you seen my car keys?"

"No, mum," he answered as he ran down the stairs, pulling on his coat. He picked up his bag and threw it over his shoulder.

She frantically ran into the lounge, kitchen, and dining-room checking all surfaces, floors and ledges, but to no avail.

"Come on mum I'm going to miss the coach," shouted Tyler from the hall.

"I'm looking for the car keys Tyler," she shouted back. "Maybe you could help, instead of standing there shouting at me." She scanned the lounge again, and investigated a shiny item that she suddenly noticed tucked down the side of the sofa. It was with relief that she quickly retrieved her car keys from their mysterious hiding place.

She dropped Abbey off first knowing, with certainty, that her daughter had missed the morning registration. The children were never late for school and although Ruth realised that Abbey was upset, she also knew that her daughter would cope well with the situation.

Five minutes later, as they pulled up outside Tyler's school, Ruth noticed, to her relief, that the children hadn't yet started to board the coach.

"I'll be fine mum," Tyler said as he hurried out of the car, "I'll go and find Mr Picker and explain why I'm late, and don't forget that I'll be home late as we still have football practice tonight after school. Bye mum see you later."

"Bye Tyler, enjoy your day and your three pound is in your bag."

Ruth watched her son as he ran in search of his form tutor, and again revelled in her son's independent nature. Had that derived from being a surviving twin? Would he have been a needier child if his brother had survived?

She decided to wait and watch Tyler board the coach, but as she glanced at her watch she realised that she was already ten minutes late for her dentist appointment. She quickly put the car into gear and made her way to the dentist.

Ten minutes later, after parking the car, she placed Lewis in his pushchair, and ran into the dentist surgery.

"My name is Mrs Cannon," she declared to the receptionist, and slightly out of breath she continued. "Sorry I'm late, but I had an appointment at nine fifteen."

"I'm sorry Mrs Cannon, but you've missed your appointment and the dentist is unable to see you now."

"Please." Ruth begged. "I know I'm twenty minutes late, but I really need to see the dentist. I've got a crack in my tooth. I've already apologised for being late, and let's be honest we both know that if I'd been on time I would still be sitting here waiting for him."

"Are you in pain?"

"Well...no...but I do need it looked at."

"I'm sorry Mrs Cannon," said the receptionist sympathetically, "but I don't make the rules. We only allow a certain time-frame for being late for an appointment, and you are well out of that time. You will also be required to make a late payment fee of twenty pounds."

"A late payment fee of twenty pounds!" Ruth reiterated. She now felt anger rising within her. "Be honest," she said, as she tried to calm herself. "Was the dentist actually sitting there waiting for me, or is he still with the patient that had the appointment before mine?"

"Mrs Cannon, as I just explained I don't make the rules. All I can suggest is that you write in explaining the circumstances why you were late, and ask for a refund."

"Write a letter! My life is in enough turmoil at this moment without worrying about writing a bloody letter, over a bloody dentist appointment." Although tears of anger and frustration were building, Ruth unzipped her handbag and retrieved a twenty pound note from her purse and, completely out of character, slapped it on the reception desk. Without another word she took hold of the pushchair, and turned to march out.

"Please wait for your receipt Mrs Cannon," the receptionist called after her.

With a sigh, Ruth returned to the reception desk, took the receipt from the receptionist, slightly nodded her head in thanks and left the waiting room.

Returning to her car, and still angry, Ruth unlocked the door and took Lewis out of his pushchair and placed him in his car seat. As she folded the pushchair to place it in the boot the anger suddenly left her. She slid into the driver's seat and turned on the ignition, but instead of starting the car she rested her head on the steering wheel. As she did so she pressed the car horn by mistake, this made her jump and Lewis cry.

The tears that had gradually built up during the course of the morning now cascaded down her face as she tried to pacify Lewis. A few minutes later, after she had calmed him and had gained some self-control, she began to pull out of the car park when she remembered that she had forgotten to take Joe's suit out of his wardrobe for cleaning. A minor incident in her day-to-day life had suddenly turned into a catastrophe and the tears, once again, flowed. Her crying quickly turned into sobs, as she again wondered why her once content and carefree life, had mutated into turmoil. Only Joe had the answer to that question, but unfortunately, the approachable, caring, happy-go-lucky Joe that she had married had changed into a different person, and one she hardly recognised.

Chapter 9

Stella realised at an early age that being greedy, materialistic, spiteful, revengeful and downright evil had given her an advantage in life. She understood her traits, and always put them to good use.

She took revenge for her unattractiveness out on Ruth, her prettier younger sister who, Stella always thought of as gullible. It didn't matter how many times Stella upset her sister; Ruth always forgave her, and if she didn't, Stella would make such a fuss until she did. Nice, friendly people, according to Stella's philosophy, didn't achieve anything worthwhile in this life.

Stella often reminisced, with glee, the time that Ruth's hamster, Errol, went missing. Stella had been fifteen years old, and Ruth fourteen. Errol was Ruth's pride and joy, and she cared for him as if she would have a dog or cat. To Stella, Errol was not a hamster but a revolting rat, and couldn't understand her sister's affection towards it. It actually made Stella feel physically sick to watch Ruth let the rodent run over her hands, arms, even her stomach and legs.

On the day Errol disappeared Ruth had been frantic. She had cleaned his cage in the morning, before school, and couldn't understand how he had escaped, when she had always been so meticulous when locking him in.

On that particular morning Stella had suffered an upset stomach, and had been unable to attend school. Her mother had been due to work a couple of hours that afternoon, but had voiced her concerns about leaving Stella on her own. Stella had reassured her mother that she was well enough to leave, and had relished in the freedom it entailed.

Later that afternoon her mother returned home just before Ruth who, as normal, went straight up to her bedroom to greet Errol. When an almighty shriek shook the house, her mother dashed up the stairs to investigate, while Stella remained in the lounge watching the television.

Ruth had been distraught as she searched the house, and once she realised that Errol had gone further afield, Ruth, her mother, and even the next door neighbour searched the outside area, but to no avail.

Stella did not offer to help in the search; it was pointless. Errol would not be found. The manhole had been backbreaking to budge, but it had been worth it. Errol would now be fighting for his life in a sewer where he belonged, and where all the other rodents hung out.

Stella also recalled the times when she would sneak into Ruth's bedroom and rifle through her belongings. She would break hair-clips, steal jewellery and make-up, and use her sister's creams and lotions. Ruth would constantly accuse her of the callous acts, but she would, indignantly, always deny the allegations.

To Stella, the fierce competitiveness between her and her sister, as children, had all been Ruth's fault. Stella could still hear the remarks made by family and friends' commenting on Ruth's dancing abilities, and her beauty. Stella had physically cringed when she had heard remarks such as: *'She's a natural dancer; It'll be a disaster if she's never discovered'; she'll break a few hearts when she gets older; she's a beauty that one.'* The only comments Stella had ever heard about herself, had been very unflattering, and usually in whisper form.

When at the age of eighteen Stella met Frank Sinclair, she thought he was the most boring man she had ever known, but soon realised that he found her fascinating. Although he was only two years older than Stella, she had learnt that he had significantly advanced in his banking career, which was useful to know. He was also a generous man, who bought her more gifts than any other man she had known, without wanting services in return.

Stella had always found younger men far too immature, who never understood a woman's wants or needs. Frank was no different, and although she had intended to keep her stock pile of men, she had also decided, in the early stages of their relationship, that she would marry Frank for security.

Stella always chose her men, in the past and today, very carefully. Of course looks and personality come into the equation, but she was more interested in what they could offer. She would often look through her 'little black book' with pride while she studied names against their occupation or side-line. None of her flock ever complained when she asked them to supply goods or a service, as they knew that the payment for their assistance would be extremely satisfactory.

When Stella had discovered she was pregnant, although not surprised, she had no idea who the father was, and had no intention of any tests being carried out to expose the true identity. Everyone, including Frank, assumed that he was the father and they married two months later.

Stella's hatred for Ruth intensified as the years passed. It was an emotion Stella had no control over, but to her satisfaction it was a passion that she thoroughly enjoyed.

Stella remembered vividly the day that Tyler had been born, a month before the due date; she had never experienced such a fuss! Anyone would have thought that Ruth had been the first woman ever to have given birth to twins. Their mother had run around as if the end of the world was about to take place, not the fact that two scrawny babies had been born, albeit one had died.

It wasn't as if they hadn't been told and, of course, they still had Tyler. Would things have been any different if it had been Tyler who had died instead of Bradley? Stella doubted it, because Ruth and Joe knew that the boys had been identical. Stella repeatedly thanked her lucky stars that both boys hadn't survived.

Where was the fuss when Jonathon had been born four months later? Of course her mother had shown excitement, but nowhere to the degree of when Tyler had arrived. It also annoyed Stella that Tyler was the first to accomplish each milestone. He had smiled first, crawled first, walked first and talked first. She would always point out that it was only natural as Tyler was four months older than Jonathon, but her mother would always insist that Tyler was an extremely forward child. She was in no doubt that her mother favoured Tyler over Jonathon, and although her mother categorically denied it, nothing would convince Stella otherwise.

When the boys were younger, Ruth had often accused Stella of turning their playtime together into a competition sideshow. Jonathon, being much bigger of the two, and encouraged by his mother, would try to push Tyler over whenever possible, and to brutally punch and pinch him. Stella had tried to explain to Ruth that healthy competition between them was natural, but Ruth was adamant that the unhealthy competition that her sister had created was downright dangerous, not only physically but emotionally, and had refused to let Tyler take part.

Tyler was the sporty grandchild in the family, and his love of football was often the topic of conversation when the family got together. He not only played for a local team, but was also his school's star player and captain of the team. Ruth's parents watched as many of his games that they were able to attend and praised him non-stop, which infuriated Stella immensely.

Stella wouldn't have minded so much if it had been Abbey that her mother favoured, but she was not prepared to sit and watch her sister's blue-eyed boy being favoured over her son. She made notes in her diary of all the occasions where her mother favoured Tyler over Jonathon, and had every intention of using this ammunition one day.

***

It was the day after she had argued with Ruth over the red dress that Stella sat on her bedroom window seat reading. She had over an hour before Jonathon was due home from school, and Frank had phoned earlier to inform her that he had a meeting after work, and couldn't give her an exact time when he would be home.

When Frank had originally suggested installing a window seat in their bedroom, ten years earlier, Stella had rejected his idea. She had thought that window seats were unfashionable and tacky, but when, by co-incidence, she had seen an article in a magazine a few months later, saying that window seats were now fashionable with celebrities in Hollywood she immediately changed her mind.

Upon recommendation of an acquaintance, Stella had employed the services of an interior designer, and had insisted on being involved with every step of its construction. Within four weeks they had produced the most beautiful window seat that Stella could have ever imagined and Frank, horrified at the cost, had mumbled to himself that it wouldn't look out of place in any royal household, and had deeply regretted suggesting the idea of a window seat.

Over the years, Stella had taken outright control of all the household decorating, and the only room that she had no control over was Frank's office. Frank had stated on the day that they had moved into the house that the small fourth bedroom would be converted into his office, and that no one would be allowed entrance without his permission. Stella had never entered the room since the day of completion, and had no interest in doing so.

Stella had employed her first cleaner many years ago, and after many hires and fires had recently found Marjorie who, she was ecstatic to discover, had standards as high as her own. Although Frank did allow her in his office to clean, he was not too impressed with her as she constantly moved everything around.

Stella enjoyed time reading, and would normally transport herself into the world of her historical romance book that she loved to read, but not today. Her thoughts kept returning to the quarrel she had with her sister yesterday.

How dare Ruth accuse her of buying that gorgeous red dress out of spite. She had heard the shop assistant state that they didn't have the dress in Ruth's size, although the assistant had advised her to try next week, Ruth had not explicitly stated that she would return to the shop, and if she did, Stella had not heard her. The fuss! After all, it's only a dress; albeit the most beautiful dress she has ever owned, but how dare Ruth call her malicious.

Ruth, Ruth, Ruth how that name grated on Stella. When Ruth had first introduced Joe to the family, Stella had taken an instant dislike to him. He was an arrogant, cocky man, who in her eyes, had never changed.

Even though Stella had despised Joe at first sight, her wish was that her sister would marry him. She hoped Ruth would have a terrible life with him because he was an upstart going nowhere, so she had encouraged her sister all she could, and had shown genuine excitement when they had announced their marriage. Stella knew that Joe would be her sister's downfall, and still believed that to this day.

Her mother and father had, without realising, helped her mission. They adored the fun-loving, handsome, man who their daughter had brought home for them to meet, and accepted him into the family with open arms.

Frustration had overwhelmed Stella when Ruth had announced her first pregnancy, being the eldest she had desperately wanted to have a baby before her sister. When, three months later Stella discovered that she was pregnant she had decided to make a grand announcement at her mother's house, only to discover on her arrival that Ruth had already broadcast that she was expecting twins.

Her parents were fond of Frank, of that she had no doubt, but she knew that they found him somewhat dull. Although he was the most boring person she knew, Frank was the business man in the family. He had worked for the same bank for twenty years, and she knew, without a doubt, that Joe would never have survived in that environment.

Stella laughed when she thought of Joe, the so-called prosperous business man, sitting in a poky little warehouse selling junk. A man, she had heard, who was never at home these days. Although Ruth had not divulged any information, Stella had her own means of finding out what was happening in the life of Joe Cannon.

How she disliked her stuck-up sister, and big-headed brother-in-law, they needed bringing down a peg or two, and she had every intention of carrying out that task.

When Stella heard the key in the door she glanced at her watch and, surprised at the time, realised that her boy was home from school. She sprang up from the window seat and hurried down the stairs to greet him.

The boy standing at the foot of the stairs taking his coat off was her world. He was a big lad for his twelve years both in height and weight, with a light-brown, slightly curled mop of hair that framed a freckled face. Although plump, the focus of his face, which he inherited from his mother, was his ice-cold, blue eyes that emitted no warmth or sincerity. He was a lazy, slovenly boy who expected everything done for him, which his mother did to the full.

"Hi Jonathon, how was school?" Stella greeted her son.

"Same old," he muttered.

"Please don't talk like that Jonathon, I suppose you've been playing with Tyler again."

"We don't play mum, we hang around. Are you saying I can't hang around with my cousin now?"

"Of course you can darling, but I just don't want you picking up his awful sayings."

"Give me a break mum."

"Please Jonathon, watch your manners," Stella berated, and made a mental note to have a word with Ruth about the influence Tyler was having on Jonathon.

"Do you have homework tonight darling?"

"Yes. I was going to ask if Tyler could come round tonight, so we can do our homework together."

"Not tonight sweetheart, I think he has to go out with Auntie Ruth this evening," she lied.

Stella disliked Tyler with a vengeance and didn't like him anywhere near her or her son. She was always being called to the school over accusations of Jonathon being a bully. Jonathon had told her many stories of Tyler's antics at school, so why hadn't Ruth ever been made accountable for her son's actions.

And now there was another Cannon boy to deal with in the future, who will probably grow up a replica of his brother. Why they had gone ahead and had Lewis she would never fathom out.

"Tyler didn't mention anything about going out with his mum," Jonathon said indignantly.

"Well, he doesn't have to tell you everything he does darling, now go and get changed out of your uniform while I start your tea."

'Yes he does', thought Jonathon quite irritably. "Mum........."

"Yes, what is it Jonathon?"

"Has Auntie Ruth.........Oh, it doesn't matter."

"Jonathon what is it?"

"Well it's just that........"

"Jonathon, if there's a problem with Auntie Ruth you must let me know, I may be able to help in some way."

"Well, it's just that Tyler said that his mum and dad have been arguing quite a lot lately, and he and Abbey are both really upset about it."

Stella's face brightened at hearing this news, but had to mask it quickly. "Yes I know," she lied again to her son, but there's nothing to worry about."

"Please don't say I told you, as I promised Tyler I wouldn't say anything."

"Of course not darling, your secret is safe with me. Now go up to your room and get changed."

As they both turned in different directions, the smirks on their faces were identical.

Chapter 10

Jonathon, a replica of his mother, also realised long before his twelfth year that being spiteful, greedy and downright obnoxious gave him an advantage in life. As he had no conscience, he constantly manipulated people for his needs. This included his mother, father, Tyler, grandparents, friends, and to some extent Abbey. Although she was harder to control than her brother, he admired her feistiness and often tried to bring her on his side, but without success.

A wave of annoyance had swept over Jonathon when his mother had stated that Tyler couldn't come round to help him with his homework. Tyler hadn't mentioned anything about going out, and Jonathon had explicitly told that idiot of a cousin that his science homework was due in first thing tomorrow morning. What was he going to do now? He didn't have the answer to that question, but did know that he'd make that cousin of his suffer.

Jonathon knew his mother was blinkered, and in her eyes he could do no wrong. When, a few months ago, she had questioned him about the smell of smoke on his clothes, he had convinced her it was his friends that smoked, and that he never would. Tyler would never dare tell on him as he knew his life wouldn't be worth living.

Jonathon was a bully, and when he was among his friends he had the foulest mouth of them all. He was aware that people disliked him, but this was of no concern of his.

He always thought of his father as a 'weakling' who had no gumption, and Jonathon could never remember a time when his father had stood up to his mother. It pleased Jonathon to see his father cringe when his mother berated him, and it was common knowledge that his mother, not only ruled the house, but their lives as well, and Jonathon was more than happy to go along with this while it suited him.

He always thanked his lucky stars that he didn't have any siblings to deal with. He knew how much his mother hated her sister, as he had often heard his mother run her down to whoever was on the other end of the telephone line. She of course thought he was in his bedroom, when in fact he was hiding, listening to all she said. He also realised that most of what his mother said about her sister wasn't true. Although he knew his Aunt Ruth disliked him, he had always admired her in the same way he did Abbey.

He also enjoyed lying to his mother about Tyler. He loved to see her face light up when he told her about his bullying ways, and his disobedient antics at school, especially when Jonathon recalled how much he and his friends torment Tyler for being such a teacher's pet. Jonathon saw his cousin as a feeble and frightened halfwit, who was the easiest of them all to control. Tyler was his gofer. Whatever Jonathon wanted Tyler would get or carry out for him, and that included homework, any alibi he may need, and of course the most important thing; money. Jonathon wasn't bothered where it came from, as long as it was available.

Jonathon wasn't frightened of anyone, especially his mother, and he would stay her beloved little boy as she was his saviour when he found himself in situations from which he had no escape.

***

Frank was unhappy at home. He no longer loved his wife, and, with a heavy heart, accepted that his son was a cheating, lying, deceitful boy. He had tried many times to convince Stella of their son's depraved disposition, but to no avail. Jonathon was Stella's life, and Frank often looked at the boy to try to see something of himself in him, but he couldn't. He now found himself wondering if Jonathon was actually his, and knowing of Stella's past and current activities, he fully intended to find out.

He had loved Stella in the beginning, but that love had faded over the years. He had realised in the early stages of their relationship that Stella was a manipulative, cunning and selfish person, but he had looked past these traits because he had loved her. Or had it been infatuation?

Even after all their years of marriage, Frank was still confused with regard to his wife's many facades. She was the devoted mother to Jonathon; bitch of a wife to him; vindictive, malicious sister to Ruth; dedicated daughter to her mother and father, and fun-loving, carefree, generous woman to her acquaintances. Stella would be the first to admit that she had acquaintances and not friends; she had neither the need, or time for them.

Stella's main aim in life, apart from being better than anyone else, was to spite her sister. Frank had never understood the issues between the two women, but knew that all the disputes and rivalry were Stella's doing.

Elaine had been his saviour; his beautiful Elaine. For over five years he had loved and adored her, and although they thoroughly enjoyed their time together, Elaine had made it clear, from the beginning of their relationship, that because she had a severely disabled child she would never leave her husband. Frank accepted this, and never put any pressure on her.

They first met when they had both jostled for the last table in a busy coffee shop in the West End of London. Although Frank had arrived at the table just seconds before Elaine, he had insisted that she occupy it when he noticed the amount of shopping bags she was carrying.

When Elaine had suggested that they share the table, Frank, although normally a very private person, readily agreed. The conversation between them started sketchy and shy, but quickly began to flow, and Frank soon realised that he had never divulged so much information about himself to anyone as much as he had that day to Elaine. She in turn told Frank about her loveless marriage, and her one year old disabled daughter, Cassie, who would always be her main concern. A wonderful love affair grew from that day, and they spent as much time as was physically possible together, and both enjoyed every minute of it.

Although not a sporting man, golf was Frank's other saviour. It gave him the chance to relax, and be away from his wife and son. He had played golf with Joe on a couple of occasions, and although Frank was loath to admit it, he was jealous of his brother-in-law. Joe had the life that Frank craved. He often wondered how different his life would have been if he had met Elaine instead of Stella. Would his life have been similar to Joe's? Would he have had a beautiful wife, adorable children, a happy home and maybe even a job that he enjoyed and was proud of?

Ruth, like Elaine, was a natural beauty, with a great personality. Stella was a plain woman, with a malicious personality, but with the ability to turn an ugly duckling into a beautiful swan.

Tyler, Abbey and Lewis were children to be proud of. Jonathon was a miniature of his mother; a bully and a cheat. Joe's home was exactly that; a home. Not the cold, unloving, show home that he had to endure.

As a financial adviser with a bank in the City of London Frank received a good wage, but detested his job. Although he gave advice to friends and family, he had often considered starting up his own financial advice service, but Stella had been against the idea, and even refused to discuss the subject; greed obviously being her reason.

He was also aware that she regularly stashed money away in her secret bank accounts, but Frank was about to put a stop to that. What Stella didn't know was that Frank was embarking on a change of career, which would dramatically change their lifestyle.

With regard to Stella's pastime activities, he had many years ago, questioned her on the subject and she had categorically denied it. He now didn't care, they had no married life or physical contact together, and of late he wondered why he had stayed with her. He was a plodder, always had been, but although that was about to change it was to his advantage only.

Chapter 11

Ruth had just finished giving Lewis his mid-morning drink when the sound of the doorbell startled her.

She placed Lewis in his chair, and strapped him in as the unwanted guests of two nights ago immediately entered her head. She decided not to open the door until she knew the identity of her visitor, so cautiously she walked to the lounge window where she had a good view of the front of the house.

It was with overwhelming relief that she saw her friend, of many years, waiting on the doorstep.

"Gill," she exclaimed, as she hurriedly opened the door to greet her.

"Why are you so surprised to see me after our telephone call this morning?" Gill said as she kissed her friend on the cheek and entered the hallway.

"Oh, you know me, forever the drama queen," said Ruth.

"No Ruth, you're not a drama queen, and that's why I'm here," stated Gill.

"Go into the kitchen, Lewis is in the lounge and I'm just going to put him in his cot for a nap," Ruth said, and added. "Put the kettle on."

Gill had rung Ruth earlier that morning, and had worried when she heard about Ruth's recent visitors, and the worsening situation with Joe. The anguish in Ruth's voice was evident, so it was without hesitation that she decided to call on her friend.

Ruth and Gill had met in the first year at secondary school, and had remained friends ever since. They listened to each other's problems, celebrated success, and, more important, laughed together. Stella had tried, on many occasions, to destroy their friendship, but without success.

Gill had married Malcolm when she became pregnant at the age of seventeen. The pregnancy had gone well, but sadly their son, Thomas, had been born with a respiratory disease and had died just before he reached three months. Although devastated, they had remained together and were still happily married, but they never had another child.

"Thanks for coming over Gill," Ruth said as she entered the kitchen and sat at the table with her friend.

"Why didn't you ring me earlier to let me know that things have got worse?" asked Gill.

"I don't know. Some things you feel you have to deal with yourself." Ruth rose from her chair as she heard the kettle boil. "Tea or coffee?" she asked her friend.

"Tea please. You are so independent Ruth Cannon, I could scream at you sometimes."

Ruth laughed, and nodded her head in agreement as she poured the boiling water into the teapot.

She placed the teapot, a jug of milk, mugs and a plate of biscuits on a tray and took them to the table. "I just wish I knew what was wrong with Joe. He's moody, has no interest in the kids, especially Lewis, and he's started to stay at work longer than he's ever done.......Oh Gill," Ruth began to cry, "I could go on and on."

Gill took hold of her friend's hand to comfort her, and hesitated before she said. "I've got to be honest Ruth, Malcolm and I have noticed a change in Joe recently."

"But what do I do about it? We don't talk anymore, and the main reason for that is because he's never home. He's spending more and more time at work, and when he is at home he's up in his office. He's ratty with the children, and I don't think Lewis even recognises him as his father."

"Ruth, I don't like to say this...but...do you....."

"Think he's having an affair," Ruth interrupted. "Of course I've thought of that."

"Well, they do say the wife is the last to know."

"Thanks Gill. You're supposed to be my friend and helping me here," Ruth replied pulling her hand away from her friend.

"Sorry, sorry, but I had to say it."

"Yes I know," Ruth sighed, "and of course you're right to mention it, if you can't say it to me, who can?" Ruth said taking hold of her friend's hand again. "I don't know what to think anymore, sometimes I wonder if he's not well and frightened to say something to me," Ruth said as she released Gill's hand again to fetch a box of tissues from the worktop.

"Well, you can't carry on like this, it's not doing either of you any good," Gill exclaimed, and glancing around the kitchen continued. "I mean, look at what the two of you have built up here."

Ruth agreed with her friend, her and Joe had spent years working hard for all they had achieved. Although in the early years Joe's business had struggled, they had both persevered. Money had been scarce, but Ruth had always coped to feed and clothe the family on the little they had.

She smiled to herself as she thought of the fun they had together. They were not only man and wife, but friends. Good friends.

"Do you remember the day we moved here?" Ruth asked her friend, as she poured the tea and milk into the mugs.

"Remember," Gill laughed. "How could I forget? What could have gone wrong – did!"

"I can still see my mum's face when I went to pick the children up and told her all that had gone wrong," Ruth laughed as she began to count the disasters on her fingers. "The removal van was late. All the electrics in this house had fused. The water had to be turned off because there was a leak in the kitchen. We had an accident in the car as we followed the removal van, and to top it all, the removal men dropped and broke the crystal vase my mum bought us for our first wedding anniversary."

Both women were now laughing. "But you didn't let it get you down," said Gill. "You cope so well with things. I don't think you realise what a strong woman you are."

"I don't feel it at the moment," replied Ruth thinking of Joe again.

Seeing the forlorn look on her friend's face Gill suggested. "Why don't you give him an ultimatum?"

"What kind?"

"Tell him if he doesn't buck his ideas up he can pack his case, leave and come back when he's sorted his head out."

"No! I couldn't do that, anyway, it's not got to that stage yet."

"Just thought it might give him a kick up the backside, he obviously needs one."

"No, there's something wrong with him, I'm convinced of that. You know him Gill, and the Joe I live with at the moment, is not the Joe we both know."

"Have you told Stella about your problems?" Gill asked sheepishly.

"No! She'd be in her glory. I wouldn't be able to stomach the smug look on her face, if she found out that we had problems. I know how much she dislikes Joe, but then Joe's not that keen on her, but thinking about it, who is?" she laughed.

"Let's be honest, she doesn't like Frank that much either," Gill laughed, and on a more serious note continued. "It's such a shame that you two don't get on,

I know I don't get on with her, but then she's not my sister."

"Aren't you the lucky one! Do you know what she's done now? I'm not giving any prizes for guessing though," Ruth said jokingly as she pointed her finger at Gill. "Very foolishly, I told her I was buying mum an e-book reader for her birthday. Not only did I research into which one would be best for her, I even told Stella which one I was buying! How stupid am I?"

Gill gasped. "She didn't go and buy her one?"

"Oh yes she did," Ruth replied in a sing-song voice. "But, not only did she buy the one I mentioned, she gave it to mum before her birthday, so she got in first. I'm furious with her, she swears black and blue she didn't know I intended to buy her one, but I know full well that I told her. We had a terrible row, and as usual I wound up apologising to her! Of course it didn't help when mum rung to tell me how thrilled she was with her present, and what a thoughtful daughter Stella was."

"She's unbelievable," Gill stated. "But you've enough going on without worrying about her antics."

"I know, but she's so infuriating. She's like a Jekyll and Hyde, one day she'll come across as the most caring sister anyone could wish for, the next she's the bitch from hell."

"But she's always been the same," Gill said. "Look at how many times she tried to cause trouble between us."

"Yes, but thankfully that's all stopped. I wouldn't say she's thick, but I think after all these years she's finally got the message that she would never come between us," Ruth laughed.

"When you think about it she's never had her own friends," Gill stated.

"No, she doesn't have friends, she has acquaintances. You have to commit yourself, even if only slightly to a friend, and Stella is not capable of that," Ruth stated and laughed as she continued. "But she's obviously run out of acquaintances, because she phoned me the other night to invite me out for an evening."

"You going?" asked Gill astonished.

"I started off by saying no, but came off the phone with all the arrangements made," Ruth said as she shook her head. "How does she do that? She cajoles you into doing something that you had no intention of doing, but the frightening thing is she's so clever at it you don't know she's doing it. I'm going to volunteer her brain to science if she dies before me," Ruth said quite seriously and added. "And as if it's not enough to put up with my sister, we now have Jonathon to contend with."

"Is he still as bad? I thought age might have helped him."

"Age!" exclaimed Ruth. "He gets worse with age, and is getting as devious as his mother. He's a cheat, a liar, a thief and above all, a bully. I hate Tyler and Abbey having anything to do with him, but there's not much I can do about that."

"Stella doesn't see him as a bully though," Gill stated.

"That boy can do no wrong in her eyes. She doesn't see him for the horrible kid he is. I was talking to one of the mums yesterday outside the school, and she's going to make an appointment to see the headmaster. She's convinced that Jonathon is not only bullying her son, but stealing his dinner money."

"Will you warn Stella?" asked Gill.

Ruth laughed. "You must be joking. She would accuse me of instigating the whole thing. She even had the cheek the other day to tell me that she thinks Jonathon is being bullied at school. That boy knows he could be in big trouble, and is covering his back already," Ruth said. "Believe me when I tell you, that boy is evil, and I'd worry if he was mine. Did I tell you about the purse incident last week?"

"No," replied Gill shaking her head.

"Jonathon had a friend round for tea after school. Stella says it helps them to do their homework together." Ruth now laughed. "Homework together, more like the boy will be doing Jonathon's homework for him. I know he gets Tyler to do his homework, and that's something I've to sort out with Stella. Anyway, later that evening Stella noticed that she had a ten pound note missing from her purse. Her very words were *'my Jonathon would never, ever take money from my purse, so it must be his friend'*. Jonathon, conveniently, had told her that he had seen his friend go into the kitchen for a drink just before the boy's mum came to collect him. The following morning she went straight to the school and demanded that the headmaster call the mother to the school or she would involve the police."

"What happened?"

"It's still an ongoing investigation and both boys have to make a statement. I know what will happen, Jonathon will bully that poor boy into confessing." Ruth laughed as she continued. "When he was a toddler I used to look for the six, six, six symbol on him, I'm sure it's there somewhere. Either that, or horns will eventually grow out of his head."

Both the women now laughed as Ruth rose from the table to re-fill the kettle for another hot drink.

"It's good to see you laughing," Gill said.

"Yes, but it's not really a laughing matter is it, when you hate your own nephew. It's Frank I feel sorry for, having to put up with Stella and Jonathon."

"I wonder what that poor sod did in a previous life to deserve them two," Gill said.

"I don't know, but it must have been something horrendous," Ruth laughed.

When Ruth returned to the table, Gill said. "Changing the subject back to Joe, I was wondering if you'd like me to have a word with him. I don't mean ask him outright what's wrong, but maybe tell him I'm a bit worried about you." Gill hesitated before she continued. "I've got to be honest Ruth you do look a little washed out so I wouldn't be lying to him."

"No, but thanks anyway Gill. We'll sort it out, I'm sure."

As Ruth said these words, both women knew that she had not said them with the conviction required to carry it through.

Chapter 12

Ruth had stood outside the busy underground station for at least fifteen minutes waiting for Stella to arrive. Although annoyed, Ruth was not surprised. Her sister never arrived early or on time, for any meeting or appointment. Not because she wasn't dressed or ready in time, but because being late was one of her little pleasures; to deliberately keep people waiting. She was probably still at home slowly sipping a glass of chilled, white wine knowing full well that Ruth was already at the arranged meeting place waiting for her.

When Ruth eventually saw Stella propelling her way through the crowd, anger crept over her, and all thoughts of lateness disappeared. As her sister approached, Ruth demanded. "Why are you all dressed up?"

"I'm not all dressed up," Stella rebuked.

"Not all dressed up! I'm sorry Stella," Ruth reprimanded as she scrutinised her sister's outfit. "But an off the shoulder, figure hugging black dress, stiletto heels, that a stilt walker would be proud of, and your hair all piled high on top of your head, in my books, is all dressed up!"

"Well, I know I said to wear jeans, and of course I was going to, but I had a good clear out of my wardrobe the other day, and when I began to get dressed earlier I realised that my one and only decent pair of jeans were in the wash."

"Oh come on Stella, for a start you could never survive with only one good pair of jeans, and you decide what you're going to wear, for any occasion, at least a week before the event."

"What are you saying Ruth that I told you to dress in jeans on purpose? Why would I do that?"

"I don't know, but..."

"Ruth, what is the matter with you these days, you are so jumpy and irritable. Tyler was saying..."

"What do you mean Tyler was saying? When does my son talk to you?"

"See! This is what I mean, no one can say anything to you without you jumping down their throat."

Why did Stella say that? Ruth knew she had hid her unhappiness from the children, but she was also certain that she had never shown Stella any signs of her worries.

"And why you always think the worst of me I'll never know," Stella continued. "Of course we have our differences, what sisters don't, but you must know I would never do anything to hurt you in any way."

Ruth surveyed her sister, and apart from the fact that she could write a very long list of why she always thought the worst of her, she had to remember that they were out for the evening, and realised that fighting with Stella was futile. "All right, I'm sorry. Come on let's go and have a good time."

"That's the spirit," replied Stella as she hooked her arm through Ruth's.

Both sisters giggled as they made their way to the wine bar.

"Do you use this wine bar often?" Ruth asked as they approached the building.

"Err...not very often," Stella replied evasively.

Situated in a large building, Calyx Wine Bar was on the first floor, and Ruth followed Stella up the steep steps. Stella stepped inside and passed a heavily built bald man, but as Ruth approached him, he put his hand in front of her, palm facing, as in a halt sign. "Sorry Miss, no jeans allowed."

"But..."

Stella quickly turned round and practically pushed Ruth back down the stairs, "Go back down and wait."

"Stella!"

"Go back down and wait," Stella replied sternly.

Ruth, reluctantly, made her way back down the stairs, and as she reached the bottom she glanced up towards the door to see her sister deep in conversation with the doorman. What was there to discuss? She was wearing jeans, and wouldn't be allowed in the wine bar.

As she was about to call to Stella to suggest that they find somewhere else, her sister motioned for her to come back up.

"Come on Ruth, you can come in," Stella shouted, but when Ruth made no effort to move Stella called her again. "Come on Ruth, the wine's getting warm."

Hesitantly, she made her way back up the stairs, and passed the doorman who completely ignored her. Once inside she pulled Stella by the arm and demanded. "What was that all about?"

"What does it matter, you're in aren't you?"

"That's not the point. If you knew we were coming to this wine bar, why did you tell me to wear jeans? And what did you say to him? If you don't use this place that often how come you know him that well?"

"So many questions little sister. Does it really matter? Come on Ruth, let your hair down and enjoy yourself."

Ruth was about to question her sister again, but Stella noticed someone she recognised. Ruth felt her sister grab hold of her hand and pull her as she practically sprinted over to him.

"Hi Greg," she squealed as she let go of Ruth's hand.

"Hi Stella, good...good to see you again," he replied sheepishly.

"This is my sister Ruth."

He nodded his acknowledgement at Ruth, and turning his attention back to Stella asked. "Been here long?"

"No, just arrived, haven't even got a drink yet," Stella stated.

"Oh, can I get you one?"

"That's lovely of you Greg," Stella squealed. "Two dry white wines, please."

"Right...okay...be back in a moment."

When Greg turned to make his way to the bar Ruth pulled at Stella's arm. "Why did you let him buy us drinks? You almost pounced on him to say hello, and he looked so embarrassed!"

"Calm down Ruth. It's quite obvious you don't go out enough. We'll get our drinks from him, then go and find a table."

Why was Ruth so surprised at her sister's attitude? Stella was ruthless and possessed the power to control people, which she used to its full advantage.

As they waited for Greg to return with their drinks, Ruth took the opportunity to take in her surroundings. It was a relatively small bar, with crimson red leather, high-backed chairs placed round dark oak tables, with an artificial orchid in a crystal vase placed in the centre of each one. The seductive wall lighting gave it a cosy, relaxed feel, and it was just as Ruth was about to comment on this to Stella that a woman interrupted her.

"Hi Stella," she said as she passed them on her way to the bar.

"Oh, hi....," Stella replied as if unable to remember her name.

"Stella! Lovely to see you," shouted another as she waved from the other side of the bar.

Stella waved back and muttered to Ruth, "God, I can't remember any of their names."

"For someone who doesn't use this bar much, you're quite well-known," Ruth said sarcastically.

"You know me, charming, likeable Stella. By the way I meant to ask you, who's looking after the kids tonight?"

"Err...Mum."

"Where's Joe?"

"He's working late, but he'll be home fairly soon."

"I hear he's never at home these days."

Ruth was about to retort when Gregg approached with their drinks.

"Thanks Gregg," Stella said practically snatching the drinks from his hands. "We're going to find a table, come and join us later."

"Thanks Stella, will do," Gregg answered as Stella turned from him.

"Thanks for the drink, and I apologise for my sister," Ruth said before she followed Stella.

"Did you see the way he looked at you?" Stella said excitedly as they found a table that a couple had just vacated.

"What?"

"Greg, did you see the way he looked at you?"

"He didn't look at me in any way!"

"That's not what I saw," Stella answered defiantly.

"Stella, you didn't stay talking to him long enough to see him do anything, let alone look at me."

"Well, I think you're in there."

"In there! What are you talking about?"

"Oh come on Ruth, don't be naïve."

As Ruth was about to answer, Stella's hand shot in the air, waving and shouting. "Scott, Scott, come and join us."

A small, fair-haired man with bulging eyes and a turned-up nose approached their table.

"Hi Scottie," Stella said. "Why don't you buy us a drink, and then sit with us."

"Err..."

"Two dry, white wines please," Stella interrupted him.

As Scott turned to make his way to the bar, Stella rested her head against Ruth's and said. "He works for one of the biggest jewellers in London, and I'm hoping to get the most beautiful white gold diamond solitaire pendant I've ever seen. He says he can get it for me at a very good price. I just need to keep in with him."

"Stella, you are unbelievable, you just use people. Tell me, what does good old Gregg get for you? Work in Harrods does he?" Ruth asked sarcastically.

"No my darling sister, he works in a betting shop, and gives me very reliable tips, I've earned a fortune," Stella answered smugly as her eyes gazed at a man who had appeared behind Ruth. "Hello Mitchell," she said seductively. "I didn't think you were going to show up."

"What, miss seeing you," said a sultry voice as he came round to face them both. "Who's this?" he asked studying Ruth.

"This is my sister, Ruth."

Ruth just nodded her acknowledgement at the tall, dark-haired, masculine man standing before her.

You joining us?" asked Stella.

"Let me get a drink first."

As Ruth watched him walk away she asked Stella. "Not asking him for a drink?"

"Oh no my dear sister, I only use him for one thing, and that's definitely not buying me drinks," Stella said as she nudged Ruth laughing.

On impulse Ruth asked. "Why did you invite me out with you?"

"Do I need a reason?"

"Yes, especially when you knew I would see your other life, obviously the life that Frank or Jonathon know nothing about."

"Jonathon is my twelve-year-old son, so he has no need to know. Frank is my husband, and is not interested, just as I'm not interested in what he does. You must know that we lead separate lives."

"Well...yes, that's quite obvious, but I really don't understand it. If you're not happy with Frank then leave him."

"Leave him!" Stella shrieked. "What leave my lovely home, my lifestyle, the man who supports me and lets me do anything I want. You mad?"

"But why does he let you do what you want?"

"Because he doesn't love me anymore, and can't afford to leave me. He has quite a few assets, and he knows I'll take him to the cleaners, and he can't afford for me to do that."

As Scott approached the table with their drinks, Stella smiled sweetly at him and said. "Oh thanks for the drinks Scottie, but I have just seen someone who I have to talk to urgently and in private. You don't mind do you? I'll look for you later, and we can have a drink together."

"Err...no...that's fine. I'll see you later. I have some news about your jewellery."

"Oh brilliant Scott, definitely see you later then."

Ruth stared at her sister. How did she gain so much power and domination over people? What did she give them in return for their favours?

As Stella pushed a glass of wine towards her Ruth said. "I don't want it."

"Why not?"

"I'm not like you Stella. I can't just take things from people as if it's my right."

"Oh, do stop moralising Ruth, and just drink it."

Ruth quickly stood up, and pushed the glass towards her sister. "You drink it, I'm going home."

"For crying out loud Ruth, will you please just sit down, and drink your wine."

Ruth was about to tell Stella exactly what she thought of her, and her way of life when Mitchell returned to the table.

"Hello again, sorry I didn't ask you girls if you wanted another drink," he said as he pulled a chair out from the table and sat down.

The two sisters momentarily stared at each other before Stella spoke.

"She's leaving."

"Why?" asked Mitchell as he turned to look at Ruth.

"Because she's miserable and too old before her time," Stella answered.

"No, I'm not Stella. What I am is stupid. Stupid for thinking that my sister wanted to spend time with me, and even more stupid for forgetting what a manipulative, devious, sly, scheming person she is."

"Woe, hold on girls," Mitchell said holding his hands in front of him, palms forward as if in retreat. "Let's not have a scrap here. Come on Ruth sit back down, and drink your wine."

"No. I'm going," declared Ruth and walked away without glancing in Stella's direction.

"What was that all about?" asked Mitchell.

"Oh, take no notice of her," Stella answered flapping her hands in Ruth's direction as her sister practically ran to the exit. "She's a hypocritical, sanctimonious woman whose, so-called, prim and proper world is about to come crumbling down on her."

Chapter 13

Joe's life was in turmoil, and he now found home life arduous. He was unable to look Ruth in the face, and he found himself submerged into a guilt ridden, shameful depth of anguish. He couldn't remember the last time they had made love, and knew that he had turned his family and their lives upside down. It was months since, as a family, they had sat and talked or laughed together, or even had an evening meal.

As he found it so uncomfortable at home these days, he spent more time at his warehouse office than normal, and now tried to concentrate on the last of this month's invoicing that desperately needed processing. He opened the file that was in front of him, and without even glancing at the documents, he pulled open his desk drawer and removed the packet of tablets that Charley had given him. Taking four tablets from their individual sealed compartments, and although he was certain they were being of some help, he was aware that he was using more than the suggested dosage advised on the box.

As he was about to reach for the bottle of vodka, also in his desk drawer, a rustling sound at the door made him glance up. Joe could not believe his eyes when he saw her standing there.

"Hello," she said.

He would have recognised her voice anywhere. He studied the woman who had been his wife for five years, and who he had loved more than life itself.

"Karen!" he exclaimed. "What are you doing here? How long have you been back? How did you find me?"

"Wow, you training for the police force? So many questions," she said.

As he heard a slight giggle in her voice he shouted at her, "So many questions! My biggest question is how did you get pass by secretary?" Anger overwhelmed him as he snarled at her. "And don't you think I've a right to ask fucking questions, after what you did to me?"

"Yes of course Joe, I'm sorry. I told your secretary that I was your cousin, and I wanted to surprise you."

"So, you're still a liar then," he snarled and made a mental note to have a word with Laura not to let anyone through to his office without his knowledge, especially now that Barry was on the prowl for his blood.

Joe studied the woman standing at his office door. She was still beautiful, and the sixteen years that she had been out of his life had been kind to her. She had lost weight, although only a little, but enough for Joe to notice.

"What do you want?" Joe asked.

"I just wanted to say hello, and see how you are. I went back to our old haunt last week and met Jimmy Maloney. He gave me this address, and said to say hello to you."

"Did he," Joe said. He would call Jimmy later, how dare he give her this address without consulting him first. "Well, you've said what you wanted to say, and yes I'm wonderfully happy, so you can go now."

"I hear you have three children."

"Do you. Well you seem to know a lot more about me than I do about you. But to be honest I'm not interested in you, so why don't you and Pete fuck off from where you came from, and leave me in peace."

Joe noticed her advance slowly into his office as she said, "I'm not with Pete."

"Find someone else to run off with did you? Another best friend was it?"

"No," she laughed. "It didn't work out between us, and I left him. I know I really hurt him, but...he wasn't you." There was a pause before she continued. "I didn't mean to hurt you Joe."

"Well you did, but that was a long time ago, and naturally I've moved on. I'm now happily married and I want you to leave this office, shut the door behind you, and never come back." Turning his face away from her, he grabbed the vodka bottle from the desk drawer, and unscrewed the bottle top, and throwing all four tablets into his mouth he swallowed them with one gulp.

"How's Ruth?" asked Karen.

Joe began to choke on the liquid that gushed down his throat, and unable to speak, he watched Karen glide into the office and take the seat opposite him.

"Look Joe, I haven't come back to make trouble for you, I just need a little help."

"What help?" Joe asked as he gained control of his voice.

"I'm just a bit short of cash. All I've got to my name is an old banger of a car that is forever breaking down, and I used the last of my money to put a deposit on a flat, well it's a bedsit really, and by coincidence not far from where you live."

"How do you know where I live?" Joe asked anger sounding in his voice.

"I've done a little digging Joe, but you must believe me when I say I'm not here to cause trouble for you."

Joe didn't respond. How could he believe her, when she had destroyed his life all those years ago? Although the woman sitting before him appeared unchanged, there was no guarantee that he still knew her after all this time.

"Buy me a drink lunchtime, I just want to talk to you."

"No Karen, I have enough problems at the moment without adding you to them."

"What problems?"

Joe could hear the surprise in her voice. "That's none of your business, now just leave Karen."

"Could you lend me some money? It looks like you're doing quite well here."

"Well I'm not, so get back into the hole that you've just crawled out of."

When he noticed the tears trickle down her face, he slammed his fist on his desk and shouted. "Don't start all that crying lark with me, it won't work. It might have done in the past, but not now."

"Please Joe, you don't know how desperate I am, and you're my only hope."

"Well that's too bad, because your only hope has just vanished."

"Joe."

Although he could hear the pleading in her voice, he ignored her, and for effect, studied the invoices on his desk.

"Joe."

"You still here?" he enquired without glancing up at her.

"Joe!" she now shouted.

"What?" he shouted as he raised his head to look at her.

"Pete's dead."

"Dead!" he repeated, bewildered. "But you just said you left him."

"I did, please Joe give me a chance to explain."

Joe, feeling slightly disorientated, nodded his head.

"We stayed in France for about ten years, and then moved back to England and rented a flat up North. If I'm honest, I was never happy with Pete, and left him about five months ago. He stayed in the flat and I moved in with a friend..."

"That sounds about right," Joe interrupted.

"A female friend," she added. "Then two months later I received a telephone call from him telling me how unhappy he was, and practically begged me to try again.

We arranged to meet the following week to talk, but the day after the telephone call he had a heart attack and died."

"Christ," Joe replied, shocked at this news.

"I just thought you had a right to know, him being one of your best friends."

"Best friend!" exclaim Joe. "What kind of best friend runs off with his friend's wife?"

"Please Joe can't we try to put all that behind us? If not for our benefit, then for Pete's."

"Why have you decided to tell me now? Joe asked. "If you still regard me as his best friend why didn't you tell me when it happened? At least I could have gone to the funeral."

"I know, I should have told you then, but I couldn't."

"You couldn't tell..."

"Please Joe," she interrupted tears slowly running down her face. "You don't know how hard these past few months have been for me. I've had terrible arguments with everyone where Pete's concerned. His mum and brother, his friends, they all insisted I had no right to voice an opinion because I had hurt him so much. They wouldn't even let me attend the funeral, and his brother even threatened me, saying to watch my back if I was seen anywhere near."

Joe studied her as she paused and opened her handbag to remove a tissue to wipe her face.

Returning the tissue to her handbag and placing it on the floor beside her she continued. "I felt so humiliated, I know that Pete was not the love of my life, but I knew him better than most. I suppose I couldn't tell you about his death because for some reason I felt embarrassed."

"Is that embarrassed because you left me for him, or embarrassed because it didn't work out for you?"

"I don't know why. But what I do know is that I'm here now asking you to help me."

Joe had refused Karen's original request to have a lunchtime drink, but had relented after hearing the news of Pete's death. Karen had again expressed that the purpose for the drink was to talk, and had promised not to make any demands on him.

The Crossed Arms Tavern was in a side street, next to the industrial park, and on entering the pub, Joe and Karen made their way to the bar where Joe ordered their drinks. Although Joe did not frequent the pub often, and was certain he would not be recognised, he suggested that they find a table in the corner to enable them to talk privately.

Ironically, it was Joe that did most of the talking, and had managed to tell Karen all his problems. He knew he was wrong talking to his ex-wife and not Ruth, but he found it so easy to confide in Karen.

"Did you go to the police about this Andy?" she asked as he finished his story.

"No."

"Don't you think you should?"

"Yes of course I do, but I haven't told Ruth the full story yet. If I go to the police, then she will have to get involved, and I'm not ready for that."

"But she has a right to know what's happening Joe, especially if it goes the worst way and you have to sell the warehouse."

All of a sudden Joe felt tears well up in his eyes, and silently reprimanded himself. He glanced at Karen and realised that she had noticed.

"Come on Joe, don't upset yourself."

"Sorry," he said, and wiped the tears from his face with his hands.

"Don't apologise. You can cry in front of me, we have history and that counts for a lot."

Joe began to laugh as he said, "So if you came here to tap me for a few bob, you've got the wrong person."

"Oh, don't worry about that, I'll get by, I always do. It's you I'm worried about now, and I want to help in any way I can. Even if it's just a shoulder to cry on, I'll be there for you Joe."

Taking hold of her hand across the table Joe said. "Thanks Karen, I appreciate that."

Joe again studied Karen, and for the second time that day realised that she was still as beautiful as the day he had married her. Her auburn coloured, thick, soft textured hair, perfectly accompanied her pale, unblemished skin.

They had met in their last year at school when Karen had been new to the area. Although Joe had played the 'boy about town' character, he had loved Karen from the first time he had caught sight of her.

As Ted had been profusely dating Heather, Joe had spent time with another friend named Pete Boston. Fortunately, Pete and Karen got on well, and Joe was happy for the three of them to spend time together.

At the age of eighteen, Joe and Karen had rented a one bedroom flat together, and although friends and family all advised them that they were far too young, Joe thought his life was complete when they married a year later. They had often discussed having children, but both had decided to wait until they were, at least, in their late twenties.

Although Joe and Karen had a good relationship and a busy social life together, they also had separate interests. Joe had his sport and fishing, and Karen, a social worker by profession, had her keep-fit regime. She had been a keep-fit fanatic, and would spend her spare time either, running, attending aerobic classes or at the gym.

Joe had lived in absolute bliss for about five years during which time Pete had met and married a girl called Lindsey and had moved to Essex. Joe and Pete kept in touch, and Karen and Lindsey became relatively good friends.

Joe and Karen's birthdays had only been a couple of months apart, and because they hadn't celebrated their twenty-first birthdays in style, they had decided to go to the Maldives for their twenty-third, and as it was also Pete's twenty-third birthday the same year, they invited Pete and Lindsey to join them.

Although the holiday had been a success Joe and Karen had noticed Pete and Lindsey's constant arguing. So it was no surprise when Pete arrived on Joe and Karen's doorstep three months later saying that he and Lindsey had parted.

They had both agreed that Pete could stay with them for as long as he needed while he searched for alternative accommodation, but three months later, he was still living with them.

As Pete had also been a keep-fit enthusiast, Joe had become concerned about the amount of time that Karen and Pete spent together. Naturally, this had caused tensions to manifest between him and Pete, so Joe demanded that he leave.

Joe had questioned Karen, many times, on the developing relationship between her and Pete, and she had categorically denied any emotional involvement between them. When Joe came home from work one evening to find the flat practically empty of all Karen and Pete's clothes and personal belongings, it confirmed his deepest fear.

He later discovered that they had left England to live in the South of France and, until today, assumed they were still there.

Now Karen, sitting opposite him, had returned to England and Pete was dead. How many times had he wished them both dead? Countless times, especially in the days shortly after they had left.

"Ruth can't know you're back," Joe stated suddenly.

"I told you Joe, I'm not here to make any trouble for you." She hesitated before she spoke again. "What were the tablets you were taking in your office earlier Joe?"

"Headache tablets."

"That's not what it said on the packet?"

"Who are you, Sherlock Holmes or something?" he laughed.

"No, but I do know that those tablets are not good to take unless prescribed by a doctor, and if I know you Joe, you didn't go to the doctors."

"Karen, don't nag. You're not my wife anymore, remember?"

"Oh, I remember Joe, but I'm sure if Ruth knew you were taking them she would be worried."

"Leave Ruth out of this! It's none of your business," Joe said, anger sounding in his voice.

"Sorry, I don't mean to interfere," she answered meekly.

Joe stood up quickly and realised it had been a mistake to tell Karen all his problems. "I had better go," he said as he pulled his coat on.

"Can I see you again?" she asked.

"No," he said abruptly. "This was a one-off drink, and I'd appreciate it if you don't mention it to anyone."

"Of course Joe, if that's what you want."

"Yes it is," he said sharply, and with his tone softening added. "Thanks for listening Karen, I do appreciate it, but that's as far as it goes. Take care."

As he left her and walked towards the door he hoped and prayed that Karen wouldn't take this encounter any further, and that this would be the last that he saw of her.

Joe returned to work that afternoon with his mind in turmoil. He had enough problems to cope with, and now Karen had reappeared in his life. What a fool he'd been to divulge all his problems to her. Could he trust her? Would she use this information against him? Would she try to contact Ruth? He did not have an answer to any of these questions, or any of the others tormenting his mind.

Although Pete had hurt him, and Joe had not seen or thought of him for many years, the news of his death had still come as a shock. It did cross Joe's mind that if a similar fate happened to him, at this precise moment, it would solve all his problems.

He arrived home from work that evening at around seven-thirty. He glanced in the lounge and saw Tyler and Abbey were watching the television, so said hello to them but exchanged no other words.

He heard Lewis crying in the kitchen and when he entered he saw Ruth pacing up and down with Lewis in her arms trying to soothe him.

"He's been crying for over an hour now."

Joe knew he should go to Lewis, take him from Ruth and help try to soothe him, but he didn't; he couldn't. "He's probably just over tired," was all he suggested. "I'll be in my office, I've had to bring a lot of work home."

"Joe! Joe!" Ruth shouted as he left the room.

He completely ignored her and made his way up the stairs. As Lewis needed Ruth's attention, he wasn't surprised when he didn't hear her footsteps following him to engage in one of their many arguments; arguments that were entirely his fault because he knew that, single-handed, he was destroying their marriage.

On entering his office he immediately opened his briefcase and took out his tablets. He opened his desk drawer and retrieved a bottle of vodka, and put four tablets in his mouth and swallowed them with a mouthful of the spirit straight from the bottle.

How had his life come to this? What solutions did he have? Realising he couldn't answer any of these questions he continued to swig the vodka from the bottle and eventually fell, with his head on his desk, into a deep drunken sleep.

Chapter 14

Ruth woke the following morning feeling exhausted as she had not slept well. Apart from her anguish over Joe's behaviour, Lewis had also cried on and off all night and it was around four-thirty that she felt Joe fall into bed.

When Lewis had eventually fallen asleep yesterday evening, a couple of hours after Tyler and Abbey had gone to bed, she went up to Joe's office to check on him. Disgust and shock overwhelmed her to see him slouched on his desk, fast asleep, with an empty vodka bottle in his hand. She had tried to wake him, but without success, so left him there to sleep it off.

She realised that this masquerade they called a marriage could not continue, and decided, whilst in bed last night, to take Gill's advice and give Joe an ultimatum. He either confessed all that was troubling him, admit to any wrong doing, or he left.

She realised that the only place she could trap Joe, and insist that he talk to her, was at his warehouse office, and that was what she intended to do.

Unfortunately, all her plans changed when Lewis woke, earlier than usual, not only with a temperature but still crying. So instead of visiting Joe at the warehouse once the children were in school as intended, it was a visit to the doctor's surgery with Lewis instead. It was after an hours wait to see the doctor, that he diagnosed an ear infection and prescribed antibiotics.

Ruth eventually returned home to put a sleeping Lewis into his cot. As Ruth shut Lewis's bedroom door she heard her mobile phone ring, so hurrying down the stairs and into the kitchen to retrieve it, she noticed, with dread, that it was Stella's name showing on the screen. Her first thought was not to answer, but knew, through experience, that her sister would persist until spoken to. So it was with trepidation that she answered her phone.

"Hello Stella."

"Glad you're home, I'm popping round for a coffee."

Ruth, surprised at her sister's words, didn't immediately reply. As Stella never normally just 'popped' round, especially as she lived a good twenty-minute drive away, she obviously had a reason to visit. It was either a new purchase to gloat about, some gossip needed, or a favour wanted.

"Okay, see you in a while," Ruth eventually replied, and with her sister's voice still ringing in her ears she said goodbye, and placed her phone on the kitchen table.

Why hadn't she made an excuse? Told Stella that she was on her way out, that she had a dentist appointment, that an alien was on its way to abduct her, anything to get out of having a coffee with her, but she couldn't. She had never been able to treat her sister as her sister treated her.

Although the house was already clean and tidy, Ruth quickly swept the front doorstep, cleaned the kitchen sink and draining board and completely cleared the worktops, took the children's paraphernalia that was in a corner in the dining room up to their bedrooms, straightened and plumped up the cushions on the sofa in the lounge, and ensured that the downstairs toilet was spotless. Although Stella had a cleaner, and had rarely cleaned her own house personally, she always frowned on people who, in her opinion, did not keep their house scrupulously clean.

Stella's obsession with colour co-ordination in her home had always fascinated Ruth. Her lounge walls were mint green and white, the kitchen black and white, the dining room burgundy and white, the bathroom pink and white, her bedroom lilac and white, Jonathon's bedroom poppy red and white and the spare bedroom sky blue and white. All the accessories in each room were in exactly the same colour as the walls, and if any room required new items, and Stella could not find them in exactly the right colour, she would have the pieces made. Ruth would often shudder at the cost, especially when they could be bought at a fraction of the price in the local shops.

Frank worked hard and earned good money but Ruth knew he was feeble when it came to Stella. She ruled the house; the finances, the decor, when and where they had their holidays. Stella did not discuss any decision-making matters with Frank: she told him. It was a golden rule in their house that whatever Stella wants, Stella gets.

Ruth's stomach did a double somersault when she heard the doorbell ring, knowing her sister was standing on the other side of the front door. She checked her reflection in the hall mirror, and quickly tidied her hair and straightened her clothes before letting her sister in.

"Hi," Stella shrieked, kissing Ruth on both cheeks in Mediterranean style.

"Hi," replied Ruth, shrinking slightly at her sister's touch.

Stella walked past Ruth, down the hall and straight into the lounge. Ruth closed the front door and followed her sister and watched in amusement as Stella quickly inspected the room before leaving and made her way to the kitchen.

"I thought you were going to decorate," stated Stella, as she surveyed the walls and floor before seating herself at the dining table. "I would help. I have a flair for decorating as you well know."

"I don't remember saying I was going to decorate," Ruth said as she surveyed her own decor. "I don't think it needs doing, but if I did I would get someone in to do it. Joe is far too busy," Ruth continued as she went to the sink to fill the kettle.

"Did you want coffee, or a cup of tea?" asked Ruth.

"Err. I'll have tea, I've already had a few cups of coffee this morning. I tried to ring you earlier, but your phone was switched off."

"I was at the doctors with Lewis."

"Lewis...oh..." Stella replied, as if she had forgotten her nephew existed. "What's wrong with him?"

"Ear infection."

"Poor thing..." she said, sounding not in the least bit concerned over her nephew's health. Stella waited for Ruth to return to the table before she asked. "Why did you leave early the other night?"

Ruth laughed at Stella's question. "Leave early! Stella, we may be sisters, but we have completely different ideas with regards to a night out. Don't get me wrong, I enjoy a wine bar as much as everyone else, but not to take drinks from everyone I say hello to, and flit from person to person whenever it suited. I was silly enough to think we would spend some time together, but never mind."

"Well, I enjoyed myself, and yes, you're right we're different, but still sisters," Stella answered with a smile, and added. "How's Joe by the way?"

"Why do you ask? You've never normally got a good word to say about him, let alone ask how he is," said Ruth.

"Of course I have. You know I think the world of him, it's just that we don't always see eye to eye."

Ruth laughed. "I think that's an understatement don't you! I've never heard you two agree on anything."

"Well, I don't think it hurts to have rational, sensible, discussions."

"Rational, sensible, discussions," exclaimed Ruth. "More like heated, aggressive arguments."

Stella shrugged her shoulders in defeat. "Anyway, you didn't answer my question, how is he?"

"Why the interest in him all of a sudden Stella?" Ruth waited a few seconds for her sister to answer, but when none came, Ruth asked. "Well?"

"It's...it's just that Tyler was saying to me...."

"Tyler was saying to you?" Ruth questioned. "You mentioned the other night about Tyler talking to you....whenever has Tyler spoken to you. I never see you even acknowledge my son, let alone talk to him."

"Ruth, how can you say that? I think the world of Tyler," Stella answered, not very convincingly. "Anyway, Tyler just mentioned that hearing you and Joe arguing so much is upsetting him."

"Tyler said that to you?" Ruth felt hurt and betrayed. "When did he start talking to you?"

Stella realised that she had taken this lie a little too far, and stumbled slightly with her answer. "Well, it's not that he talks to me on a regular basis....he just looked a little forlorn when he came home with Jonathon for tea the other evening, and I just asked him if there was anything wrong. I thought he may have problems at school."

Ruth couldn't believe that her son would talk to Stella on such a delicate subject; but why would her sister invent this? "What else did he say?" asked Ruth reluctantly.

"Just that...well... things weren't the same at home and....."

"And?"

"And that you and Joe are arguing non-stop."

Ruth was confused, how could they argue non-stop, Joe wasn't at home enough, and when he was he buried himself in his office.

When a puzzled look appeared on Ruth's face, Stella regretted her exaggeration on the last remark, so added.

"I must admit, I did take that remark with a pinch of salt, I knew if things were that bad you would have said something to me by now."

Ruth wanted to reply '*You would be the last person I would talk to,*' but said nothing and waited for Stella to continue.

"Look Ruth I'm not prying, I just want to know you're all right. I know you think there's always an ulterior motive for my actions, but I'm genuinely concerned about you. All of you...even Joe."

Ruth studied her sister and suddenly noticed a different hair style. Why hadn't she noticed it when she had first entered the house? Ruth knew the reason; she was always on the defence when Stella was around. She was always waiting for the catty remark she knew would eventually come, or the sneer at something new that Ruth may have bought for the house, or a glance at some minuscule morsel of dust or smudge on a surface she may see. Ruth smiled at her sister. "Your hair looks nice Ella."

"Please don't call me Ella you know how much I hate it."

"Sorry," Ruth replied laughing to herself.

"Ruth, how about another evening out, and I promise it will be just the two of us this time."

"Why?" Ruth asked surprised.

"Well...because you're right. I shouldn't have behaved as I did, and I want to make it up to you."

Ruth had no intention of going out with her sister again, but to stop Stella hounding her she said. "I'll see."

An awkward silence prevailed over the kitchen and was, thankfully, broken by the sound of the kettle boiling. Ruth immediately jumped up from the table and, using cups and saucers instead of mugs, made the tea. It was as she placed the cups on the table with a plate of biscuits that the telephone rung.

Ruth quickly, without looking at Stella, made her way to the lounge. She was hoping that is was Joe calling to apologise for last night, so to make sure that Stella couldn't hear her conversation, she decided not to answer the telephone in the hall.

To her disappointment it wasn't Joe, but a woman's voice she didn't recognise.

"You don't know me Ruth, but my name is Karen Cannon."

Hearing that name sent Ruth's mind in a whirl. Karen Cannon! Joe's ex-wife? She lives in France. Is she back? Does Joe know she's back? Maybe it's a different Karen.

"Not...not Joe's Karen," Ruth stumbled, regretting her words immediately.

"Well, I don't think of myself as Joe's Karen anymore, but if that helps you to know who I am then yes, Joe's Karen."

It's a hoax, was Ruth's immediate thought. Someone was playing a dreadful joke on her. "I don't know who you are, but I would appreciate it if you would stop this now before this stupid joke goes too far."

"Ruth, I know you are really surprised to hear from me, but I can assure you this is no joke."

Ruth felt resentment as her heart began to race. "What do you want? Why are you ringing me?"

"I just thought it would be nice to meet the woman who Joe married, and the mother of his children that's all, nothing sinister."

Did she have a sneer in her voice? Ruth, convinced she did, asked. "What do you mean 'that's all'? What kind of person rings their ex-husband's wife to say hello after all these years? Why would you want to meet me?"

"I just happen to say to Joe yesterday, while we were having a drink, that I don't see any reason why we shouldn't all be friends."

"Having a drink..." Ruth shouted.

"Yes, nothing much, just a lunchtime drink, and a chat."

Trying to calm herself, Ruth said. "Look, I don't know what you want, but let me tell you this, I definitely don't want to be your friend, so I would appreciate it if you never call this number again, and stay away from my husband. Do you hear me? Stay away from him."

"Ruth, you have it all wrong. I'm not here to make any trouble between you and Joe, don't forget we were married, best friends and lovers for the best part of five years, I would never do anything to hurt him or you."

"I don't care what you would or wouldn't do, just stay away from my family and fuck off back to where you came from!"

She pressed the 'end call' button on the telephone so forcefully that a sharp pain shot up her finger. She was shaking from head to toe, with so many thoughts and questions invading her mind. If Karen was back in the country how did Joe know? Who suggested having a drink? Why would a man go for a drink with his ex-wife of nearly sixteen years, and not mention it to his wife of thirteen years? It suddenly dawned on her the reason for Joe's recent behaviour; he was having an affair with his ex-wife.

The more Ruth thought about the situation the more she became confused. She knew how much Karen had hurt Joe all those years ago, and the fact that Joe had always said he could never forgive her.

Ruth's mind was racing, when she suddenly remembered Stella. She decided to go up to the bathroom to calm down before returning to the kitchen. As she turned to leave the lounge she didn't notice Stella hurry back to the kitchen from the lounge door where she had listened to Ruth's telephone conversation. Nor did she see her sister return to the lounge, pick up the telephone and make a note of the last incoming telephone number before she quickly returned to her seat in the kitchen.

On Ruth's return, Stella asked. "Are you all right? Not bad news I hope."

"No...I'm fine." Ruth answered, still feeling slightly shaken. "Just an old friend who wants to meet up," she lied.

"I thought I heard you shouting."

"She was on her mobile, and couldn't hear me properly."

Stella admired her sister's quick thinking and said. "I could have sworn I heard you threatening someone."

"Well you never, so can we change the subject please."

"Okay...okay..." Stella said, putting her hands before her as if in surrender. "You were saying about Joe...."

"What is it with you and your obsession with Joe at the moment," Ruth shouted. "His name never normally passes your lips unless you're slagging him off."

"I never slag him off," Stella said most indignantly.

"Stella, you've never liked Joe from the minute you first met him, but I must confess I've never known why. He's always tried to be civil to you, and he's helped in family matters whenever he can."

"Ruth, you have it all wrong. I'll be honest, I didn't like Joe in the beginning, but I've nothing against him now," she lied convincingly.

"Then you have a strange way of showing it."

Ruth again rose from her chair as she heard Lewis cry. "I'm going up to Lewis. I maybe a while if he's still tired and needs to be settled back to sleep."

Stella ignored her sister's remark, but took a piece of paper from her trouser pocket. She studied the telephone number she had retrieved from Ruth's phone, and held the piece of paper to her chest. She felt a surge of excitement come over her, as she thought of the fun she was about to have.

Chapter 15

Karen sat on the tatty sofa and surveyed the grotty bedsit. Damp peeling wallpaper, flaking paint, electric sockets hanging off the walls, a brown stained kitchen sink, two gas burners of which only one worked, a toilet cistern that only flushed now and again, and threadbare carpets. These items were at the top of her list, should the owner ever decide to return her telephone calls.

A roof over her head was a necessity, and this hovel was all she could afford. It had taken every penny she had to secure the deposit, and pay one month's rent in advance. She sighed deeply, and thanked her lucky stars that at least the roof didn't leak; she glanced at her watch, and hurriedly put her coat on.

Five minutes later, sitting at her vantage point, Karen recalled how ecstatic she had been to see Joe yesterday. It had confirmed that, not only was she still in love with him, but the chemistry between them had endured. Although his immediate reaction towards her had been rude and obnoxious, she had fully expected this.

Although she had originally planned her surprise visit to ask Joe for his help, money and emotional support, the reverse had happened; she had been his pillar. Joe had problems; big problems. Problems that Ruth had no idea existed.

Karen had been honest with Joe when she had told him that she had no intention of causing trouble for him, but thought that Ruth had a right to know that she was back in the area, and Karen knew for certain that Joe wouldn't tell her.

Karen loved Joe so much. So why did she leave him for Pete? She had asked herself this question so many times over the years. Their relationship had begun not long after Pete had moved in with them, and developed gradually over the weeks. The time they had spent together had been fun, and although Karen had never lacked attention from Joe, Pete's attentiveness had been lavish.

It had been three weeks into their relationship that Pete had surprised Karen one evening after a session in the gym. He had taken her to a flat not far from where they lived, and confessed that he had secured the accommodation not long after he began to live with her and Joe, but hadn't moved in because he couldn't bear to be apart from her. When he had suggested they move into the flat together Karen had declined. She wanted a life somewhere different; not just around the corner from her old life, although they did use the flat on many occasions when Joe thought they were at the gym.

Had she love Pete? Yes she had, but different to the way she loved Joe.

She wrote to Joe just months after she had left, begging his forgiveness but she never received a reply. The only letters that she ever received, regarding Joe, were from his solicitor citing her for a divorce on the grounds of adultery.

How she had missed him. Joe had been the love of her life, and leaving him had been the biggest mistake of her life. Although her love for Pete had diminished over the years, she had stayed with him, selfishly, for security.

On the day that she discovered that Joe had re-married, Karen had been heartbroken, and now thirteen years later, they were still together and had three children.

Ruth intrigued Karen, but what had started out as mere interest had quickly turned into an obsession. Was there a difference between stalking and a healthy interest in a person? Karen hoped so.

Karen had discovered where Joe and Ruth lived by following him home from work one night about three weeks ago, and although not surprised, she had stared at the house in admiration. She always knew that Joe would be successful and prosperous one day.

She had sat in her car and watched Joe approach his house, and hoped that Ruth would come to the doorstep to greet her husband, and had been bitterly disappointed when she didn't. As she drove home that evening, Karen had become aware of her infatuation with the woman who had captured Joe's heart. She desperately needed to see her, and assured herself that just a glance would suffice.

The day following her first encounter to Joe's house, Karen had risen about seven o'clock, and quickly showered before she ate her breakfast. She had assumed that Ruth wouldn't leave the house before eight-thirty to take the children to school, so at eight-twenty prompt, once again, she had sat in her car across the road from Joe and Ruth's house.

As the front door opened, Karen had watched anxiously as Tyler and Abbey weighed down with school bags appeared, followed by Ruth carrying the baby. Utter astonishment overwhelmed Karen as she stared at Ruth, and she was in no doubt as to why Joe had fallen in love and married her; she was beautiful.

Once Ruth left to take the children to school, Karen had hastily drove home, and failed to erase Ruth from her thoughts for the rest of the day. At eight-twenty the following morning Karen, again, had sat in her car across the road from the Cannon house, but instead of returning home once Ruth and the children had left as she had the previous morning, she followed Ruth as she took the children to school. The first stop was Tyler's school and Karen had watched as Tyler shouted his goodbyes to his mother, sister and baby brother.

The next stop was Abbey's school, and to Karen's surprise, when she had been unable to find a parking space she felt bitterly disappointed. She drove home and hoped that her interest in the woman who had married Joe would now fade, but she had spent the rest of the day wondering how Ruth spent her time.

Karen realised that Ruth had a young baby to care for, and a big house to keep clean, but she was curious if Ruth helped Joe with his paperwork, or took the baby to a park, or saw friends for coffee. Where did she grocery shop? Where did she buy her clothes? Was Joe in her thoughts when she bought her clothes? Did she have special clothes that she wore for Joe when the children were in bed? Karen did not sleep well that night, her mind whirling with questions; questions that she had no answers to.

The following morning Karen had driven to Abbey's school early and found a parking space to wait for Ruth to arrive. It was ten minutes later that she had watched Ruth get out of her car and walk to the back passenger door, which she opened for Abbey, before she unstrapped Lewis from his car seat.

Karen now found herself following Ruth constantly, and knew nearly every aspect of Ruth's daily events. Why had she started this quest? More importantly, what would she gain? What were her feelings towards Ruth? Was it hate, jealousy, contempt? Karen had no idea, but she now realised that Ruth Cannon had the life that should have been hers.

She now sat and watched Ruth, for the umpteenth time in the last three weeks, walk out of her house for the daily school run. She had admonished herself for contacting Ruth yesterday, and decided that her obsession with Ruth would end today. She would not follow her around the supermarket watching every item that she placed in her trolley. She would not follow her as she pushed Lewis in his pram around the park. She would not wait outside her friend's house, whilst they sat inside drinking whatever it was they drunk. She would put an end to it; it had gone on long enough.

She watched Ruth as she strapped Lewis into the car, and with as much willpower as she could muster, she reversed her car and drove off in the opposite direction to which Ruth would take.

With her entire body trembling she drove to the park to calm down and clear her head. She parked her car and as she slowly walked through the park to the cafeteria for a coffee her mobile phone rang. She retrieved her phone from her handbag and glancing at the screen, was surprised to see 'unknown number'.

"Karen!" She heard as she answered the phone.

"Yes? Who's this?"

"Hi Karen, you don't know me, my name is Stella, I'm Ruth Cannon's sister."

Karen could now feel her heart beating faster and faster with every ticking minute. She had seen a few women enter Ruth's house when she had often set up surveillance outside the premises, but wasn't sure which one, if any, were her sister. "What do you want?" she asked quickly.

"I was at Ruth's house when you phoned yesterday, and I'll be honest with you Karen she was so distressed when she come off the phone, it took me quite a while to calm her down." Stella lied.

"That wasn't my intention, and although I'm sure my call was a shock to her, there was no need for her to be that rude to me."

"Yes, I agree she was rude, but let's be honest, you don't expect your husband's ex of sixteen years to ring out of the blue. Imagine how you would feel. Look Karen, Ruth is very vulnerable at the moment. She and Joe are having a few problems and let's just say that there's a lot going on that I shouldn't really discus with

114

you. Ruth always confides in me, and would be furious if she finds out I have called you."

"Then why did you?"

"Can we meet?" asked Stella.

"Why?"

"Because it will be easier to talk, and I have something I want to discuss with you."

Panic now engulfed Karen. Had Ruth discovered that she was stalking her? Had she decided that Stella would be the judge and jury? There was only one way to find out. "All right," she finally said, "but I say where and when."

"That's fine with me," Stella replied.

"Bates Coffee Bar in the town at ten-thirty tomorrow morning,"

"One thing Karen, I think we should keep this meeting to ourselves, nobody else needs to know. I'll look forward to seeing you."

"Wish I could say the same," Karen said as she ended the call and threw the phone back into her bag.

As she made her way to the cafeteria, she tried to formulate a plan. If Ruth, or her sister, had discovered her foolishness she would need an excuse as to why she had embarked on her pursuit of Ruth. If they haven't, then she had no idea why Stella had requested this meeting, and if she was honest it was the latter that worried her more.

She entered the cafeteria, ordered a coffee and found an empty table by the window. As she sipped her coffee she recalled her phone call to Ruth yesterday. The phone call had purely been on impulse, and no thought or reason had gone into it. If Ruth had told Joe about the call, Karen knew she would have heard from him by now as he would be furious with her, and demand that she stay away from his wife and family.

This latest development confirmed that her stalking antics must now stop, and with great restraint she decided that once she had finished her coffee she would go home, and stay there for the rest of the day.

The following morning, after a restless night's sleep with thoughts of Joe, Ruth and Stella invading her mind, Karen woke later than usual. After breakfast and a quick shower, she searched her sparse wardrobe for an outfit to wear. She eventually decided on a black, belted slip dress, cream stiletto heeled shoes and a cream jacket.

She checked herself in her full length mirror for the umpteenth time, as she realised she had to make a good impression. She left her bedsit and walking to her car, she felt as if she were a lamb going to her slaughter.

***

Stella had also found sleep hard to come by that night. She lay in bed and listened to Frank's steady breathing while she recalled the events of the day. She had thanked her lucky stars that she had been at Ruth's when the telephone call from Karen had come through, and a plan was immediately devised.

For her plan to work she would have to come across to Karen as a caring, devoted sister who would go to any lengths to ensure her sister and brother-in-law's happiness and wellbeing. The surprise call to Karen had been a good tactic, as Stella immediately heard the worry and concern in the other woman's voice.

When her bedside clock displayed the time as six-thirty, she rose from bed and put on her favourite silk robe. Stella had always been an early riser as it gave her the chance to enjoy a leisurely shower, and meticulously perform her daily skin care regime before she prepared breakfast for Frank and Jonathon, and lay out Jonathon's school uniform.

Once Frank and Jonathon had left for the day Stella, like Karen but from a far wide-ranging selection, chose very carefully what she should wear. She settled on a pair of black linen trousers, a sleeveless black and white striped top accompanied by a long black lace cardigan, and black suede kitten heeled shoes. It was at exactly ten minutes past ten that she left her house feeling confident that the morning would go exactly how she had planned it to.

***

Karen arrived at the coffee bar half an hour before their scheduled meeting time to make sure she was the first one there. She felt this would give her the upper hand, and after ordering a cappuccino sat at a table in the middle of the room.

Karen took one glance at the woman who had just entered the coffee bar, realised it wasn't Stella and returned her attention to the menu that was in front of her. It was only when she felt a presence beside her that she lifted her head again and saw the woman standing there.

"Karen?"

"Yes," she answered bewildered.

"Hello, please to meet you," Stella said, as she took a seat at the table and added, "I'm Stella."

Shocked, Karen studied the woman sitting next to her. How could two sisters look so different? Karen's immediate thought was of Cinderella and one of the ugly sisters, but an ugly sister who knew how to make the best of her unattractiveness.

"I should imagine you are curious as to why I wanted to meet you."

"Well yes, you could say that," Karen said. How she now regretted her interest in Ruth and realised that it had become quite unhealthy.

"Let's order first, another coffee?" Stella asked indicating to Karen's now empty cup.

"Cappuccino please," Karen said and watched as Stella rose from the chair, and seem to glide towards the counter to order the drinks.

As Stella left the table, Karen could not see the broad, smug grin that appeared on Stella's face.

On her return, Stella placed the tray of coffees on the table, sat down. "I'm worried about Ruth and Joe."

"Is that the reason you wanted to see me?" Karen asked, relief flooding through her as she realised that this meeting had nothing to do with her stalking Ruth.

"Yes, but first I must apologise for my sister's rudeness on the phone, but she's in a bad way, and as I said, I'm worried about her."

Karen made no comment on this statement, but watched Stella slowly stir her coffee, and as she had no intention of dominating this meeting waited for Stella to continue.

"Ruth and Joe have a few problems, and I have every intention of helping them, but I can't do it all on my own. I did think of asking Ted, Joe's friend, but he has enough to cope with looking after his wife. Then I thought of Gill, Ruth's friend, but decided it would be best not to involve anyone who is close to them, so when you rang Ruth the other day it was a Godsend. You are the perfect person to help me."

"Me! How can I help? I'm not exactly in any of their good books," Karen stated.

Stella smiled. "They won't know you are helping, you will be in the background so to speak."

Karen, feeling totally confused, stared at the woman sitting next to her, and with agitation sounding in her voice said. "I have no idea what you're talking about, and I'm not getting involved."

"Please Karen let me give you a little idea of what's going on. Ruth is convinced that Joe has a problem that he's not sharing with her. Now it could be anything from a health problem, to a business problem, to a woman problem, and believe me Karen your name has been bandied about since your phone call. I understand that you had a drink with Joe."

"Yes, but nothing went on!"

"No, no, I'm not here to accuse you of anything, this meeting is purely to ask you to help me watch over my sister and her husband while they go through this bad patch."

Karen noticed that Stella paused before she asked the next question.

"Did Joe tell you or give you any hints of what his problems are?"

"No," Karen lied, realising that she had answered too quickly. "No, it was just a drink, I had some news for him, but it has nothing to do with any problem Joe may have now."

"Have you made any plans to meet again?"

Karen shook her head. "You've got to understand that Joe is still angry with me for what I did to him all those years ago."

"Yes I do, but you need to gain his confidence. All I want you to do is keep an eye on him. Pop into the office now and again. Suggest another drink, you never know he may open up to you."

"What if he tells me he never wants to see me again? He might do if I keep appearing out of the blue."

"I'm not asking you to stalk him..."

"Why did you say that?" Karen interrupted, anger sounding in her tone.

"What?"

"Stalk him."

"No reason...I'm just making a point that I don't want you to go over the top where Joe is concerned. Are you all right Karen? You've gone quite pale."

"I'm fine, thanks," Karen said and picked up her handbag as if to leave. "I'm not sure about this."

"Please Karen, listen to me. All I'm asking is for you to keep an eye on Joe. No more than that, and if anything occurs then you ring me and I'll deal with it."

"What do you mean if anything occurs?"

"Well...anything out of the ordinary. Look Karen, it won't be forever just until they sort themselves out."

Karen placed her handbag back on the floor and said. "I'll think about it." She watched as Stella, who had placed her handbag on the chair next to her, rummage through it and produce a pen and piece of paper. She wrote a mobile phone number on it and handed it to Karen.

"Ring me anytime."

Karen took the piece of paper from Stella, and nodded her head in agreement.

"Err...Karen...can I ask why you came back here?"

"No, you can't," replied Karen. "But, I have a question for you."

"What?" said Stella surprised.

"Where did you get my telephone number from?"

"Err...I've got to be honest, I retrieved it from Ruth's phone without her knowing. Wrong and deceitful of me I know, but as I said I will do anything to help my sister, and her husband." Stella said, and hesitated slightly before she continued. "Well, I have to go. It's been lovely meeting you Karen, and I hope, between us, we can do some good. Ring me whenever you need to. Speak soon, bye."

Surprised at her abruptness, Karen watched as Stella grabbed her handbag, hastily rose from the table, and practically ran out of the coffee bar. Karen looked at the piece of paper in her hand with Stella's mobile phone number on and shuddered. She had taken an instant dislike to the woman who had emitted no warmth or tenderness when she spoke of her sister who, she claimed, she wanted to help.

***

Stella had been jubilant when she had first entered the coffee bar and seen Joe's ex-wife. Karen was everything that Stella had expected and hoped for; tall, slim and very attractive, and she had just given her a licence to pursue the man who, Stella had no doubt, she was still in love with.

Although pleased with herself, she had momentarily panicked, and had to leave the coffee bar before Karen could ask any more awkward questions. Her unrehearsed performance had been satisfactory, and the encounter had gone to plan, and although Karen had been on her guard, Stella had been fully expecting this.

Stella now sat in her car and recalled how the colour had drained from Karen's face when the word 'stalk' had entered the conversation. Was she already stalking Joe? Or maybe even Ruth? Enthralled at the prospect of this, Stella checked her make-up in the car's rear mirror as a shudder of excitement, again, ran through her where Karen was concerned.

121

Chapter 16

Joe thought relentlessly, night and day, about the man who had penetrated his life and had brought him to imminent bankruptcy and ruin. Andy Bolan. Joe was now convinced that he was part of a syndicate, because the whole scam had been too professionally carried out. How had they chosen him? Had they stalked him? Was it possible that they had hacked into his computer? These questions constantly whirled around in his mind, but there was one main question that he needed an answer to: Why him?

As soon as he had realised it was all a scam, his first step should have been to contact the police, his second, to post it all over the internet before some other poor soul fell for it. Although he had every intention of pursuing both those avenues, they would have to wait. He first had to find the finances to pay off Barry McGraw, not only the fifty thousand pounds but the interest that was accruing.

Joe sat at his desk contemplating the one last option left open to him; one that would shatter his pride. He picked up the office telephone to tell Laura not to disturb him for the next fifteen minutes, and counted to ten before he hesitantly picked up his mobile phone that lay on his desk and dialled the number.

Although brother-in-laws, Joe and Frank were not friends, and both men had known for years that the blame lay with Frank. Joe had never questioned why Frank disliked him, and just accepted the situation because it was of no consequence to him. Frank was financially affluent, and Joe hoped that a little conscience would rear its head, and his brother-in-law would come to his rescue.

As he listened to the ringing tone and waited for Frank to answer his call, Joe's heart was pounding, a feeling that he was experiencing more these days.

"Frank Sinclair speaking."

"Very business-like I must say," Joe said, a nervous laugh escaping from his throat.

"Hi Joe, what's wrong?"

"Does there have to be something wrong for me to ring you?"

"Of course, you never ring me," Frank answered, bewilderment sounding in his voice.

"You don't exactly make me welcome."

"What do you want Joe a song and dance."

This conversation was not going to plan. "Look Frank, I know we don't always hit it off, but we are family. I really need to talk to someone, and don't have anyone else to turn to."

"The answer is no."

"Come on Frank, you don't even know what I want."

"If it's nothing to do with our wives or children, then you must want money. I have no control over my wife or child, but I do have control over my money and I can't lend you any."

"Frank, I really do need to talk to you." Joe could hear the panic in his own voice.

"I'll talk to you Joe, but let's get this straight from the beginning, I won't be lending you any money."

"Please Frank, just listen to what I have to say, and I'd appreciate you not saying anything to Stella about me ringing."

"Joe, whenever do I say anything to Stella?"

"I know, but this is a very delicate situation I'm in Frank, and I desperately need your help," Joe said, and heard Frank sigh at the other end of the line.

"I'll meet you in the Fox and Arms at around seven tonight."

"Thanks mate, I appreciate it," Joe said.

Frank terminated the phone call without any form of a farewell.

Joe lay his phone back on his desk and run his fingers through his hair. Frank was his ultimate saviour, without him he was doomed.

He opened his desk drawer and reached for his tablets. He glanced at the box as he tried to remember when he had last used them. Had he taken three or four doses already today? Common sense told him not to take them if he wasn't sure, but desperation overpowered his sound judgement. He removed the tablets from the packet, popped them into his mouth and swallowed them with the help of his usual mouthful of vodka.

The clock on the wall displayed the time as five-twenty. He realised he should call home to tell Ruth that he had a business meeting after work, but knew from recent experiences that this would just result in another argument. He decided to use the time to formulate a plan with which to convince his brother-in-law how desperate he was. He also decided to write down a couple of repayment proposals for Frank to peruse.

As he pulled a pad of A4 paper from his tray a text notification on his mobile phone came through from Frank, so it was with his heart pounding, again, that he opened the message.

'Sorry Joe I'm cancelling tonight have no intentions of lending you any money, and not really interested in listening to any sob stories'.

Mortified, Joe re-read the text twice. Frank had not even given him the chance to explain his predicament. So it was with shaking hands that he tapped out his reply: *'Please Frank hear me out. Am in the shit & only you can help. Please'.*

Frank's answer came through almost instantly. *'Sorry Joe, I can't. I'm in the middle of something myself and no spare cash'.*

Frank had been his last hope, and that hope had now been eliminated. Joe put his head in his hands and sobbed. He sobbed like a child; a child that was lost with no hope of finding his way. His whole world had suddenly come crushing down on him. His life, as he knew it, was over. How many times had he asked himself how could he have been such an idiot to fall for one of the oldest scams that had ever been invented? How could he have fallen for it so easy? He came to the same conclusion every time he asked himself this question; greed.

Once Joe's sobs had abated slightly, his thoughts turned to Barry McGraw and his boys who had paid him a visit at his office yesterday. They had explained, in very few words, that Barry was still waiting for this month's payment, and that he was not prepared to wait any longer. Joe, having convinced himself that Frank would come to his aid, had promised them that he would have Barry's money by the end of the week; he would now have to break that promise.

Although the call to Frank had shattered his pride, his next course of action was sole destroying. A meeting with Barry would have to be arranged to ask for an extension on this month's payment while he put his warehouse on the market.

If Barry refused, Joe understood the consequences explicitly, but he had to admit to himself that, at this precise moment, the thought of his body lying underneath a concrete slab had more appeal than explaining his situation to Ruth.

Chapter 17

Joe was finding it hard to breath, and little pockets of sweat were appearing on his face. He loosened his tie, and undid the top button of his shirt. Suddenly, nausea and thirst overwhelmed him and as he noticed a water cooler in the corner of the office, he rose from his chair and, although unsteady on his feet, made his way towards it. He could sense Barry's eyes watching him walk, unsteady, across the office. Filling a plastic cup with water, he gulped the liquid so quick that it caused him to have a coughing fit.

Barry finished his telephone call, and stared at Joe as he made his way back to his seat. "You all right Joe? You don't look too good."

"Yes, I'm fine. You actually sounded a little concerned for me there Barry," Joe said, trying to bring a little light-heartiness into the proceedings.

"Don't kid yourself Joe I just can't afford to have the Old Bill sniffing around just because some idiot decides to die in my office." Barry laughed at his own joke, and in a more serious tone continued. "I take it you are sitting in that chair because you have some money for me."

Joe had called Barry earlier this morning, and Barry had been reluctant to see him unless he had at least a month's money, in cash. Barry had relented when Joe had pleaded with him.

"No Barry, I told you on the phone earlier that I haven't," Joe said. Although he felt slightly better, he could still feel his heart pounding throughout his body.

"You had better explain yourself Joe, because I don't like the sound of this."

"It really is quite simple Barry. I haven't got your money, and I'm here asking you to put it on hold why I try to sell my business," Joe said trying to force confidence into his voice.

Barry began to shake his head. "That's not how it works Joe, you know that."

"Well, you had better finish me off now. I don't have your money Barry, and won't have it until my business is sold."

"Finish you off Joe? I don't know what you're talking about."

Joe laughed. "What will you do, send the boys round tonight?"

"Again Joe, I don't know what you're talking about. This is a respectable estate agent where I help a few friends out."

Joe laughed again. "It's all right Barry I haven't got a listening device on me."

Barry now stood up, anger showing in his face. "I think you had better leave my office Joe."

Joe realised that the meeting had not only finished, but had not gone to plan. "Come on Barry give me a little breathing space, that's all I'm asking for."

Barry took his seat once more, and without glancing at Joe said. "Close the door on your way out."

Joe studied the man before him, and wondered how any human being could be so callous and cold-hearted. There had never been a truer saying than 'money was the route of all evil'.

Joe slowly rose from his chair, and made his way to the office door. It was as he put his hand on the door handle that Barry's words came to him.

"Give my regards to the family Joe."

Anger now overwhelming him, Joe ran back to the desk and snarled at the man sitting behind it. "You leave my family out of this. You lay one finger on any of them and you're dead."

"Please Joe," Barry said, a smirk appearing on his face. "This is a respectable office, there's no need to talk like that."

To the surprise of the staff in the outer office, as Joe left the building he slammed the door behind him so hard that they felt the vibrations tremor through the premises.

Barry stayed seated at his desk before he picked up his mobile phone to make a call. Once that call had ended, he made another. "Leave Joe Cannon alone for a couple of weeks, let him sweat for a while."

***

As soon as Joe left the estate agents another panic attack struck him. He hurried to his car, and once inside took deep breaths to try to calm himself. What was he to do? He couldn't think straight. He searched his glove compartment for some tablets but soon realised he had none in there. He now had a regular order of tablets placed with Charley, and although he had his last delivery two days ago, he didn't put any in his car's glove compartment as normal.

After five minutes and feeling slightly composed he drove back to his office. He ignored Laura when she tried to talk to him, and made his way to the office. Although it was a cold February day, Joe did not switch on the two bar electric fire as a fiery heat already penetrated his body. He made his way to his desk and as he sat down he took his tablets and a small bottle of vodka out of the drawer. Placing four tablets in his mouth and swallowing the vodka, he waited, with his head in his hands, for the panic attack to completely subside.

Would Barry hurt his family? Surely not. Barry saw himself as a respectable business man, and respectable business men didn't go around maiming or killing women and children. It was him that Barry wanted, not his family.

The loud knock on his office door abruptly brought Joe back from his thoughts. He looked up as he saw Laura enter the room, and heard her gasp as the cold in the office struck her. He watched as she slowly walked towards his desk, her eyes not leaving the bleak looking, unlit two bar electric fire.

"Yes Laura?"

As Laura turned her attention to Joe, she placed a pile of papers in front of him and answered. "This week's purchase orders." She rubbed her hands up and down her arms and said. "Joe it's freezing in here."

Ignoring her remark he asked. "Anything else?"

"Yes there is. Did you remember to put last month's purchase orders through with Western Products? Alf said stocks are extremely low, and not all the orders can be filled."

"Of course I did," he snapped. "Why haven't you chased them?"

"I did. They said they have no record of last month's order."

"Well get back to them, and tell them if the order is not here by tomorrow we'll be changing suppliers," he again snapped.

"But Joe, they can't supply what you didn't order."

Joe stared at Laura and said stiltedly. "I placed the order with them, and I'd appreciate you not questioning me. Now, is there anything else?"

"No," she sighed but added. "It's so cold in..."

"Thanks Laura," he interrupted, and added. "Get onto Western Products and speak to the manager if you have to. Close the door behind you please, and I don't want any calls for the next hour."

"Joe!" she exclaimed.

"Laura, will you just do as you're told," he shouted, and regretted his actions immediately. He had never had cause to talk to Laura in such a rude way, and had always considered her more a friend than an employee. He noticed the tears fill her eyes, and watched her turn and leave the office without another word.

Guilt overwhelmed him, but in reality that was the least of his worries. An upset secretary was insignificant compared to the problems that now faced him.

Chapter 18

It had been two days since Joe's last conflict with Barry, and he was equally pleased and surprised that he had not had another visit from the 'boys'. He tried, relentlessly, not to involve Ruth and the children, so he spent as little time at home as was possible, but being five-thirty on a Friday evening, and with no plausible excuse that he hadn't used many times, he had no choice but to go home.

Joe had noticed a change in Ruth over the last couple of days. She had not only ignored him completely, but it seemed that she was unable to look him in the face. He must try to make amends this weekend, not only with Ruth, but the children as well.

On his arrival home he hung his coat on the stand in the hall, and as he entered the kitchen immediately noticed that the dining table had been laid for their evening meal, and could hear Tyler complaining.

"But I'm not hungry mum. Can't I eat later?"

"No. We are going to sit down as a family to eat tonight," she replied, and as she observed Joe enter the kitchen she added. "Of course that only includes people who regard themselves as part of this family."

Joe ignored the remark and smiled at his wife, but she ignored him as she carried on preparing the meal. Joe said hello to Tyler and ruffled his son's hair before he left the kitchen with the excuse of going up to the bathroom to wash his hands before dinner.

He sprinted up the stairs to his office, and going to his desk drawer suddenly remembered that he had taken tablets just before he left the warehouse. With his hand hovering over the bottle of vodka, he quickly picked it up, unscrewed the top and took two large gulps of the liquid. He waited a couple of minutes before he took another.

The meal, unfortunately, had been an arduous event. Tyler grumbled all the way through it that he wasn't hungry, Joe, as much as he tried, couldn't summon the energy to talk to his family, Abbey, seeming to sense the atmosphere ate her meal as quick as possible, and Ruth just pushed her food around the plate.

As soon as the meal had finished, Ruth demanded that Tyler and Abbey go straight to their bedrooms to finish off the rest of their homework. Without a word to Joe, or glancing in his direction, she unstrapped Lewis from his baby chair and followed the children up the stairs with Lewis in her arms.

With a heavy heart, Joe watched his family mount the stairs before he made his way into the lounge. He sat on the sofa and pulled a newspaper in front of him, but soon realised that not a single word had penetrated his brain. He heard Tyler and Abbey calling goodnight to Lewis, and it dawned on him that Ruth had not offered him the opportunity to say goodnight to his youngest son. When he eventually heard Ruth, an hour later, descend the stairs, he decided against challenging her on the subject, as he knew it would turn into another argument.

It was after Ruth had finished loading the dishwasher and had tidied the kitchen that she finally entered the lounge.

"Have the kids gone to bed?" Joe asked surprised as he watched Ruth sit in an armchair and pick up a magazine.

"Yes, they've had a busy week, so they've gone to bed to watch television," she answered not looking up from her magazine.

"What did you want to do this weekend?" he asked as light-hearted as possible.

She ignored him.

"Ruth, did you hear me?"

"Yes I heard you Joe, but I'm wondering what you're up to."

"I'm trying to make amends here, and make up with you."

"Make amends! You have turned this family upside down since before Christmas and you think a nice cosy weekend will do the trick."

"What do you want me to do?" he shouted at her. "I think you've made your mind up that you're not going to give me a chance."

"I've give you more chances than you'll ever know, but now I know that you are a lying cheating bastard."

"I've had enough of this," he yelled as he rose from the sofa and turned to leave the lounge.

"Don't you dare turn your back on me, and leave this room," Ruth snarled at him as she jumped up from her chair.

Surprised and shocked at her tone, Joe stopped and turned to face her.

"I've had enough of all this Joe, and I want answers from you. I know there's something wrong, and I now know what it is. But I'm sick and tired of listening to your lame excuses. All I hear you say is, 'I'm tired', or 'I've had a bad day at the warehouse', 'a delivery didn't turn up', 'too many people reported in sick', or whatever other excuses you give me. Now, I want the truth, and you are not leaving this room until I hear it from your mouth. I want to hear you admit it."

"I don't know what you're talking about. I'm just going through a bad patch at work."

"A bad patch at work! That's not a reason for being so moody and bad-tempered all the time. You've got no patience with the kids, especially Lewis. When was the last time you picked him up for a cuddle or played with him? As for the other two, they ignore you now as much as you ignore them, and I won't even begin to talk about our relationship Joe, because we don't have one!" She paused to study his face, and although her anger ebbed slightly, she asked him with sarcasm sounding in her voice. "Enough to be going on with, or shall I carry on?"

When he didn't respond she said. "Look Joe, I know you're having an affair so let's get it out in the open and finished with."

Joe laughed inwardly, and thought to himself *'if only it was that simple'*. "Ruth, I'm not having an affair, you are the only woman I want, and you know that."

Joe watched as Ruth lowered her head, as if in defeat, and slowly sat back down again. It was the tears in her eyes that Joe first noticed when she looked up at him again.

"What about Karen?"

"Karen?"

"Yes Joe, Karen. You know...your ex-wife," she answered sarcastically. "I know she's back on the scene, so don't lie to me."

"It's no big deal she just turned up at the office the other day," he said taking the seat next to Ruth.

Joe saw the immediate change in his wife when she again stood up and shouted. "No big deal. Your ex-wife turns up out of the blue, you have a drink with her, and conveniently forgot to tell me, and that's no big deal."

"How do you know she's back?" Joe asked.

"She phoned me."

"She phoned you?" Joe questioned, anger sounding in his voice.

"Yes Joe, so the next time you see that slag, tell her to leave me out of it." She paused, and tried to calm herself before continuing. "The sad thing about it Joe is that I've been waiting for you to tell me, so if it's no big deal, as you say, then why didn't you?"

"I didn't give it much thought."

Anger again welled up in Ruth. "Not much thought! Your ex turns up after ....how many years...and you didn't give it much thought? Do you know the sick thing about it?" When Joe didn't respond Ruth continued. "She called saying that she wanted to meet me, and didn't see why we all couldn't be friends."

When Ruth began to cry, Joe tried to take her in his arms again as he said. "Please Ruthie, you have to believe me when I say I'm not having an affair with anyone."

"Well I don't! I've put up with your moody behaviour for weeks, but at least now I know it's because you've been shagging your ex-wife," she screamed at him as she struggled free, and ran out of the room and up the stairs to her bedroom.

On hearing their bedroom door slam, Joe sat on the sofa with his head in his hands. Can things get any worse? He should have told Ruth about Karen's return. It would have been one less problem to deal with. More puzzling; why had Karen called Ruth? She had promised him faithfully that she hadn't returned to cause him any trouble.

Joe now laughed to himself. He wished his problems were as easy as having to admit to Ruth of an affair, rather than he was about to lose the business that he had worked so hard for, and the possibility of losing their home. Even more frightening was the fact that if Barry McGraw doesn't receive a payment in the immediate future, she will also be a widow.

He recalled how hard he had worked to build up his warehouse business, and how he had started his working life on a market stall, selling women's clothes for one of his father's friends. With his good humour and slightly cocky personality he had been a natural, and within a year, he was managing the stall single-handed. He selected and bought the stock from the wholesalers, set the prices to ensure a good profit, and set up the stall each market morning with the flair of a window dresser. His wages were minimal, with the repeated promise of pay rises that never materialised. Joe could have quite easily put an extra pound or two in his own pocket, but dishonesty had never been part of his nature.

Joe knew he was a competent salesman so when, at the age of twenty, a job opportunity arose for a sales agent with an insurance company, he applied and, to his amazement, received a letter informing him that he had been the successful applicant. Within eighteen months Joe was their top-selling agent.

During his time at the insurance company Joe had begun buying and selling his own merchandise. He would buy any good quality household items at a reasonable price, and sell them on for a sufficient profit. Start slow and build gradually was the rule that Joe always applied in his younger days. He had also tried to encourage Ted into setting up a warehouse business as partners, but Ted had just started his own landscape gardening venture, which after years of hard work, was now very lucrative.

It was on Joe's twenty-sixth birthday, that Ted told him of a warehouse that had come up for lease at a reasonable price on the London/Kent border.

Six months later Cannon's Household Supplies emerged. It had been Joe's pride and joy ever since, and the thought of losing it was not only heartbreaking, but pure devastation.

***

After slamming her bedroom door shut, Ruth flung herself on the bed and cried as she had never cried before. Water erupted from her eyes, her nose and her mouth. She had been a fool to give Joe the benefit of the doubt. She had waited for him to tell her that Karen was back in the area, but he hadn't. Deep down she had convinced herself that Joe would never have anything to do with his ex-wife, especially after the way she had hurt him, but obviously she didn't know her husband as well as she thought she did.

When her crying abating slightly, waves of convulsions cascaded through her body as her weeping turned into sobs.

She slowly sat up on the bed and glanced around the room. For the first time since she had lived in the house, she wished she had a lock on the bedroom door as she did not want Joe anywhere near her. He would either have to sleep on the sofa tonight, or find somewhere else to rest his deceitful, lying head.

The thought of Karen coming back into their lives had never entered Ruth's head. Although she often wondered if an affair was the reason for his unusual behaviour, Karen had not entered the equation. Why would she? She lived in France, a woman who was long gone out of Joe's life and would never be seen or heard of again.

How could Joe have done this to her? They were in the thirteenth year of their married life; obviously those thirteen years meant nothing to Joe. She began to sob again. She sobbed the tears of a woman whose heart had just been torn in two by the man she loved more than life itself.

Once her sobs subsided, anger took over. She rose from the bed and roughly pulled Joe's suitcase from the top of the wardrobe. She threw it on the bed and angrily unzipped it. She pulled open his wardrobe door with such a force that the door bounced off the wall and came back and hit her on the side of the head. She gasped in pain, and vehemently cursed as she pulled some of his clothes off their hangers, and threw them into the suitcase. She then pulled his underwear drawer out of its bracket and tipped the drawer upside down so the contents fell into the case. She zipped the case up and dragged it off the bed.

Surprised at the weight and catching her breath, she pulled the case across the bedroom and opened the door. Unfortunately, she didn't notice Tyler standing by the stairs, rubbing his eyes through tiredness.

"What you doing mum?"

"Oh..." she exclaimed. "Your...your dad has to go away tomorrow so I've just packed a case for him."

"Away where? Dad never goes away," Tyler said, suddenly appearing wide awake.

"I know darling, but a business opportunity has come up and he doesn't want to miss it. I'll explain it more to you in detail tomorrow. Now go back to bed."

"Will I see dad before he goes?"

"Yes...yes, of course," Ruth replied, not expecting this question. "Now, go back to bed, or you'll be tired in the morning."

"All right, good night mum."

"Good night darling."

In all her upset and temper she had not given the children a thought. What a mess. What has Joe done to this family? These thoughts were whirling around her mind like a Catherine wheel with no ending as she dragged the suitcase down the stairs to confront its owner.

Chapter 19

Stella was aware that Frank had returned home from his early morning Saturday walk to the newsagent in a mood. He entered the kitchen, threw the newspapers on the table, filled a glass of ice-cold water from the refrigerator's dispenser, and left the kitchen mumbling that he was going up for a shower and a change of clothes.

She laughed to herself as she watched him leave, and as she was about to pick up one of the newspapers from the table she noticed a mobile phone on the floor beside the refrigerator. On investigation she discovered that it was Frank's that somehow must have dropped out of his pocket unnoticed.

Frank was never more than three feet away from his mobile phone, whether in bed, in the bathroom, and even on the extremely rare occasion that they had sex, his phone was always at hand; but out of Stella's reach.

This had never bothered her, because she knew if she ever did scroll through his texts there would be an array of messages from Elaine. Sweet, stupid Elaine as Stella thought of her; Frank's mistress, who he assumed his wife knew nothing about.

That Frank had a mistress was of no concern to Stella. Frank gave her the lifestyle that she considered rightfully hers, and his relationship with that woman gave her the freedom she craved. She had been stockpiling money into her secret bank accounts for years, and also had her cache of men who were always available, and every one of them had a use, which Stella used to her advantage.

She quickly picked up the mobile phone and placed it in her trouser pocket, and hurried out of the kitchen to the bottom of the stairs where there was no sign of

Frank. She returned to the kitchen and retrieved the phone from her trousers, turned it off, and returned it to her pocket as Jonathon entered the kitchen.

"Breakfast darling?" she asked her son.

"Yes please mum, then I'm going out."

"Are you?"

"Yes mum, but I'll be back in time for lunch though."

"Oh...oh...alright darling, I'll have something nice ready for you."

"Thanks mum, love you."

Why did no one else ever see this loving side of Jonathon? Although if Frank had witnessed it he would have said that the boy was up to something.

Jonathon gulped down his breakfast, and as he kissed Stella on the cheek he said. "See you later mum."

"Jonathon, I really think you should tell me where you are going."

"Just out with friends mum, bye," he said as he ran from the kitchen.

"Jonathon, come back here, I want to speak to you," Stella shouted as she followed him, but heard the front door slam shut just as she entered the hall. Stella shook her head and laughed to herself. How proud she was of her son, a strong-willed boy who, thankfully, showed traces of knowing what he wanted out of life, and would stop at nothing to achieve it.

Stella was still laughing to herself as she returned to the kitchen to clear the breakfast dishes, when she heard Frank behind her.

"Have you seen my mobile phone?" he asked as he searched the worktops.

"The only place I ever see your mobile is in your hand," she laughed.

"I've searched our bedroom, my office and the bathroom, and I can't find it," he said, ignoring her remark.

"Well, I haven't seen it, and I'm going up to change my clothes," she said as she left the kitchen. Once in the bedroom, she quietly closed the door and opening her wardrobe pulled all the items from the top shelf to reveal a steel box with a combination lock, which she used to stash money away until she had time to go to the bank. She unlocked the box, and placed the mobile on top of a pile of money, but quickly locked it and placed it at the back of the shelf together with all the other items as she heard Frank's footsteps on the stairs.

"Stella," he shouted. "Are you sure you haven't seen my phone, I can't find it anywhere."

Stepping out of the bedroom Stella responded. "Frank, if I had found it don't you think I would have told you by now? When was the last time you had it?"

"If I knew that, I'd know where it was!"

"I'm only trying to help."

"Well you don't!" he snapped as he walked into the bedroom.

"I'll get my phone and ring it for you, so at least you'll know if it's in the house." She left him in the bedroom rummaging through the dirty washing basket and ran down the stairs to the kitchen to fetch her phone. As she retrieved his number from her list of contacts she pressed the call button and walked to the bottom of the stairs where Frank was on his way down. "I think it's been turned off, as it's saying you're not available and to try again later."

"Turned off! I never turn it off."

"Maybe you've left it in the office, and the battery has run down."

"I've not left it at the office, I used it last night," he shouted. "You know how much I need that phone for work. It's never turned off, and it's charged all the time."

"Please don't talk to me like that Frank I'm only trying to help."

Without saying another word he suddenly turned and ran back up the stairs. Frightened that he may have already discovered her box she quickly followed him. When he entered Jonathon's bedroom and started searching through his chest of drawers Stella exclaimed. "Frank what you doing?"

"What does it look like I'm doing?"

"Jonathon wouldn't have your phone!"

"Stella, I don't trust that boy as far as I could throw him. At some time this morning he must have hidden it before he went out."

"Frank," she shouted. "That's your son you're talking about, not some stranger." She had never seen Frank so angry and forceful, and slightly regretted hiding his mobile phone.

Frank suddenly stopped searching and swung round to face Stella. "That's where you are wrong he is a stranger to me. I don't know our son. I don't think I have ever really known him. I've tried, even you must admit to that, but he just doesn't want to know me, and to be honest I've grown used to that now."

"You still have no right to rummage around his room, so stop now," she demanded.

Frank glared at his wife and said in a quiet, but stern voice. "I have every right this is my house, and if I think my phone is in this room I will search it until I find it and God help him if I do." As Frank was about to continue his search he asked. "Where did he go by the way?"

"Out."

"I could have told you that! Out where?"

"I don't know, he just said he was going out."

"Didn't you ask him where he was going? A twelve-year-old boy and you let him have that much freedom?"

"Me! I never see you showing any concern for our son's welfare, all that nonsense about him being a stranger to you, that's just a good excuse for you not to be bothered with him. Since when have I had full responsibility for our son?"

"Since the day he was born and you shut me out, but I'll ask you again. Where did he go?"

"Out with friends, but said that he'd be back in time for lunch. Frank, you should be proud of him, he's an independent, strong-willed boy."

"Strong-willed boy! He's a deceitful, lying, pain in the arse."

Stella turned from Frank and left the room. She stood at the top of the stairs holding the banister for support before she made her way down. How dare Frank say those things about their son. Frank was jealous of Jonathon, always has been, always will be.

Five minutes later, seated in the lounge, she heard Frank descend the stairs. As he entered the lounge she immediately noticed that his face was stern with rage. He had a magazine and an envelope in one hand, and a locked box which, coincidentally, had a striking resemblance to hers, in the other.

She noticed that the front cover of the magazine was of a pornographic material so asked nervously. "What have you got there?"

"This," he said, waving the magazine in the air, "I'm not worried about, its normal, but what is in this envelope I'm disgusted at. I dread to think what's in this box."

"What's in the envelope?"

Frank threw the envelope at her which landed on her lap. As she picked the envelope up, photos slid from it and sprawled in front of her. Glancing at the photos she gasped out loud and caught her breath. "What are these?" she asked with repulsion in her voice.

"What do they look like to you my sweet?" he asked sarcastically.

"They're disgusting! They can't be Jonathon's."

"I'm sure he'll say they're not, and we'll soon find out. What time did you say he was due back?"

Stella glanced at her watch before replying. "In a couple of hours."

"Good," he said, as he placed the box on the coffee table and fiddled with the lock.

"You can't open that box Frank!" she exclaimed.

"Who says?"

"It's Jonathon's personal stuff."

"I don't give a shit about it being his personal stuff," he shouted.

Frank picked up the box, walked out of the lounge and made his way to the kitchen. He pulled open a drawer and rummaged through it. When Stella followed him, still holding the envelope, she saw that he had taken a small screwdriver from the drawer.

"What are you doing?"

"Opening the box," he stated.

"You can't, it's wrong."

"Will you stop telling me what I can and can't do."

"I just think you are invading our son's privacy."

"At the age of twelve and living in this house he has no privacy." Frank answered as he wedged the screwdriver under the lid to prise it off. After a couple of minutes the lid came off to disclose not only a vast amount of loose change lying at the bottom of the box, but ten and twenty pound notes tied into small bundles. Frank took a handful of the bundles out of the box, and snatched the envelope from Stella's hand. With the envelope in one hand and the money in the other, he moved each hand up and down as if weighing them and stated. "He's selling those disgusting photos."

"No!" she shouted. "He would never to anything like that. I just can't believe they belong to him."

"Well you can bet they do, but I'm sure he'll deny everything and blame someone else, he always does."

Stella was about to retaliate when they heard Jonathon's key in the front door. Stella immediately ran to greet him and Frank pick up the box and followed her.

"Why are you home so early?" Stella asked her son.

"That's not important Stella. Jonathon, come into the lounge," Frank demanded as his son entered the hall.

Stella noticed Jonathon's eyes widen as he stared at the items in his father's hands, and glanced at her before he followed Frank into the lounge. "You've been in my room!" he accused his father.

Frank turned to face his son, and held the photos and box in the air. "Explain!" he demanded.

Jonathon completely ignored him and asked. "Why have you been in my room?"

"That's not the issue here, I want explanations regarding these," Frank replied still waving the items in the air.

"You had no right to be in my room, you must have been searching."

"I have every right to be in your room, and I'm not standing here explaining myself to you. Now Jonathon, explain these disgusting photos and the money in the box."

Stella studied her husband and son. She had never seen Frank so angry with Jonathon, and had never seen Jonathon so frightened of Frank.

"They're not mine," Jonathon answered hastily.

"There, I told you so," Stella said with relief and satisfaction sounding in her voice.

"I'm going to ask you just once more to explain where these have come from, and why they were in your room."

"They're Tyler's," Jonathon suddenly stated. "He said he thought Auntie Ruth was going to have a good clean out in his room, so he told me to look after them for him," he lied.

"He told you to look after them!" Stella repeated. "What do you mean, 'told you'."

"Mum, you don't know him. He can be so mean...and...he's…"

"And he's what darling?" Stella asked sympathetically.

"A bully."

"He's bullying you?" she questioned with anger rising within her.

"Do you really think I want those horrid photos in my room," he said crying as he ran to Stella, and flung his arms around her waist, burying his face tightly into her body.

Stella immediately cuddled her child, and with anger overwhelming her she stared at her husband. "Didn't I tell you so? I knew it would be something like this, and I for one am not surprised that Tyler is involved in this, I've never liked that boy."

"Please mum," Jonathon pleaded as he pulled away from his mother. "Please don't say anything to Auntie Ruth, let me sort it out with Tyler myself. Please mum promise me."

"All right darling," she replied pulling her son back towards her. "Don't upset yourself anymore, we'll talk about it later, but I promise I won't say anything without you knowing."

Frank stood and watched dumfounded as the theatrical piece between his wife and son took place. Jonathon could have told his mother that an alien had planted those items in his room and she would have believed him.

Frank stared at the back of his son's head. "Jonathon, look at me," he said, but when there was no response he shouted. "Jonathon, look at me."

Jonathon slowly turned and stared at his father.

"Exactly what would Tyler have done to you if you had refused to look after this stuff for him?"

"Frank! Don't you think he's been through enough?" Stella admonished as she again pulled Jonathon towards her.

"No Stella, I don't think he's been through anything. You've just stood there and accepted everything he's told you, so I'm sure he can answer my question."

Jonathon lowered his head to stare at the floor, and in a subservient, quiet voice answered. "He would have got his gang onto me."

"His gang? What gang?" Frank asked.

Jonathon turned and stared at his father again as he answered. "Dad you don't know him."

"No son, it's not Tyler I don't know, it's you." Frank replied as he threw the photos, money and box on the sofa and walked out of the room.

"You believe me mum, don't you?"

"Of course I do darling, and don't worry I'll speak to your father later, naturally he was upset to find those things in your room." As she ran her fingers through his hair, and motioned her head towards the sofa, she asked. "Now, what are we going to do with those awful photos and that money?"

"I don't want to get Tyler into trouble mum. Let me give the photos and money back to him, and I'll tell him that you and dad know what's going on. I'll tell him that if he carries on selling them you'll tell his mum and dad, but that you are willing to give him one last chance."

"Oh Jonathon, that's such a good idea. You are such a thoughtful boy."

"Thanks mum," he said with a smile on his face. "I knew you'd believe me, and you know I would never do anything like that don't you?" he added nodding towards the items on the sofa.

Stella kissed her son on his forehead and cuddled him. "You're my son Jonathon, and I probably know you better than you know yourself. Now, you take all that stuff back to your room, and then go wash your hands and face. It's a bit early for lunch, so why don't I fix you a nice mid-morning snack."

"Thanks mum."

As Stella was about to leave the lounge she turned and said. "Jonathon, you will make sure that those photos and money are removed from the house today."

"Of course mum, I'll ring Tyler after lunch," he answered.

"There's a good boy," she said, and made her way to the kitchen to make her son his favourite mid-morning snack.

***

Frank retreated to his office, and locked the door behind him. It was a known fact that although most mothers had an unadulterated love for their children, they also had the ability to recognise their children's faults; but not Stella. In Stella's eyes Jonathon had no faults, and although it was obvious that those photos belong to their son, no amount of discussion would convince her of that. That boy ran rings around her, and she would follow those rings to eternity.

Frank again searched his desk for his mobile phone, knowing full well, after a previous extensive search, that it was not in his office. Whilst on his walk to the newsagent earlier, he had received a disappointing text from Elaine to inform him that she couldn't meet him this afternoon, and he had also checked for any further texts from her when he had reached home. So if Jonathon didn't have the phone, then it was in the house somewhere.

Although he would have no problem buying another phone, and had, in foresight, made a copy of all his personal and business telephone numbers, his computer login passwords, and all his other important notes, it was losing all Elaine's wonderful love poems that she had text him that upset him the most, and prayed that she had copies of them.

His thoughts, as they often did recently, now turned to Joe, and the text messages from him. He could tell by the tone of them that Joe was in trouble, and as much as Frank was often hostile towards him, he didn't wish him any harm, but Frank had his own future to consider, and was reluctant to lend Joe money that he may possibly need himself.

Although Frank had denied Joe his request for money, a heavy guilt hung over him for not helping his brother-in-law.

Chapter 20

Frank had been in a sulky mood all weekend, and Stella wondered why he didn't go out on Saturday afternoon as he had originally told her he was. Stella confirmed her suspicions that it had something to do with Elaine when she had checked the texts on his mobile phone later that evening.

He had complained all weekend about losing his phone, and was still searching the house on Sunday evening. Stella had ignored his childish behaviour as she had more important subjects to consider.

She had promised Jonathon that she wouldn't divulge the discovery of the photos and money to Ruth, and although she had never broken a promise to her son before, she fervently felt that Tyler had to be punished. Naturally, she realised that Ruth would deny her son's involvement, and would place all the blame on Jonathon.

All over the weekend her thoughts had been constantly on this dilemma, and by Sunday evening, and not because of any sense of duty to her sister, Stella had decided to honour her promise to her son.

Stella also decided over the weekend that, as much as she thought the time was right for some meddling in her sister and brother-in-law's affairs, she would avoid her sister for the next couple of weeks and wait for Karen to achieve that goal for her.

However, that all change on Monday afternoon when Jonathon had come home from school and told Stella that Tyler had been crying. He had told Jonathon that his dad had gone away on a business trip, but Tyler had heard his mum and dad argue, and felt sure that his dad had left home.

Stella had been jubilant at this news, as she couldn't imagine why Joe would have to go on a business trip. To where? She felt sure that Joe would buy all his cheap, shoddy products locally, or via the internet.

So the following morning, once Jonathon had left for school and Stella had calculated that Ruth would be home from the school run, she decided to pay her sister a surprise visit. She would have to put her best actress skills to the test, and show surprise, concern, and even a little sisterly love.

***

Ruth had an abysmal weekend without Joe, and had somehow managed not to cry in front of the children. She had told them that Joe had gone on a business trip, and although Abbey had accepted all that Ruth had said, Tyler had questioned her about the argument he had heard that night. She had tried to convince him that he hadn't heard them arguing, and that he must have dreamt it.

She had tried to act as normal as was physically possible over the weekend, and had taken the children out on Saturday to a local fun-fare, and out for lunch on Sunday. Joe had phoned every night to talk to the children, and although Ruth had answered the phone she had been unable to talk to him. She had gone to bed early every night since Friday with question after question whirling around her mind as she cried into her pillow.

Joe had been gone three whole days now, and she missed him desperately. This morning she had taken Tyler and Abbey to school as normal, and as she now sat crying at her kitchen table deciding on her course of action she heard her doorbell ring. She quickly wiped her eyes, and as she was not expecting visitors, she cautiously opened the front door to see her sister standing on her doorstep.

"You've been crying!" Stella stated.

"No I haven't. It's hay fever."

151

"What, at this time of the year? Rubbish. Don't use that old excuse on me Ruth. I know you've been crying." Stella replied as she walked past Ruth, and made her way along the hallway into the kitchen.

Ruth closed the front door and followed her sister.

"So why are you crying?" Stella asked when Ruth entered the kitchen.

Momentarily ignoring Stella, she approached the sink and whilst filling the kettle said. "Nothing in particular, just a few problems."

"What problems?"

"Just a few personal problems, that's all."

"With Joe?"

"No...yes..." Ruth answered stammering her words.

"Come on Ruth," Stella interrupted. "I know we don't always get on, but I am your sister and you know I would never do anything to deliberately hurt you. If you can't tell me, who can you tell? And please don't say Gill, I know she's a good friend, but she's not family."

"Stella!" Ruth admonished as she turned to face her sister. "How can you say that? She's more than a good friend, as you well know."

"But, she's not your sister is she? Oh Ruth, don't get me wrong, I know you think the world of Gill, but sometimes you're better off with family rather than friends helping. Now come on, tell me what's wrong."

Ruth laughed to herself as she listened to Stella's words. Gill had been more of a sister to her than Stella could ever imagine, and although Stella was placed firmly at the bottom of Ruth's consoling list, she decided to confide in her sister rather than she learn about it from a gossipmonger.

"Joe's gone."

"Gone! Gone where?" Stella asked.

"I don't know, and I don't care. That two timing bastard is having an affair with his ex-wife."

"No..." Stella replied, shock visible on her face.

"Yep, can you believe it?"

"When did he leave?" Stella asked.

"Friday."

"Oh Ruth, why didn't you ring me? You've been all on your own since Friday? I can't bear to think of you suffering like that."

Ruth, feeling slightly uneasy to see genuine concern on her sister's face, admonished herself not to cry. She finished making the coffee and took it to the dining table where her sister had settled. She began to disclose the whole story, and Stella, to Ruth's astonishment, asked questions at appropriate places, and had shown great concern.

Once Ruth had finished, Stella said. "Well, I can't believe this. What made her come back?"

"I don't know, and really don't care."

"Has Joe admitted to it?"

"Of course he hasn't. He is denying the affair, but then he would, wouldn't he?"

The two sisters sat in silence for a short while before Ruth asked. "You always phone me before you come round. How comes you didn't today?"

"No special reason, I was out shopping, and just thought I'd take the chance you were in."

Ruth studied her sister, and realised that she was lying. Stella didn't shop locally in the area that Ruth lived, and she never came to see Ruth without ensuring she was at home first.

"You were out shopping early, it's only nine forty-five now," queried Ruth.

"Yes...well...I haven't actually been shopping yet, thought I'd come and see you first."

"I'm sorry Stella, but you're lying, and I have enough on my plate at the moment without you adding to it," Ruth said sternly.

"Ok. Jonathon came home from school yesterday saying that Tyler had been crying and thinks Joe has left home. So naturally being concerned, I came round to see you."

"To gloat, more like."

"No Ruth, I can't bear to see you so unhappy, and I'll do all I can to help you."

As Ruth studied her sister, she once again wondered if her sincerity was genuine.

"Thanks Stella, but only me and Joe can sort this out, and I'd appreciate it if you would keep it to yourself."

"Of course I will. Are you going to tell mum and dad yet?"

"No, I don't want to worry them, and of course I don't want the kids knowing yet. I've a lot of decisions to make."

"Ruth I'll do all I can to help, even if it's only looking after the children why you try to sort yourself out."

Ruth suddenly began to cry and ran into her sister's arms. "What am I going to do Stella? I can't imagine my life without him."

"It's not come to that yet," Stella replied stroking her sister's hair. "It will all work out fine in the end, I'm sure, because you and Joe were made for each other."

Stella also had decisions to make. For her plan to work, Stella must convince Ruth that Joe would not lie to her with regard to the affair.

For her to bring about their demise together, they must stay married.

Chapter 21

Joe had spent the last three days between a hotel and his office at the warehouse. When Ruth had packed him a suitcase on Friday night he knew he had no other choice but to leave. He was too tired and drained to fight her, although he had no idea where he would go. His first thought had been his parents, but he did not want to worry them with his matrimonial problems. His second was Ted's, but knew that his friend had enough problems with Heather's health.

He suddenly remembered that he had received a couple of missed calls from Ted, and although he had replied by text, it had been very curt, promising to call him as soon as possible. He now realised, with guilt, that he hadn't returned Ted's calls, and hoped that his friend hadn't needed him urgently. He had always admired Ted's loyalty towards Heather and his determination to protect her.

Remorse suddenly overwhelmed him as he realised that over the last few months he hadn't protected his family as he should have, in fact, he had been blatantly ignoring them, and had selfishly put them in danger.

Joe had asked Ruth if he could see the children before he left on Friday night, and through tears she had told him of her conversation with Tyler earlier that evening. When Joe eventually spoke with Tyler he felt sure that he had convinced his son that it was a business trip he was going on, and that he would be home soon. Abbey had been sound asleep when he entered her room, so he had gently kissed her on the forehead and whispered how much he loved her.

When he had entered his baby's room and studied Lewis asleep in his cot with his arms and legs in a spread-eagle position, Joe had cried. He cried for the happy times, and recalled the day his youngest child had come into this world. He also cried with guilt, due to the lack of attention and love that he had failed to bestow on his baby. He stroked Lewis's head and told him how much he loved him, and that he would make it up to him one day. Joe didn't know how, but if it was the last thing he did he would make sure his children, and Ruth, knew how much he loved them.

Ruth had shut herself in the bedroom while Joe had made his exit, and although he had seen the bedroom curtain move slightly as he got into his car he didn't acknowledge this. He had driven around the corner and parked the car, while he searched the internet for a local hotel, and chose one that was close to home and his warehouse.

Although he had spent his days in his office, his concentration was at such low ebb he didn't achieve any productivity. He had returned to the hotel around seven-thirty each evening, purely to lay his tired, weary body on the bed. He had no need for food as his appetite had completely diminished. He had called and spoke to the children every night, but Ruth had refused to speak to him.

He now pulled his computer towards him and clicked on the correct programme that started a slide show of family photos of last year's holiday in Majorca, and it was while he studied them that he heard a text notification on his mobile phone. Hoping it might be Ruth he quickly picked up his phone, but to his surprise noticed that the message was from Frank.

'I don't know how much you were going to ask me for but am assuming it was quite a lot, I'll lend you 15k. No more. Send me your bank details and I'll transfer the money right away'.

Joe read Frank's text many times before the message actually penetrated his brain. Although taken aback, a huge flourish of relief overwhelmed him at the same time. He had been bitterly disappointed in his brother-in-law when Frank had originally refused to help, because although they didn't always see eye to eye, they were family.

He was slightly disappointed that Frank hadn't suggested a meeting to discuss the amount, but realised that fifteen thousand pounds would keep Barry content for at least a month or two, and it also gave him a little breathing space to get the rest of the money.

He also hoped that Frank would be lenient with regards to the monthly repayments and time of the loan, so he text his brother-in-law to thank him and to enquire about the arrangements.

As he sat at his desk, drum rolling the top of his fingers on the surface waiting for a reply, it dawned on him that this turn of events could not only save his business, but his marriage too. Ruth believed that Joe was having an affair with Karen, so his main objective now was to convince Ruth that he would never cheat on her, especially with his ex-wife.

He would be honest and tell Ruth that Karen had contacted him to borrow money, but he had turned her down, he would also tell her about Pete. Joe knew that Ruth would bring up their lunchtime drink, and he would have to convince her that he agreed to this purely to talk to Karen about Pete's death.

The reply from Frank arrived five minutes later. *'Will text terms later. Don't worry Joe I'll go easy on you'.*

Joe jumped up from his chair, ran to the office door and opening it hurried into the reception area where Laura, working at her desk, looked up at him in alarm.

"Joe!" she exclaimed. "What's wrong?"

"Nothing is wrong my wonderful secretary," he laughed. "In fact everything is absolutely perfect. Can you phone Ruth for me please, and tell her I'm on my way home."

"Of course," she replied, a puzzled look on her face.

"Laura, I need to apologise to you for my behaviour recently. I'm sure you've guessed but I've had a few problems, but I think they're sorted now."

"I know it's none of my business Joe, but it might have been easier if you had said something sooner."

"Maybe Laura, but hopefully things will go back to normal now."

"Let's hope so Joe," Laura answered smiling as she began to dial Joe's home telephone number.

***

After taking the call from Laura, Ruth wondered why Joe hadn't telephoned himself, but soon realised that he would have been afraid that she may have refused to talk to him.

She decided that this was the opportune moment to talk to her husband, so she hurried upstairs to her en-suite to freshen up. She needed to prepare herself not only to listen to what Joe had to say, but for any battles ahead. He had categorically denied on Friday night that he was having an affair with Karen, but she hadn't believed him, and couldn't see any reason why that would change.

Ten minutes later she heard Joe's car pull onto the drive, so she quickly checked on Lewis who was fast asleep in his baby chair in the lounge. She hurried to the window and watched him get out of his car. How she had missed him, and still found it hard to believe that he had betrayed her with another woman.

She hurried into the kitchen to wait for him, but to her surprise the doorbell rang.

"Why didn't you use your key?" she asked as she opened the front door.

"I didn't think it was right, seeing as I'm not living here at the moment."

She didn't answer, but turned to make her way back to the kitchen.

She heard him close the front door, and once he entered the kitchen she asked. "Do you want tea or coffee?"

"Neither, what I want is to come home. I swear to you Ruth that I'm not having an affair with Karen or anyone else for that matter. You know I would never hurt you like that."

"No, that's the problem Joe I don't. I don't know you anymore. Your moody, irritable, and I think that me and the children don't have a place in your life anymore," she answered as tears fell down her face.

"No place in my life! Ruth, you and the children are my life!"

"Well, you've had a funny way of showing it lately."

"I know and I'm so sorry, it's just that things haven't been going well at work, and I've lost a few large orders," he said sighing.

"I'm sorry Joe, I don't believe you."

"Ruth, it's the truth. I've lost good customers, and I've had trouble getting money from most of the others. I tried to get a loan from the bank, but they turned me down."

"Why haven't you told me all this? It would have made life much easier."

"I know, but I didn't want to worry you."

"And you think your actions lately haven't been worrying?"

"You know me, I don't always think properly," he answered laughing.

Although she realised Joe was trying hard to make amends, Ruth couldn't get the image of him and his ex-wife out of her mind. "And what about your ex-wife?"

"What about her?"

"Why is she back? And don't lie to me Joe I know you've been seeing her."

"I only see her once, and I only agreed to that so she could tell me about Pete. Apparently she broke off with him and he died shortly after."

"Died!"

"Yes, all his family have turned against her, and she wasn't even allowed to attend the funeral."

"But you should have told me all this Joe. We've never kept secrets from each other, especially ones on this scale."

"I know, and I promise that it will never happen again."

Ruth stood before her husband confused. Joe had met up with his ex-wife, after all these years, and had not mentioned it to her. He had fervently denied that they were having an affair, but could she believe him? Would he stand there, with their marriage at stake, and blatantly lie to her? The Joe she knew wouldn't, but she couldn't vouch for the Joe he had turned into. She desperately wanted to believe her husband, because without trust they had no marriage.

"I don't want you to have anything to do with her at all," Ruth demanded.

"I won't, I promise, I've got no need to see her again what so ever. Please Ruth, please believe me when I tell you that I've not had an affair with anyone," he pleaded taking hold of her hand. "You are the only woman for me, and as I said before you and the children are my life. Please let me come home Ruth, I miss you all so much," he begged.

Ruth looked at the only man she had ever loved, and as the tears began to fall down his cheek she dissolved into his arms. "You have put me through hell Joe, and I won't let you do that again."

As she felt his arms wrap around her, and his face bury into her neck, she could hear him crying, and it was in between the sobs that she heard his words.

"I won't. I love you too much Ruthie, and never want to lose you."

It was at this point that Lewis woke, and Joe took the opportunity to go to his son, pick him up and cuddle him as he had not done in months.

Joe went with Ruth to collect the children from school, and both children, in turn, cuddled their father, saying how much they had missed him.

They would never know how much he had missed them, not only the last few days, but the last few months. On the way home he told the children that they were having a family day out at the zoo on Saturday, and the excitement that filled the car was music to Joe's ears.

Chapter 22

The Cannon family awoke, on the following Saturday morning, to a grey, cold, overcast day. Both Joe and Ruth realised that early March was not a good time of year to spend walking around London Zoo but, wrapped up well, they knew the children would enjoy it. Both Tyler and Abbey looked in awe at the tigers, lions, elephants, giraffes, and monkeys. They spent time in the butterfly paradise, the aquarium, the rainforest life and the penguin beach, but both children declared that their favourite had been the gorilla kingdom, and had laughed at the young gorillas, so human-like, getting up to all kinds of antics.

Ruth had suggested that they leave Lewis with her mother, but Joe had insisted that the family day out included them all.

They left the zoo as dusk began to settle, and on the journey home Tyler and Abbey had cheered loudly when Joe announced that they were going to a restaurant for their evening meal.

As the family settled down to dinner, Joe felt as though he now had part of his life back, but knew he still had a multitude of problems; one of them being the neglect of his business. He forgot to place orders with his suppliers; ignored warnings from his staff of the failure to complete customer's orders; and hadn't realised how his once pleasant, courteous attitude towards his staff, and clients alike, had changed to one of arrogance and rudeness. Consequently, over the last couple of weeks he had lost two significant clients, and although he had tried to apologise and secure their custom again, it was to no avail.

He also felt that he now had no need to tell Ruth about Andy Bolan, because once he solved his money problems, it would be an episode in the past and, hopefully, forgotten.

His one other bugbear was the tablets. He didn't feel confident enough, at the moment, to cope with his dilemmas without them, but made a promise to himself that, again, once he had solved all his problems he would stop taking them. He remembered reading a quote once, by whom he couldn't remember, but found it apt to how he was feeling at the moment: *'Any idiot can face a crises, it's the day-to-day living that wears you out'.*

He now felt more positive than he had in a long time, and had applied to the bank for another loan, a smaller amount this time, as he hoped this would increase his chances of success. He had not seen or heard from Karen, and was confident that she was, once again, out of his life.

***

Karen placed the newspaper on the small coffee table after scouring it for jobs, without success. Although she knew she had no right to be fussy, every job that interested her was either too far away, or awkward hours.

Her career as a social worker had ended the day she left England for France with Pete. In France she had worked in local supermarkets and had waited on tables, although her health obsession and keep-fit regimes had remained.

It was as she was about to change into her jogging clothes that her mobile phone rang, and felt disgruntled when the name 'Stella' appeared on the screen. Her first inclination was not to answer, but if she had judged Stella correctly, she felt certain that the woman would hound her until she did.

"Hello."

"Hi Karen," said the cheerful voice at the other end.

"Oh, hi."

"How are you?"

"Fine thanks."

"You don't sound it. Anyway I'm ringing because I've not heard anything from you. Have you seen Joe lately?"

On hearing these words her stomach churned. "No Stella and I have no intention of."

"He's very down Karen, and I'm worried about him," Stella replied. "I thought we had a deal. You promised me you would keep an eye on him."

"I don't remember promising you anything."

"Look Karen, I have enough on my hands with Ruth. She is so depressed that I'm trying to get her to see a doctor. All I want from you is reassurance that Joe is all right, but it seems that you're not bothered about him because you've not kept your part of the bargain."

Could she trust this woman? Although she had no reason to doubt her sincerity, she didn't remember agreeing to be part of any bargain.

"I'm sorry Stella, but you've got to understand how hard this is for me."

"You've obviously not heard," Stella said.

"Heard what?"

"Joe and Ruth have split up. She thinks he's having an affair with you."

Dumbfounded, Karen replied. "But...we're...not."

"And I believe you Karen, but now you must realise how much I need your help."

"I'll go and talk to Ruth, make her see sense."

"No you won't, that will only make it worse," Stella replied, panic sounding in her voice.

"But I can't keep turning up at his office, we'll wind up arguing and then I'll lose all contact with him."

"Not if he thinks you're there as just a friend. I thought you knew and understood him Karen. I thought you of all people would realise that all he needs at this moment in time is a shoulder to cry on."

"I know, and I don't like to think of him suffering, but I don't know what to do about it."

"Then I'll tell you," Stella replied, impatience sounding in her tone. "Turn it around. Phone him and say you want to see him. Let him think that it's you that needs help. That way he gets to play Sir Galahad, and you can keep an eye on him."

Karen hesitated slightly as she said. "I'm not sure...he..."

"I thought you cared about him," Stella interrupted.

"I do...he means the world to me."

"Well, you have a funny way of showing it. He needs help, and you as a friend should be there to help him."

"All right, I'll arrange to meet him somewhere."

"No, he won't agree to that. He'll be afraid of someone seeing you together. Invite him to your flat. Assure him that all you want to do is talk, and that naturally no one will know about it."

"I'll try, but I can't force him."

"Please try Karen, I can't stress enough how worried I am about him."

"All right, I'll text you if I make any arrangements."

"No Karen, you text me when you have made the arrangements, not if."

"I promise I'll do my best Stella, I can hear how worried you are."

"Thank you Karen, you don't know how much I appreciate this. It really takes a load off my mind."

As Karen pushed the 'end call' button, she decided to phone Joe immediately before she changed her mind. She would look forward to seeing and talking to him again, the difference being this time she had permission.

***

Stella placed her mobile phone back in her handbag triumphantly, because she had no doubt that Karen would now make the arrangements to see Joe, although she did wonder if she had made the right decision in telling Karen of their separation.

She shrugged this doubt off and considered her plan. It was a remarkably simple one, once Karen had advised her of the date and time of her encounter with Joe, she would drive to Karen's flat, park in one of the many spaces opposite, and sit and watch her brother-in-law go into Karen's flat, and come out again.

She would add the date and the amount of time they spent together to her list of Joe's misdemeanours, to use against him when the appropriate time came.

She decided not make any arrangements for the next few days while she waited for Karen's text. How she loved a plan that eventually came together.

***

Joe, Ruth and the children had just finished their starters when Joe's mobile phone began to ring. He glanced at the screen which said 'number unknown', and feeling annoyed with himself for not turning it off, felt obliged to answer it.

"Hello, Joe Cannon here."

"Hello Joe, how are you?"

Karen's voice was the last one he expected to hear, so he looked at Ruth and mouthed the words, 'Sorry work'.

"Hello Mr Bryant, I'm sorry but I'm out at the moment, and don't have any paperwork on me, but I'm sure your order has been dispatched. I'll ring you first thing Monday morning."

"I take it you can't talk," Karen said. "When's the best time? I desperately need to see and speak to you Joe."

"Yes Mr Bryant, Monday morning. Thanks for ringing, enjoy the rest of your weekend. Bye."

Feeling angry and flushed he ended the call, turned his mobile phone off and placed it back in his pocket.

"You all right Joe? You look very flushed," Ruth asked sounding concerned.

"Yes I'm fine. Just hate being caught out like that," he assured Ruth.

"Caught out?" she enquired.

"Yes, customers ringing out of office hours, and having no paperwork on me to answer their questions."

Joe noticed the doubt on Ruth's face, and was sure she was about to question him when he noticed the glee on the children's faces as the waitress placed their meals in front of them. Ruth had obviously decided this was not the right time.

Joe was furious but tried, with as much self-control as he could gather, not to show it, although he did notice Ruth staring at him on the odd occasion. How dare Karen ring him on a Saturday, when she must have realised that there would be every possibility he would be with his family. She had no way of knowing that he and Ruth had parted recently. Although he had no interest in why she had wanted to see or speak to him, he was of a mind to call her on Monday morning to reprimand her for the contact, and pointedly remind her that she was not, and never would be, part of his life again.

The rest of the meal was very enjoyable, and Joe realised how much he had missed his family, not just over the few days he had been apart from them, but the few months that he had not been part of their lives. Although he had spent money today he could hardly afford, he did not regret one penny of it. It had, he hoped, brought him back to the heart of his family where he belonged.

They arrived home around eight-thirty that evening, and Joe immediately opened a bottle of wine. As Lewis was already asleep Ruth put him straight into his cot, and both Tyler and Abbey were absolutely exhausted, so they also decided to go to bed.

Joe and Ruth spent the next couple of hours talking, and Joe felt ashamed of how much he had neglected his children over the last few months as Ruth updated him on their schooling, leisure time and general pursuits.

She also brought him up-to-date about Stella and her antics, including her sister buying the red dress, and the e-reader Ruth had intended to buy for their mother. She also told him about Jonathon and the missing money, and being brought before the headmaster for bullying.

Joe was surprised to hear that Ruth had received two visits recently from her sister, the last one being just this week, and although Stella had phoned a couple of times since then, Ruth had been vague with her, and hadn't yet told her that Joe was back living at home. They had laughed at the fact that she must be foaming at the mouth for information about them.

When Joe enquired why Ruth hadn't told him all this before, she replied that some of it she had, but he obviously had his mind elsewhere and hadn't heard her.

That night they made love for the first time in months, and Joe made an oath to himself that he would never let anything come between him and his family again; no matter what.

Chapter 23

The following Monday morning Joe was sitting in his office at the warehouse at six thirty. He had become aware over the weekend just how much effort and time would be needed to get his business back on track. He hoped to hear from the bank with regard to his loan within the next week which would allow him to buy fresh stock which was urgently needed. He also had decided to set up meetings with the two clients that he had recently lost.

It was just after seven o' clock when he took his first dose of tablets of the day and his mobile phone rang.

As the screen did not show the caller's name, Joe said. "Hello, Joe Cannon here."

"Hello Joe, sorry about my call on Saturday," replied Karen.

Anger now engulfed Joe. "So you should be," he shouted into his phone. "How dare you ring me, especially on a Saturday when you know full well that there'd be every chance I was with my family."

"I thought you'd split from Ruth."

"Where did you hear that?" he demanded.

"Oh...err...I'm not sure now. Have you split from her?"

"No...yes...It was only for a couple of days, but it's all been sorted now. You still had no right to call me over the weekend, or any time for that matter."

"I know, and I'm really sorry, but I desperately need to see you Joe."

"Well I don't need to see you. Now piss off Karen and leave me alone."

"Please Joe," she pleaded. "Just give me half an hour, I really need to speak to someone."

"Then call the Samaritans."

"All I'm asking for is half an hour of your time. Pease Joe, just this one meet, and I'll never bother you again."

He listened to the plea in her voice which worried Joe slightly, and realised he didn't want to be responsible if she were to do anything stupid to herself.

"Okay, when and where?" he sighed.

"I don't mind, but as soon as possible. We could meet in a bar somewhere."

"No. I don't want to take the chance of being seen with you."

"Come to my flat then."

Joe contemplated this suggestion for a few seconds. "Give me your address and I'll be round at eleven-thirty, but don't expect help from me Karen I've enough problems of my own."

"Just an ear to listen that's all I need. Thanks Joe."

After Karen had given him the address, Joe ended the call and placed his phone on the desk. What was he letting himself in for? Why had he agreed to meet her? He thought he had heard stress and despondency in her voice, but Joe knew his main reason for meeting her again was to make sure that she hadn't come back into his life to cause him trouble. She had already phoned Ruth, so at least he knew that he couldn't trust her.

He wanted to make it quite clear to her that she was no longer a part of his life, and that this would be the last time they saw each other. His attitude towards her would be harsh and cold and he would show her he meant every word.

He arrived at her second floor flat promptly at eleven-thirty only to discover, to his annoyance, that she wasn't in. He rang the bell and knocked on the door three times, and was just about to leave when she came running up the stairs apologising.

"Sorry Joe, I bumped into a woman who said there's a job available in the shop she works, and is going to get me an application form," she said excitedly.

He had no interest in her news, so did not offer an opinion. He stood there, impatiently, waiting for her to retrieve her keys from her pocket and open the front door. He followed her in and noticed, with surprise, that the entrance of the flat led directly into a room which contained a small lounge area, her bed and a kitchen. He assumed the door leading off to the left was the bathroom and toilet. Although the room was clean and tidy, shock overwhelmed him at the poor condition of the property.

"You want to get in touch with the landlord. Look at the state of this place. It needs decorating and a complete refurbish," he said as he walked over to the electric wall sockets. "These need looking at, they're dangerous and a fire hazard."

"I've called him a couple of times, but he's refusing to do anything."

"Then get in touch with environmental health, they'll sort him out," he offered with no emotion in his voice.

As he removed his coat, she offered him a seat on the tiny, uncomfortable looking sofa, and began to prepare a pot of coffee. She placed a plate of croissants on the table and said. "I'm sorry I wasn't here when you arrived, but I popped to the shop to get these, I remembered how much you liked them."

Again he proffered no answer, and watched as she poured the coffee and settled herself on the chair next to her bed.

"Please don't be angry with me Joe, and believe me when I say I have no intentions of making any trouble for you. I know how much you love your wife, and wouldn't do anything to spoil that."

"You keep saying that but you phoned my wife the last time we met. Remember?" he answered with a sarcastic tone in his voice.

"I know, and I can't apologise enough. I don't know what made me do that. I honestly think I had this silly notion in my head that we could all be friends, but of course I realise now that it would never work."

"No Karen it wouldn't. This is the last time we will see each other, and I mean it this time. An ex-wife coming back on the scene is quite frowned upon by the current wife, especially when they know there's been contact."

"Joe, I can't apologise enough, please forgive me, and I promise never to ring you again."

"Why did you want to see me this time?" he asked.

"To set the record straight and apologise for ringing Ruth, and because I didn't want us to part on bad terms again."

Although still angry with her, he could sense how unhappy she was, and suddenly felt his attitude towards her resolve slightly. "Do you miss Pete?" he asked, and noticed her surprised reaction to this question.

"Yes...no...I do sometimes," she hesitated. "You've got to remember that we were separated for a short while before he died, and if I'm honest...he was not the love of my life."

Joe didn't respond to this statement, as he was afraid of where it would lead. He took an offered croissant that she had spread with butter and jam; just the way he liked them.

"Do you intend to stay here?" he asked glancing around the room.

"It's all I can afford at the moment," she replied. "But once I find a job, and get some money behind me, the first thing I'll do is find somewhere more decent to live."

It did cross Joe's mind that one of their packers had just given notice, but dismissed the thought immediately. He wanted Karen out of his life, not working in his warehouse.

For the next hour their topic of conversation ranged from Joe's business, his family, and her time living in France. It was when Karen touched on the subject of their past relationship that Joe glanced at his watch. He immediately stood up and grabbed his coat. "Christ, its one o'clock," he said. "I've got to run, I've an appointment at two, and I've got to go back to the warehouse first."

"Thanks Joe, I appreciate you coming to see me," Karen said as she rose from her chair.

"That's all right, but we agree no more contact between us."

"None, I promise. I've a life I need to get on with."

"I really hope you do Karen, you deserve to be happy."

"Thanks Joe."

He kissed her slightly on the cheek and said. "Look after yourself."

She accompanied him to the front door, and he left without any further communication between them. As he walked along the landing, he hoped and prayed that he had not made a mistake by coming to her flat today and spending time with her again. He was absolutely convinced he could trust her with regard to not contacting Ruth again, but knew he would have to bear the consequences if she did.

He buttoned up his coat as he ran down the stairs, and made his way to his car. He was deep in thought as he unlocked his car door, so he didn't notice Stella sitting in her car opposite, watching his every move.

He hadn't intended to spend so long with Karen, and now wished he had brought the particulars with him for his afternoon appointment. Arriving back at the warehouse he quickly checked on the details, and made his way to see a Douglas Wrotham who was the head buyer of a group of shops scattered over South East London, and a potential customer.

After the meeting, even though Douglas had mentioned reports of Joe's recent loss of clients, Joe felt more positive than he had in months. If he were to win this contract and have his bank loan application approved, his problems would greatly decline. So it was with a bottle of wine, flowers, and chocolates in hand, that he decided to go home early for a family evening with Ruth and the children.

He woke the following morning in a positive mood, and was again in his office at six-thirty. It was about eight-thirty that he switched on his computer to read his emails and immediately noticed one from Douglas Wrotham. With his heart thumping he opened it up and to his horror read that he had not been successful with the contract.

Joe was about to reply to Douglas to request another meeting, but realised that not only was it unethical, but he was in no mood for begging, so it was with shaking hands that he pulled the bottle of vodka from his drawer to accompany his tablets.

He spent the rest of the morning trying to organise an advertising campaign through a trade magazine, at a cost he couldn't afford.

Laura had taken the morning off for a dentist appointment, and when she knocked and walked into the office, just after lunch carrying the post, she noticed Joe taking tablets.

"Got a headache Joe?"

"Err...yes," he lied.

"Do you want me to go through the post if you have a bad head?"

"No, that's all right. I'll do it. Thanks Laura."

As Laura walked out of the office, Joe pulled the post towards him and quickly glanced through the pile. He noticed a letter from his bank, so with a pounding heart for the second time that day, he opened the letter and read it.

Anger surged through him, as he screwed the letter into a tight ball and threw it across the room. They had again rejected his application for a loan. If he was to protect his family from Barry McGraw, he either had to sever all ties, or greatly reduce the amount he owed him, and to do this he desperately needed to borrow at least another twenty or thirty thousand pounds.

His life was a roller coaster of emotions; up one hour, down the next. He suddenly felt his grip on life slipping away again, and although he had only just taken four tablets, he reached for his desk drawer, took out another two and the bottle of vodka.

Chapter 24

Once completed, the house adaptations had a slow but sure effect on Heather. She gradually regained her confidence and began to cook meals, complete daily housework chores, and manage her own personal hygiene without any help.

Ted could leave Heather alone in the house for longer spells than he had previously been able to, which enabled him to concentrate and, hopefully, re-build his landscape gardening business.

It was just over two months after the start of their new life that Heather started to complain of a slight headache. It was when the headache worsen that she began a course of painkillers which, unfortunately, did not lessen the pain. Heather mentioned the ailment to her doctor, two days later, whilst at a routine check-up, and he diagnosed stress. He explained that although her lifestyle was now easier, she still had to cope with the changes, and prescribed stronger painkillers.

Two days later, the pain had become so intense that Ted immediately took her to the accident and emergency department at their local hospital, where the doctors carried out a thorough examination, and immediately admitted her.

An inoperable brain tumour was diagnosed, with just days to live. Devastated at hearing this news, Ted stayed at Heather's hospital bedside refusing to leave her. The doctors and nurses had all insisted that he go home for some rest, and although he knew his own health was suffering, he had rejected their request. He watched, helpless, as the woman he loved suffered and changed, personality-wise, overnight as the doctors had warned.

Ted had cried. He cried as he had never cried before. He was going to lose his wife, his best friend, his soul mate, his Heather. He had tried to ring Joe on a couple of occasions during the last few days, but had received no answer, except for a short text saying he would contact him soon.

Ted needed his friend as he had never needed him before. Maybe he should have text Joe informing him how ill Heather was, but felt that would have been a cold and heartless action. He would call him again tomorrow, and if he still received no response he would phone Ruth. Although Heather and Ruth had never been close, she still had a right to know that Heather was dying.

Heather had been in and out of consciousness all day, but sadly did not recognise Ted when she was awake. As the night veered towards the early morning Ted sat and lovingly held her hand. The nurses had checked on Heather all through the night, and it was as Ted noticed the sun rising that he decided to climb on the bed to lay with his wife. He gently put his arms around her, and it was as he whispered how much he loved her that Heather peacefully died in her sleep.

It was two hours later when Heather's body had been removed and the paperwork completed that Ted, lethargically, gathered Heather's possessions from the hospital room, trying not to look at the empty bed. He left the hospital a lonely, sad man with no one around to comfort him. As he walked out of the entrance he again tried Joe's mobile phone, which went straight to the answer machine. In anger he typed out a text message informing Joe that Heather was dead and added, sarcastically, that he hoped all was well with him.

He regretted sending the text as soon as it he had pressed the 'send' button.

***

When Ted answered the door to Joe later that evening, Ted didn't greet his friend but walked back to the lounge, leaving the door open to enable Joe to follow.

Joe closed the front door behind him, and humbly entered the lounge. "I'm so sorry mate I don't know what to say."

Ted stood, with his back to Joe, at the patio doors staring out to the garden. "Where were you Joe?"

"I've got some problems," Joe answered meekly.

Ted swung round to face his friend. "Have you recently watched your wife suffer in so much pain, and couldn't do anything to help her?"

"Err...no..."

"Have you sat at your wife's hospital bed and watched her personality change into someone you don't know?"

"Ted..."

"Is your wife dead Joe?"

"Ted..." Joe said again.

"Is your wife fucking dead Joe?" Ted now shouted.

"No...no, she's not."

"Then...don't...tell...me...you've...got...problems," Ted said, emphasising every word. "You don't know the meaning of the word."

"I'm so sorry, I don't know what to say to you."

"Nothing Joe, there's nothing to say, so shut the door on your way out."

"No Ted, I know I wasn't there for you when you needed me, but I'm here now."

"I don't need you now Joe, I needed you when Heather was dying. I needed you to cry with, I needed you to shout and curse with. I need to be on my own now. I'll ring you when I've arranged the funeral. Give Ruth and the children my love."

"Let me help you with the arrangements. You still need me. Please Ted, don't shut me out."

Suddenly, as if reality had just hit him, Ted crumbled to the floor, curled into a foetal position and cried like a baby. Joe quickly lay down beside his friend and cried with the man who he had always thought of as a brother. Joe cried for the loss of Heather, he also cried for all his own problems, but mainly he cried for his friend, and the fact that he hadn't been there for him when he had needed him the most.

***

Sitting in the lounge now with a bottle of whiskey and a bottle of vodka open, Joe listened to his friend as he explained what had happened over the last couple of weeks. He also explained how Heather had only just got used to the house adaptations. Ted laughed as he told Joe that she had never had so much room to manoeuvre, but had still kept bumping into things, including the furniture and doorways.

Joe had called Ruth earlier, and told her of the devastating news. She had been very upset, and agreed that Joe should stay with Ted for the night.

Although Ted insisted he had no appetite, Joe ordered a Chinese take-away, which had just been delivered, so Joe now dished the meal onto plates and passed one to Ted.

"So what problems have you had?" Ted asked his friend as he took the plate.

"Nothing compared to yours."

"Come on Joe tell me, it might help me take my mind off Heather for a while."

Joe took a swig of vodka before he said. "Remember Andy Bolan and the fifty thousand pounds?"

"Of course I do, I panicked every day until that money was back in the bank. Has it paid out yet?"

"No, and it won't," Joe said shaking his head.

"Back a wrong one, did you?"

"I didn't back anything, it was a scam," Joe answered, and proceeded to tell Ted all that had happened.

"Joe! I can't believe you went to Barry McGraw for the money," Ted exclaimed.

"I had no choice," explained Joe.

"But Barry McGraw Joe, he's notorious. The amount of people he has apparently hurt for not paying back his money is unbelievable."

"Thanks Ted, you're a great help," Joe said with a slight smile on his face. "I only wanted the money for about nine months," he continued. "Barry's a hard man, but I had no one else to turn to. Now I can't pay him back, and whether Barry gets to me first or not, you could say I'm stuffed."

"Why didn't you tell me? We could've sorted something out. I feel guilty now."

"No Ted, you needed that money for Heather. There's only one person to blame and that's me."

"I can't believe you haven't told Ruth," Ted said as he scraped their untouched meal into a carrier bag.

"I know, and as time goes on I find it harder to tell her. But you've not heard the rest of it yet." Joe said, and filled up both their glasses before he continued. "Karen's back."

"Karen…"

Joe again continued with his story, telling his friend all the details of Ruth accusing him of having an affair with Karen.

"Wow," Ted said when Joe had finished. "Are you and Ruth all right now?"

"Well…let's just say she's watching me like a hawk," Joe laughed.

"And you say Frank has now lent you fifteen thousand pounds."

"Yes, and I'm waiting to see him to sort out a repayment plan. I intend to ask him if I can borrow another twenty thousand, or more if he can afford it, then I won't owe Barry so much and I'll be able to keep the payments up every month."

"Do you think he will?"

"I've no idea. He turned down my first request then changed his mind, so I might be in with a chance."

"That's a lot of money to pay out every month."

"Believe me it won't be as much as I have to pay out now."

"What about the tablets Joe?"

"What tablets?"

"Joe, you've only been here a couple of hours and I've seen you take two lots already."

"They're headache tablets."

"No they're not, they're benzodiazepines. Heather was on them a few years ago when life got too much for her, but they would only let her stay on them for a few weeks."

"They help me Ted."

"How long you been on them?"

"About six weeks."

"So your doctor should start to wean you off them now."

"Yeah, I'm due to go back next week," he lied. "Will you stay in this house Ted?"

"I've not even thought about that. This place was adapted for Heather, so I'm not sure."

"Sorry Ted, bit insensitive to ask at this time."

Ted now studied his friend. "I'm glad you're here Joe. I don't know how I'm going to cope without Heather, but knowing you're here for me really helps, and I know you have problems, and believe me mate, I intend to be there for you.

***

Joe arrived back at his office the following afternoon feeling absolutely exhausted. They had sat up until around four in the morning, and Ted had cried as he talked of Heather and his future life without her. Joe had listened to him, and promised to do all he could to help his friend.

Joe still couldn't believe that Heather was dead, and worried for his friend's state of mind. He had offered to go with Ted to make the arrangements for the funeral, but Ted had insisted he did this unpleasant task on his own.

Although Joe would worry about his friend, he still had his own problems, the main one being where could he possibly obtain at least another twenty thousand pounds. Joe knew that his time was running out where Barry McGraw was concerned, and that Frank, again, was his only hope.

Later that afternoon, Joe, thankfully, received a text from Frank asking to meet him. Although he knew that Frank's main aim would be to agree a repayment plan for the money he had already borrowed, Joe's main aim would be to borrow more. Frank suggested a bar that Joe knew well, and they arranged to meet at twelve-thirty tomorrow lunchtime.

Joe eagerly awaited this meeting with Frank, and a chance to talk to him. To explain to his brother-in-law what an idiot he had been, and maybe, just maybe, Frank would see his way to lending him at least another twenty thousand pounds or more, with hopefully, a considerate repayment plan, which would solve most of Joe's problems.

Feeling slightly elated now, Joe took his coat and scarf from the stand, put them on and left the office. He intended to first pay a visit to Ted before he went home for an evening with his wife and children.

Chapter 25

For Joe's liking, the bar was busy; far too busy for a weekday lunchtime. He had arrived early for his meeting with Frank, and strained his neck to observe everyone who entered the bar.

He had decided to confess the whole truth with regard to his idiotic venture into the money world to his brother-in-law, as he felt sure that Frank would not divulge the information to Stella, and hopefully, would have empathy with him, and offer a further advance.

Joe had enjoyed his evening with Ruth and the children last night, and feeling confident about this meeting with Frank today, he had promised Ruth a luxurious summer family holiday to make up for his unreasonable behaviour of late.

Joe noticed the familiar figure as soon as she entered the bar. Did she normally use this bar? Maybe she was with Frank. With his heart pounding he surveyed her as she glanced around; she was obviously here to meet someone. As their eyes locked she waved and smiled at him, and to Joe's utter amazement she made her way towards him. As she approached, she kissed him slightly on the cheek, and took the sit next to him at the table.

"Dry white wine please," she said as she retrieved a mobile phone from her handbag to glance at it, and returned it to her bag. "Twelve forty-five, sorry I'm late, the traffic is atrocious."

Dumbfounded he asked, "Late. Late for what?

"Our meeting of course, that's why you're here isn't it?

"But...but I'm meeting Frank here."

"Frank? I don't think so, now be a good boy and get me that drink."

"No! Not until you tell me what's going on," he replied defiantly.

When she didn't respond, he pulled his mobile phone from his pocket and dialled Frank's mobile number. When a ringing tone sounded from inside Stella's bag, she retrieved it to answer the call.

"Hi Joe," she said into the phone with a dreary tone in her voice, and stared at him with no emotion or expression on her face. As he was about to rebuke her, she quickly interrupted him with a menacing tone penetrating her voice. "Joey boy, if you know what's good for you, you'll get me that drink now."

Joe was about to speak again, but Stella's body language and facial expression implied that he should play down this confrontation, and as he didn't want to make a fuss in such a crowded bar, he stood up and very reluctantly fought his way to the busy bar.

Whilst waiting to be served question after question whirled around his mind. Why was Stella here instead of Frank? Wouldn't Frank have told him if he was sending Stella instead? Why did she have Frank's phone? Were they now working as a partnership? He didn't think so. As far as Joe knew, Frank sometimes disliked his wife as much as everyone else.

After waiting at least ten minutes to be served, he ordered a wine for Stella and two double vodkas and a pint of beer for himself. The first vodka he snatched from the barman's hand and threw down his throat, the second was swiftly behind it.

Stella had laughed to herself as she watched Joe march to the bar, pushing a few people out of his way. She laughed again, but this time out loud. She now had the almighty Joe Cannon just where she wanted him; eating out of the palm of her hand. She also had the added pleasure of the fact that he hadn't realise it yet.

Joe returned to the table, and as he placed the drinks down he demanded. "Now, you explain what's going on here, because I've had enough of your silly games."

Stella completely ignored him, took a couple of sips of her wine and pulled a disgruntled face at the taste of it and, with composure, placed the glass on the table. She pulled a packet of cigarettes out of her handbag and placed it underneath her nose to inhale the aroma of the tobacco, and returned them back to her bag.

"I didn't know you smoked," Joe said taken aback.

"There are a lot of things you don't know about me Joey boy," she said as she picked up her glass again to sip her wine. "I take it Barry was pleased with the fifteen thousand you've just repaid him," she continued, and took great pleasure as she watched the shock expression appear on her brother-in-law's face.

Joe now stared at Stella totally bewildered. How did she know about Barry and the loan?

"I was so pleased when Barry called me and said you'd been to him for a loan. Of course I had already warned him that you might, and I insisted that he gave it to you, at a reasonable rate I might add.

Joe was about to question her, but realised he didn't know where to begin.

She laughed at him. "Not like you Joey Boy to be lost for words. I thought cocky Joe Cannon always had something to say."

Joe stared at his sister-in-law, and with shaking hands he picked up his drink and gulped it down as if all the answers lay at the bottom of the empty glass. He had hoped it would quench his insatiable thirst, but sadly the liquid made no contact.

With anger and confusion now overpowering him, he banged his glass on the table, which he noticed made Stella jump slightly, and snarled at her. "Okay Stella, my turn now, I want an explanation to what's going on, I'm not playing anymore games with you."

She regained her composure after his slight outburst and replied. "Believe me Joe, I'm not playing games, and err...just out of interest did you manage to borrow the rest of the money?"

He didn't answer her, he couldn't answer her; his mind was racing. What was happening here? He had received a text from Frank requesting to meet him, but instead of Frank he was sitting across a table with his sister-in-law who, Joe was absolutely convinced, was the devil's daughter.

Stella moved her wine glass to one side, leaned across the table and put her face so close to Joe's that their noses practically touched. Very seductively she began to stroke his face and said. "You know, there was something else I had to tell you, but can't for the life of me think what it was."

Joe grabbed hold of her wrist and forcibly yanked her hand away, but keeping hold of her arm he studied his sister-in-law. She was a plain-looking woman, but with a skilful knowledge of cosmetics and dress sense. She had made countless passes at him over the years, even including an offer of money last year for services she would render, which he had blatantly refused, giving her the exact reasons why. Frank had told him many years ago that he and Stella practically lived separate lives. Had that changed now? He somehow doubted it.

"Let go of my wrist Joe," she said emphasizing each word, and waited for him to release her arm. Studying Joe, she knew why she had always admired his good looks, but his biggest mistake was not being forthcoming to her advances towards him.

As Joe freed her arm he glanced around the bar hoping that no one had witnessed their little confrontation. Satisfied nobody had, he returned his attention back to his sister-in-law.

Stella picked up her glass, sipped her wine and said. "Oh yes, I remember what I had to tell you now, Andy Bolan said to say hello."

On hearing Andy's name Joe sat bolt upright. "Andy...Bolan...what do you know of Andy?"

"You'll be surprised at what I know Joe," she said with a menacing tone in her voice.

Without any warning Joe rose from the table and went straight to the bar. On his return he placed a pint of beer for himself and another glass of wine for Stella on the table. He sat down and stared straight at her. "All right Stella, you have my attention. I know at this precise moment you definitely have the upper hand, but I would really appreciate an explanation to all this."

"Joe, Joe, Joe, you just don't realise how much of an upper hand I have."

"What's going on Stella?"

"Haven't you figured it out yet Joe? I thought you were much brighter than you appear to be at this moment."

Joe stared at her, trying to read the expression on her face. What hadn't he figured out? Why was she here? How did she know about Barry? And more to the point, how did she know about Andy?

Suddenly, as if a thunderbolt had struck, it hit him.

"Did...you...set me up?"

"Bingo Joey boy, I set you up good and proper!" she exclaimed, imitating a cockney accent.

"But how? Why?" Joe asked in disbelief.

Stella ignored these questions and said. "I had a bet with Andy that you would fall for it. I even won myself a couple of hundred pounds there. Of course I had the upper hand, knowing you as well as I do," she added with a smirk on her face.

Joe reprimanded himself as he felt the tears well in his eyes, and covered his face with his hands. Shaking his head from side to side he listened as his sister-in-law continued.

"The shame about it is Andy thought you were a really nice fellow. Although he never was a good judge of character," she added sarcastically.

"Obviously not if he's a friend of yours," Joe said quietly.

Stella again ignored him and continued. "I told him you were a greedy bastard, and would fall for it."

"How did you know that I didn't have the fifty thousand pounds, and that I would go to Barry for the money?"

"You may act like the big business man Joe, but even I know you wouldn't have a spare fifty thousand pounds. So I had a little bet with myself that you'd go to the bank for a loan, but I also guessed that you were probably already up to your neck in debt with them. Of course, if you'd got your bank loan, things would have been different."

Joe suddenly had a thought. "Where's Andy now?"

"If you're thinking of trying to find him don't bother, he's long gone. Never to be seen again I should imagine," she replied picking up her glass of wine. "Do you know, I'm going to miss him, I've known him a long time, and believe me when I say we've had some fun in the past. We also did a lot of business together, and I earned a lot of money with him."

"What screwing poor bastards like me?"

"Oh no Joe, you were a one-off. Andy, well that's not his real name of course, actually is a financial investor. Your fifty thousand just gave his coffers a little boost so he could go and disappear, which he's been waiting to do for some time now."

"Are you telling me that you don't have any of my money?"

"Not a penny. That was the deal. He did this one job for me, and he kept all the money. Worth every penny I might add."

"I'm going to the police!" Joe stated.

"Don't be stupid, I'll deny everything I've just told you. Come on Joe, are the police going to investigate a little suburban housewife, married to a wealthy business man as part of a financial scam ring." She began to laugh as she added. "They'll laugh you out of the police station."

"But why Stella?" Joe pleaded. "Why have you tried to destroy me like this?"

"Because Joe you are a big-headed, cocky little bastard who needed bringing down."

"What about Ruth? You have basically destroyed your own sister."

"Ruth! Believe me, that stuck-up cow needed bringing down more than you."

"What has she ever done to you to make you hate her so much?"

When Stella didn't answer but held up her glass to indicate she wanted a refill, Joe snarled, "Get your own!"

Anger overwhelmed her, and with her facial expression suddenly changing to one of intimidation she said through gritted teeth. "If you know what's good for you, and that stuck up wife of yours, and those bastard children you'll do as you're told." She hesitated before she continued with a lighter tone. "By the way Joe, need any more tablets?"

"Tablets?" Joe questioned.

"Yes Joe, tablets. You know the ones you are relying on so heavily. Do you know that you're probably buying more than the average local chemist?" she laughed.

"How are you involved in that?" he asked astonished.

"Let's just say that Charley owed me a big favour, and was pleased to pay it back to be out of my debt."

"I never realised you knew Charley."

"I know who I need to know."

Joe shook his head. "You are something else Stella, you are one evil cow."

"Thanks for the compliment Joe and I think another drink is in order to celebrate."

"Celebrate what?" Joe asked, the fight for survival gradually draining from him.

"Our new alliance of course, me at the helm, and you Joey boy, submerged somewhere in a deep, dark gutter that you call your life."

Chapter 26

As Joe slowly opened his eyes he noticed, apart from the pain pounding in his head, a wisp of light glowing in front of him. As the seconds past and consciousness began to manifest he realised he was in unfamiliar surroundings.

He sat up slightly, and with his hand began to fumble around on a surface to his right that, he assumed, was a bedside cabinet. He found a lamp and after a couple of seconds found the switch to turn it on. Although the light from the lamp hurt his eyes, he scanned the room but could not fathom out where he was, and as he glanced at the empty space beside him in the bed, he groaned out loud as his memory came flooding back.

Through a crack in the curtain he noticed that it was dark outside so assumed it was evening time, and noticing a clock on the wall confirmed that it was seven-thirty.

Seven-thirty! Would Ruth be worried sick wondering where he was? Or would she be ready to accuse him of going back to his old ways again. With his headache increasing in pain and nausea rising within him, he slowly got out of bed to search for his jacket, which he found thrown over the back of a chair. He stumbled back to the bed and retrieved his mobile phone from his jacket pocket. As he saw several texts, and missed calls from Ruth he groaned again.

He could not bring himself to talk to Ruth at this moment, as the shame was too much to bear. With shaking hands he sent her a text message apologising for not contacting her earlier, confirmed that he was all right, and that he would explain everything later. He would think of an excuse before he got home.

"You really shouldn't take so many of those tablets and vodka together Joe, it's not a good combination, and definitely not good for your health you know."

Looking towards the door where the sliver of light had originated, he watched as Stella emerged with a towel wrapped round her. It was as she glided across the room, and sat at an antique looking dressing table that Joe now realised how luxurious the room was. He was sitting on a four-poster canopied bed, surrounded by fine antiques and reproduction furniture. Tiny crystal droplets hung from the lampshades, wall and ceiling lights, and the corn coloured painted walls were adorned with pictures and mirrors embedded in gold antique style decorative frames.

With her back to him, but watching his reflection in the mirror, Stella noticed Joe glancing around the room. "This is like my second home at the moment, and I get it for such a good price because I'm renting it long-term."

"Is this where you bring all your victims?"

"Victims? Oh Joe, you have the wrong idea. The men I bring here do so at their own will, and believe me when I say they're not victims," she said and laughed as she continued. "In fact they have a fantastic time."

"You don't think I'm a victim?"

"No. You are my vocation, my calling, my mission in life."

"Your mission in life is to what, destroy me?"

"I haven't destroyed you Joe, I've just brought you onto my side."

"I didn't realise it was a competition."

Stella turned to face Joe. "All you had to do, in the past, was pay me a little attention."

Joe looked at her astonished. "Is that what this is all about? Because I didn't want sex with you?"

"No Joe, I told you yesterday it's because you are a big-headed, cocky little bastard who thinks he's better than everyone else, and you are married to my stuck-up-sister. I think they call that 'killing two birds with one stone'.

"What's that supposed to mean? You just can't stand the thought of me and Ruth having a good life. You've never wanted us to make a go of it, and you are just a devious, jealous woman. Do you know Stella you are the worst snob there is, and I find you disgusting."

"You didn't find me disgusting last night Joe. If my memory serves me well, you were begging for more."

"Don't kid yourself," he answered with satisfaction in his voice.

Stella stood up and let the towel drop from her body, and Joe suddenly felt embarrassed by her nakedness. She made her way over to the mahogany cabinet, opposite Joe, and pulled the door open to retrieve her handbag. Taking a DVD disc from it she went over to the television set, which possessed a DVD in-built player, switched it on, and placed the disk in the slot and waited for it to play.

As Joe watched the television screen come to life with images of him and Stella cavorting around on the bed he immediately ran to the bathroom and was violently sick. Stella listened to him being sick as she watched the screen, admiring not only her body, but her performance.

By the time Joe emerged from the bathroom, Stella had switched off the DVD, and was sitting on the edge of the bed. He walked around the bed to where he had been laying and threw himself on it.

"Feeling better?" she asked. When she received no answer she said. "I'm talking to you Cannon. You had better learn to mind your manners where I'm concerned in the future."

"Fuck off," he replied.

Stella ignored him, and began to rummage through her handbag and pulled out her mobile phone and began to press the appropriate buttons. "Aren't you interested in who I'm calling Joe?"

Joe ignored her until he heard her say. "Hi Ruth, its Stella."

He sat up so quick that his head felt as though it would explode, and a further bout of nausea rose in his throat. He quickly grabbed the phone from her hand and immediately noticed that the screen was blank. She had not dialled Ruth's number.

"Just a little warning Joe, I can tell Ruth at any time."

"So can I," he snarled.

"Come on then," she said. "Get yourself dressed, and we'll go and pay my little sister a visit. She must be wondering where you are, most likely thinks you're with the ex-wife. Karen isn't it?" When Joe didn't respond, she continued. "Very attractive woman, I must say. Completely different from Ruth though."

Joe sat with his head in his hands. What more could this evil woman throw at him, so with as much bravado as he could assemble he said. "Why am I not surprised that you've gone out of your way to find Karen? So have you finished now?"

"No, I haven't as it happens. Does Ruth know you were at Karen's flat on Tuesday?"

Taken by complete surprise, Joe stammered. "How...what..."

"Oh dear, wasn't anyone suppose to know of your little rendezvous? Is this just another little secret we share Joe?"

Joe, feeling absolutely exhausted put his head in his hands again and asked. "What do you want from me Stella?"

"I have what I want Joe, but you don't seem to have grasp the content of all this." She stared at Joe before she

194

continued. "I own you now Joey Boy. I own your body and soul."

"But…"

"No buts," she interrupted. "Now, get yourself dressed and get out of my sight."

***

As he sat on the sofa in his lounge later that evening, the noise and activities of the household felt alien to Joe. Ruth was in the kitchen preparing the children's packed lunch for school tomorrow, Tyler and Abbey were upstairs arguing who should use the bathroom first before going to bed, and Lewis was crying in order to gain his mother's attention.

Joe had lied to Ruth, again, about his reason for being home so late from work, and told her that he had met an old friend and they had gone for a drink. She had turned away from him without any comment, obviously not sure whether to believe him or not.

His whole life had now turned into a lie. It seemed that every time he spoke to Ruth these days he lied. He could never divulge the whole truth to her now; it had gone too far. She would never forgive him for not being honest with her from the beginning, and when he mentally listed all the problems, it actually made him go light-headed and nauseous. He had been part of a financial scam, and lost fifty thousand pounds; the potential loss of his business and home; Ted's involvement with the original loan; Barry McGraw and his boys ready to break as many bones in his body as they possibly could, or even kill him; no possibility of borrowing any money from his bank; his possible addiction to prescription tablets, and Karen. Joe laughed to himself as he now realised that all those predicaments went into insignificance when he thought of his new problem; Stella.

Joe was tired. Not just because he had been drinking most of the day, but tired of his life and his problems. He knew that the tablets helped, but he also knew that he was relying on them more than he should, which would eventually affect his health.

As Joe listened to the noise of his household he pulled a newspaper in front of him, but as much as he tried, no words he read penetrated his mind. No sentences strung together, and no paragraph told a story. The only capability he had at this moment was to recall the whole sordid mess that was his life.

What had he ever done to Stella to deserve this? It would seem that his only crime in Stella's eyes, apart from refusing her sexual advances, was being married to Ruth. Stella was a sick, evil woman who took pleasure in hurting others. By destroying Joe she would eventually destroy her sister, which, without a doubt, was her ultimate goal.

The ring of the telephone brought Joe out of his thoughts. As the ringing continued, and although Joe was able to reach the extension from where he was sitting, his body was unable to move.

Ruth made her way to the hall to answer the telephone, and with sarcasm sounding in her voice shouted. "I'll get the phone shall I Joe? You just sit there."

"Hello Ruth."

She flinched as she heard these words. "Oh, hello Stella." This was the fourth time her sister had called her this week.

"How's everything?"

"Fine thanks."

"Are you doing anything on Saturday night?"

"Err...no." Ruth answered with hesitation in her voice.

"Good, you can all come round for dinner then. Listen Ruth, I was really upset when you had that problem with Joe and you didn't phone me. As your sister I should have been the first one you called. I think that just proves how much we've grown apart, and I'm determined all that will change."

"Grown apart?" Ruth questioned. "Sorry Stella, I never realised we were ever that close."

"Please Ruth, let's not argue over how close we are, or are not. All I want is for us to be a family again, and I'm sure you must want that as well." Stella paused before she added. "I'm thinking of asking mum and dad over. Don't you think that will be nice?"

Ruth suddenly found herself in an awkward situation; no matter which option she chose it could be regrettable. It would be wrong, in the eyes of her parents, to refuse her sister's offer of reconciliation, but if she agreed and fell into another of Stella's traps, she would never forgive herself.

Her other main tumbling block would be to convince Joe, so to allow herself time she said. "I'll mention it to Joe and call you sometime tomorrow."

"All right Ruth, but please think seriously about what I've said. I'll speak to you tomorrow."

Ruth said goodbye, and replaced the phone back on its holder. She walked into the lounge and sat on the sofa next to Joe. "That was Stella."

"What did she want?" Joe asked with urgency sounding in his voice.

"That's the fourth time she's rung me this week, and to be honest I'm not sure what she wants. She's saying we should be much closer, she's even talking about a family meal at her house on Saturday."

"Don't be taken in by her," Joe said, anguish overwhelming him.

"Don't worry, I won't, I know her too well from old, but...maybe she is trying to make amends." Ruth paused before she continued. "I really don't know what to do, but I am wondering if we should go."

"You go, I'll stay at home with the kids."

"The kids are invited. She said she's going to invite mum and dad as she wants us all there. She thinks that we should all become close again. I don't know what she's up to," Ruth answered as she giggled and continued. "But I suppose it could be interesting."

Although Joe had showered before leaving Stella's hotel room, which was a necessity to conceal her perfume, he suddenly felt contaminated by the mere mention of her name. The thought of spending an evening with Stella made him feel physically sick. His only solace could be the presence of his in-laws, but he also worried that Stella, somehow, intended to use her parents against him.

"Well what do you think? Shall we give her one more chance?" asked Ruth.

"How did you leave it with her?"

"I said I would call her tomorrow."

Joe breathed a sigh of relief. "Let's make up our minds tomorrow, and you can phone her tomorrow evening."

"All right, but I feel we should go, purely because mum and dad are going to be there," Ruth replied.

Joe nodded his agreement but had already decided that he would contact Stella in the morning and tell her that he and his family had no intention of spending any time with her. "I'm just going up for a quick shower," he said as he rose from his seat and kissed Ruth slightly on the forehead.

It was as Joe reached the top of the landing that he felt the vibration of his mobile phone in his pocket signifying an incoming text message. Joe pulled the phone from his pocket and read it.

'See you on sat Joe, can't wait, and don't even consider not turning up!! xxxx'.

Joe slowly put the phone back into his pocket and made his way to his bedroom. He stripped off his clothes, threw them on the bed and realised that if he thought his life had been bad these last few months, then he should think again. Stella had stepped up the turmoil in his life a thousand notches, and he could see no way out.

He entered the en-suite and stepped into the shower. He turned the water on and raised the temperature to a higher level than normal. He needed Stella eliminated from his life, but, unfortunately, he had no idea how to carry that off.

Chapter 27

Joe woke on Saturday morning with a pounding headache, after a very restless night. He had read and re-read Stella's text yesterday, and although he had every intention of calling her, he would have to summon up the courage first.

Ruth and the children were eating breakfast as Joe entered the kitchen, and after finding some headache tablets in the cupboard he poured himself a cup of coffee.

"You kept me awake nearly all night," Ruth said as Joe joined his family at the table.

"Sorry."

"You had better have a sleep this afternoon if we're going to Stella's tonight."

Joe's stomach turned at the thought of this. "Do we have to go?"

"Please Joe, don't start all that again. We agreed last night to go, and I've rung and confirmed it now."

"Did we? I don't remember agreeing."

"Well we did, I suppose as normal you weren't paying attention."

The sound of the doorbell startled Joe. Although he had just paid fifteen thousand pounds to Barry, the thought that his 'boys' may still pay him a visit was always at the forefront in his mind.

As Joe opened the front door all he could see was a large bouquet of flowers.

"Please sign here," said the voice behind the floral arrangement as he handed Joe a piece of paper.

Joe signed the paper, and passed it back.

"This is certainly some bouquet," the man said as he handed the flowers to Joe.

"Mm..." Joe answered as he took the flowers and nodded his thanks.

On closing the door Joe examined the bouquet, and his immediate thought was that Ruth had carried out some good deed for a friend, and they were saying 'thank you' by way of flowers.

When he entered the kitchen Ruth looked at the flowers in amazement. "Wow," she exclaimed. "I take it these are from you?" she asked Joe.

"No, too expensive for me," he said in a deadpan voice.

Ruth took the flowers from him and placed them on the worktop. She opened the envelope and read the card. *'Just wanted to say hello, and hope to see you again soon xx'.*

"Who they from?" asked Joe.

"I haven't the faintest idea," she answered passing the card to Joe.

Joe read the card and glanced up at his wife. "They must be from someone you've met recently."

"Such as who? Where do I go to meet anyone?" she answered with a slight trace of anger in her voice.

"I don't know what you get up to while I'm at work."

Ruth stared at her husband. "How dare you say that," she snarled at him. "It's you that has the freedom. I cater for the needs of a husband and three children while you are at work. You come home every night to a clean house, a substantial dinner on the table, your clothes washed and ironed, and food in the cupboard...."

"Whoa, whoa, I'm sorry...I didn't mean that," he said taking Ruth in his arms. "It's just that they are a very expensive bunch of flowers."

"I know, and I really have no idea who they're from."

"I'm sure we'll find out one day...err...I'm popping into work for a couple of hours," Joe said.

"On a Saturday? Oh Joe, do you have to?"

"Yes, work is picking up now," he lied. "So I do need to go in and do a few bits."

"Can't you work from home?"

"No, can you believe I left my laptop there last night."

"All right," Ruth said, disappointment sounding in her voice. "Don't get home too late though, we're expected round Stella's at seven o' clock this evening."

Joe nodded, and kissing Ruth on the cheek turned to make his way up the stairs to get showered and dressed.

He had lied to Ruth again, he hadn't left his laptop at the warehouse, and work wasn't picking up. In fact, he had lost another large customer yesterday, one of his drivers had given in his notice, and he had notification from three suppliers stating that they now required cash payments before any orders could be despatched. Joe knew that he had no one else to blame but himself for this living hell that was his life.

He had to contact Stella and needed the privacy of his office to speak to her before tonight's shambles took place. He intended not to ask, but to beg her to pay off Barry the remainder of the loan, and allow him to pay her back at a reasonable monthly rate. Surely Stella has had her fun now, and must realise that even though she hates him and Ruth, this fiasco has to stop.

He suddenly realised that she hadn't mentioned to him the details for repaying the fifteen thousand pounds that she recently put into his account. Was this another ploy on her part to use against him at a later stage? Also when he had questioned Stella about using Frank's mobile phone, she would only say that he had mislaid it, and had refused to elaborate any further.

Sitting at his office desk now and assuming that she was still using Frank's phone, he sent her a text message to ask her to contact him as soon as possible. So when

202

his mobile phone eventually rung showing 'Frank' as the caller, it was with trepidation that he answered it.

"What do you want Joe?" Stella asked with no trace of emotion in her voice.

"I need help Stella. I'm begging you to pay Barry and get him off my back. If this carries on you will not only ruin my marriage, but my business as well."

"You got yourself into this Joe."

"No Stella, you set me up."

"Well if you hadn't been such a greedy bastard you wouldn't be in this position now."

"And you'd know all about greed, wouldn't you Stella?"

"I'd keep a civil tongue in my head if I were you Joe. Now if there's nothing else, I'll see you tonight for our little family get together."

"Stella, please," Joe begged. "Why are you doing this? Why destroy my family? Your family."

"Family?" she sniggered. "Do you actually think family means anything to me? The only person in this world that means anything to me is my son. No one else. Now Joe, I really am busy, I have a meal to prepare," she said with sarcasm in her voice, and added. "Do you know Joe all my friends think I'm wonderful having my sister and brother-in-law over for dinner tonight especially after all that my sister has done to me."

"You don't have friends Stella, you have people you can use. Anyway what are you talking about, all she has done to you?" Joe asked surprised.

"Oh, my dear brother-in-law, you'd be surprised at what I tell people. I should write a novel with the imagination I've got."

"You're telling lies about your own sister?"

"No, not lies Joe, they're stories," she laughed. "Quite good ones actually."

"You are one sick, evil bitch."

"Yes I know. Don't you just love me? Bye Joe, see you tonight, and don't be late," she said, and ended the call.

"Stella! Stella!" he shouted into the phone, but to no avail.

He threw his mobile phone on his desk, opened the desk drawer and reached for the bottle of vodka.

***

As soon as Frank had finished packing his weekend bag he took it down to the hall and placed it by the front door. He entered the kitchen and to his surprise saw Stella preparing quite a large meal.

"Who you cooking for?" he asked.

"Ruth, Joe and the children are coming round for dinner this evening."

"This evening?" he questioned. "But I won't be here."

"I know," she said without looking at him. "It was the only evening they were free," she lied and added. "And apart from forgetting you were going away, I didn't think you would be bothered by not being here."

"Well...no I'm not, it just seems strange you all having dinner without me here."

"You don't like Joe and my sister."

"Yes I do! Well maybe not Joe that much, but I like Ruth and the children. Anyway, what's brought this on?"

"What?"

"You know very well what I mean, Joe and Ruth coming round for dinner."

"Both Ruth and I think that it's about time we put our differences behind us and start again."

"Oh," Frank said surprised, and asked. "Where's Jonathon?"

"At Ryan's, his mum is taking them to the pictures later, and will bring him home after."

"Does he know I'm away for the weekend?"

"I don't know. You never bother with him, so I doubt it will make any difference if you're here or not."

Frank ignored this remark, he was not prepared to argue with Stella as he was about to leave for a golfing weekend.

"What time are you going?" Stella asked.

Frank glanced at his watch. "In about half an hour or so."

Stella nodded her acknowledgment, and washed her hands. She left the kitchen and returned with her jacket on and her car keys in her hand. She approached Frank and kissed him on the cheek as she said. "Just popping out for a few things I've forgot. Have fun, and I'll see you when you get back tomorrow night."

As Frank watched her leave the kitchen and heard the front door close, he wondered what his wife had planned. Stella did not invite people for dinner, unless there was a motive in it for her, and with Ruth and Joe coming round for an evening anything was possible.

***

When Joe hadn't arrived home by four o' clock that afternoon Ruth called him on his office landline and his mobile phone, and felt concerned when she received no answer from either. Although he was not as moody as past weeks, Ruth knew there was still something worrying him, but gave him the benefit of the doubt that it had nothing to do with Karen.

Joe had visited Ted every day this week, so Ruth hoped he was with him, and had either switched his phone off or the battery had run down. She had spoken to Ted on several occasions offering help and advice, and had decided that the next time she spoke to him she would bring up the subject of Joe's, still ongoing, unusual behaviour.

She again glanced at the kitchen clock before going to the bottom of the stairs to shout up to Tyler and

Abbey. "Tyler can you have your shower please, and Abbey, you can either wait for Tyler to finish or you can use the en-suite."

As Ruth made her way back to the kitchen Abbey came running down the stairs and followed her. "Mum do we have to go tonight? Me and Tyler really don't want to."

"Of course we have to go. Why don't you want to?"

"We don't want to spend time with Jonathon."

"Why not?" Ruth asked, although not surprised at her daughter's statement.

"Well, Tyler doesn't like him."

Ruth, again, left the kitchen and went to the bottom of the stairs. "Tyler, can you come down here please."

"What have I done?" he immediately shouted back.

"Nothing, I just want to talk to you."

When Tyler eventually entered the kitchen he slouched on a stool at the breakfast bar.

"Why don't you want to go tonight?" asked Ruth.

"I have to spend time with Jonathon all week in school," he answered sulkily. "So I don't want to spend tonight with him."

"Tyler, you've never said anything like this before."

"I've never had to spend a Saturday night with him before. You don't know him mum. No one likes him at school, except for his bully mates."

"Does he ever bully you Tyler?" Ruth asked.

"No," Tyler said shaking his head.

"You'd tell me if he did, wouldn't you?"

Tyler nodded his head in answer.

Ruth wondered if her son was lying, but didn't want to press the subject now. She would speak to Stella later, so to ease the situation she said. "We are all trying to become a close family again, so shall we see how it goes?"

Tyler nodded his head in agreement and left the kitchen saying he was going for his shower.

Ruth knew her nephew was a bully, but as yet had seen no signs of him bullying Tyler; apart from making Tyler help him with his homework. If Stella's true objective for tonight's get together was to bring the family closer, it would be the ideal time to bring up the relationship of their sons.

When Ruth heard Joe's key in the door thirty minutes later, relief overwhelmed her, and she ran out to greet him. "Where have you been?" she asked. "I've been trying to ring you."

"Sorry, I've been really busy," he said as he took off his coat and made his way to the stairs. "Kids in their bedrooms?" he asked.

"Yes, they've had their showers. I tried to ring your landline and mobile phone."

"I've had a couple of meetings with potential clients and turned off my mobile," he lied.

"Oh..." she said disappointment sounding in her voice. "But your mobile was ringing, and I just thought you would've called to let me know you were going to be so late."

"I'm sorry Ruth, I should've but things have been so busy and hectic I didn't realise the time. I'll go up and have a quick shower."

"Abbey used the en-suite, so I don't know how messy she's left it."

"That's fine, she's normally quite tidy. Make some coffee, will you please, I'll be down in five minutes," he said as he kissed her slightly on the cheek and ran up the stairs.

Lying to Ruth had now become second nature to Joe. He lied to her as easy as he told her the truth. Why hadn't he told her that he had slept at his desk all afternoon, and had not heard either of his phones ring.

Although he probably wouldn't have mentioned the fact that he had drunk half a bottle of vodka this morning.

He thought of tonight's dinner at Stella's with apprehension and fear, and although he had tried to think of many ways to avoid it, he felt certain that the consequences of not attending her little gathering would be worse than attending.

Chapter 28

Stella opened the door as soon as Ruth rang the doorbell.

"Hi," she squealed as she ushered them all into the hall. "Take your shoes off and come into the lounge. I've drinks and canapés all ready for you."

Quickly removing their shoes, Joe with Lewis in his arms, Ruth, and the children followed Stella into the lounge.

Stella immediately turned to Tyler and Abbey and said. "I've set up drinks for you in Jonathon's bedroom if you want to go up to him. He's playing on one of his consoles, although I'm not sure which one and I'll call you when dinner is ready."

Stella's words came as a surprise to Ruth, she had invited them to a family get together and her first act was to banish the children to a bedroom.

Ruth, carrying Lewis's bouncy chair, placed it on the floor close to where she would be sitting, and took his baby bag into the kitchen, to place his feed in the fridge. When she re-entered the lounge Joe was settling Lewis into his chair.

"Drink Joe?" asked Stella.

Joe hesitated, so Ruth quickly said. "You drink Joe, I'll drive home."

"What a wonderful wife my sister is. Don't you agree Joe?" Stella said.

Joe didn't answer his sister-in-law, but said. "I'll have a vodka and tonic please."

"I guessed you'd be driving Ruth, so I bought some non-alcoholic wine."

"Err...Oh...thanks Stella, that was very thoughtful of you," Ruth answered with surprise sounding in her voice.

"My pleasure," Stella said as she poured her sister her non-alcoholic drink.

Joe, naturally, did not trust his sister-in-law, so rose from his chair and approached the drinks cabinet to check the bottle of wine to make sure it was alcohol free.

"Why are you checking the bottle Joe?" Stella asked sternly.

"Just looking at the label to see what grape it is," he lied.

"What time are mum and dad getting here?" asked Ruth.

"They're not. I decided it would be nice for us to spend some time together, so I didn't ask them."

"Oh, I would have phoned mum if I'd known. I haven't spoken to her for a couple of days thinking I would see her tonight. Where's Frank?"

"Golf."

"What this time of night. What time will he be home?"

"He's away for the weekend."

Ruth and Joe glanced at each other, but it was Ruth who spoke.

"Why did you choose a weekend that Frank was away?"

"I forgot he was away," she lied. "And although I was disappointed, I didn't want to cancel once we had arranged it."

"So the family get together is just us three?" Joe asked.

"Yes Joe, just the three of us, and not forgetting the children of course. How cosy."

Joe realised, with dread, that Stella had chosen this weekend knowing Frank would not be here and was fearful of her objectives.

The next hour and a half went smoothly. The children came down to join them at the dinner table, but were quickly encouraged to return to the bedroom immediately after the meal with promises of ice cream, sweets and more fizzy drinks being brought up to them.

Stella had been considerate in her choice of menu, including garlic bread for starters and a roast chicken dinner, ensuring that everyone, especially the children, would enjoy it.

Joe knew that behind every kind gesture that Stella carried out there was an ulterior motive. She needed Ruth to believe that she actually meant all that she had said about being a family again, and obviously wanted the children out of the way.

Ruth pulled Tyler to one side to enquire if he was happy to return to the bedroom, and he informed her that they were having great fun, and that Jonathon was actually being friendly to both him and Abbey.

Lewis had fallen asleep soon after his feed, and the three of them were now settled back in the lounge, with Joe and Ruth sitting on the sofa, and Stella in a chair at the side of them.

"Pour me another wine Joe," Stella ordered.

Joe immediately turned to Stella and noticed that the expression on her face which conveyed, *'Do as you're told, or else'.*

Ruth sensed the sudden tension in the room and glanced at her husband. She felt sure he would rebuke Stella for the way she had just spoke to him, but to her surprise Joe rose from his chair, took the empty glass out of Stella's hand and went over to the drinks cabinet to refill it.

As he replaced Stella's drink on the side table by her chair, she nodded her thanks and asked. "Not having one Joe?"

"No, not yet," he mumbled in reply, and sat back on the sofa not looking at either Ruth or Stella.

Once Joe had settled, Stella looked at her sister and brother-in-law in turn and said. "Now tell me, are you two all right now?"

"Yes, of course we are," Ruth answered with indignation in her voice.

"So Karen is out of your lives once again," Stella stated.

"Stella!" Ruth shouted.

"I just want to make sure you are both happy, that's all. You've not seen Karen lately then Joe?"

Joe frowned at Stella. What was she up to? Surely she had no intentions of telling Ruth about him going to Karen's flat.

"No...no...I haven't seen her," he lied.

"Do you think she came back to stir trouble for you Joe?"

"No...no I don't. Can we drop this subject Stella? Karen has nothing to do with me and Ruth, so there's no point in discussing her."

"Yes of course. Sorry Joe, I didn't mean to upset you. Why don't you get yourself a drink, and get something for Ruth."

"I'm fine," Ruth snapped, and stared at her sister not understanding her intentions. If they were genuinely to rekindle the family ties, she was going the wrong way about it by upsetting Joe.

Joe again walked to the cabinet and with shaking hands poured a vodka and tonic, and realised that he should never have agreed to participate in this nightmare. His body was craving for its dose of barbiturates, which he now relied on more than ever. He had vowed to himself, he didn't know how many times, that once all his problems were over he would cease the practice and never use them again.

Having poured his drink, Joe left it on the cabinet and excused himself from the lounge. Once in the bathroom he immediately retrieved the tablets from his trouser pocket, and putting four tablets in his mouth, he cupped his hands under the tap in the sink and hurriedly swallowed the pills.

When he returned to the lounge, he retrieved his drink from the cabinet and as he settled back into his seat next to Ruth, he caught the end of Stella's conversation.

"...he mentioned something about flowers."

"Who did?" Joe enquired.

"Oh, just someone Ruth met when we went out."

"I didn't meet him," Ruth said indignantly. "You introduced him, I said hello and that was it."

"Well, you definitely made some impression on him," Stella stated.

"What were you saying about flowers?" Joe asked.

"I didn't actually catch what he was saying to be honest, it was just a passing conversation, but heard him mention the word flowers."

Joe looked accusingly at Ruth. "Were those flowers you got this morning from him?"

"Joe, I haven't the faintest idea. I don't know this man, and I wouldn't even recognise him in the street if I saw him."

"Well, I've seen him a few times since you met him, and he mentions you every time."

"If those flowers are from him, where did he get my address?"

"Oh come on Ruth, don't be naïve. In these days of the internet you can get anything you want," Stella said with a smug look on her face.

The flowers had been a brilliant idea and, although expensive, they had been worth every penny as Stella watched, with delight, Joe's reactions through the whole of that fracas. His face had shown every sign of suspicion and jealousy as they rose to the surface. Stella had now added another worry to Joe's list, and as everyone knows, each little worry grows when another appears.

Stella knew that once all Joe's secrets and lies were out in the open, Ruth and Joe's marriage would be over. Karen's intervention could have ruined their marriage earlier, if Stella had manipulated the situation further, but to Stella's way of thinking that would have been too easy and not as much fun.

Stella wanted their downfall to include not only the loss of their business and home, but the loss of their pride and self-respect.

Stella was thoroughly enjoying the evening, but decided to liven it up a little, so turning to Joe she asked. "Joe, do you know a man called Andy Bolan?"

"No...no...don't think I do," Joe said as the colour completely drained from his face, and heat penetrated his body.

Both women looked at him in alarm, but it was Stella who spoke. "Joe, are you all right? You've gone an awful colour."

"I'm fine," he answered glaring at his sister-in-law. He noticed the pleasure on her face and felt physically sick. He now realised that if he didn't rectify this situation with Stella, she would make his life hell. Which of course, he knew was her every intention.

"It's just that I was talking to him the other day, and for some reason your name came up in the conversation. He mentioned that he'd done a little business with you."

"He's probably a customer," Joe replied a little too quickly. "I don't always know their personal names, as we mostly use their business name."

"I don't mean with the warehouse Joe," Stella said, and added mockingly. "He really is a nice chap, and will help anyone. He's done me a few favours, one quite recently in fact." Stella paused to gauge Joe's response before she continued. "No, I don't think he would be a customer of yours Joe, because he's a money investor. He's loaded, and told me that he's been away for a couple of months on holiday and spent thousands of pounds. Can you believe that Joe? Thousands of pounds," she emphasised. "Anyway, he said to say hello to you."

Joe glared at Stella unable to speak or move.

When Joe made no reply Stella said. "There are some nibbles in the kitchen Joe, fetch them for me would you. Oh, and check on the kids for me please."

Stella was playing with him; a sadistic, evil game. The events of the last few days were galloping out of his control, and Joe would have to play along with her until he had the time, and the energy, to set a strategy in motion to deal with the Stella situation. Although he gathered his composure slightly, he couldn't summon up the courage to look at Ruth as he rose from his chair to obey her sister's orders.

"Refill my glass on your way back Joe," Stella ordered at the same time smiling at Ruth. "I must say Ruth, you have him well trained."

"Yes, haven't I," Ruth answered completely bewildered, not only by the conversation, but the whole evening. If she didn't know of her husband's opinion of Stella she would have assumed that there was some conspiracy between them. She had noticed the shared glances, even the glares between them, and her husband who was normally waited on hand and foot, was running around like a little skivvy.

When Joe left the room Stella immediately asked Ruth, "How are things between you two now?"

"Yes fine," she answered quickly, not wanting to broach that subject, but added with annoyance in her voice. "I must say Stella you definitely have Joe on his toes tonight."

Stella laughed. "It doesn't hurt for a man to know his place now and again."

"What place is that Stella?"

Stella ignored the question and asked. "And that Karen woman is definitely out of the picture again?"

The clank of dishes being dropped on the floor made both women look in Joe's direction as he entered the lounge.

"Joe what on earth is wrong with you tonight?" Ruth admonished.

"Nothing, I just dropped the crisps and peanuts," he stated.

"Must have been the mention of a certain person's name," laughed Stella as she watched Joe bend down to clear the mess.

"Have you seen her lately Joe?"

"Stella!" shouted Ruth as she went to help her husband. "We've had this conversation. Can we leave that subject, I'm sick and tired of talking about her."

"Sorry, I didn't mean to hurt anyone, I was just asking to make sure she's not making trouble for you both, once an ex-wife is back on the scene they can cause all sorts of trouble. You can understand me being concerned can't you Joe?"

As Ruth waited for her husband's reply, she could see the confusion and hesitation on his face.

"Err...I suppose so."

"You suppose so," Ruth repeated staring at her husband. She pointed her finger at Stella, without taking her eyes away from Joe. "You think she's concerned about us do you Joe? Since when? I don't know what's going on here tonight between you two, but I've had enough."

"Please Ruth," Stella begged. "I'm really trying hard here to bring us together, but maybe I'm going about it the wrong way. I thought if I showed concern for you both you would realise how serious I am about bringing us together again."

As Ruth stormed off into the kitchen to fetch Lewis's baby bag, Joe immediately went up to Stella and whispered. "I don't know what you're fucking playing at, but it has to stop."

"It stops when I say so, and not before Joey boy and you will do yourself a favour to remember that," she replied with harshness in her voice.

When Ruth came back into the room Stella went up to her, and taking hold of her hand said with sincerity in her voice. "I apologise if I've upset you in any way Ruth. Please let's start again."

Ruth did not reply, but went back to her seat and sat there looking at Lewis who was fast asleep in his chair, wishing she was at home and out of her sister's snare.

"Don't the children play well together," Stella stated light-heartedly as she returned to her seat.

Ruth decided that this was the opportune moment to bring up the subject of Jonathon's bullying, so taking a deep breath she said. "I meant to ask you Stella, did you have to see the headmaster about Jonathon's behaviour?"

"How did you know?" Stella snapped.

"Oh...one of the mums..."

"Are you listening to gossip about your own nephew now Ruth?" Stella interrupted, but realised she had sounded rather harsh so lightened her tone. "I'm sorry Ruth, I'm sure you weren't. Sometimes we get dragged into gossip, and it gets out of our control. But you're right, I did get called into the headmaster's office about his behaviour, but it was all hearsay. They had no proof of any of the allegations. I told him that my son was not a bully, and if he accuses him again, without any proof, I will have him up in front of the board of governors."

"What did he say to that?" asked Ruth.

"Nothing, what could he say. I'm sick and tired of people picking on Jonathon. That boy wouldn't hurt a fly, and as I told the headmaster, if he is behaving out of character he would only be doing it in self-defence." Stella now laughed as she added. "I bet Tyler is more of a bully that Jonathon. Don't you agree Joe?"

When Joe didn't answer, both Ruth and Stella glared at him. Ruth waited to hear her husband announce, quite proudly, that Tyler was not, and had never been a bully. Stella waited, with anticipation, to see Joe cringe and wince as he agreed with her.

Joe was furious with Stella. He had no doubt that she had achieved her aim of the evening, and he had helped her in every way, but how could he slander his son. Whichever way he decided to answer, he would receive the wrath of either his wife or the woman who had every intention of making his life hell.

"Well, boys will be boys," he said and hoped he had appeased both women.

"Boys will boys!" Ruth screamed at him. "What does that mean? Since when have you ever thought Tyler was a bully?"

"I don't think Tyler's a bully."

"Then tell her."

"Come on Joe tell me," Stella said, taunting him.

"I've had enough of this," he shouted, and turned to Ruth. "Get the kids, we're going home."

"So soon," Stella said with menace in her voice, as she sipped her wine.

Ruth glared at her sister as she unbuckled and snatched a sleeping Lewis into her arms. She gathered his belongings and left the lounge with Joe following closely behind.

Stella followed them into the hall where Ruth was at the bottom of the stairs, calling for the children to come down.

"Ruth, what on earth is wrong with you? You have no sense of humour these days," Stella said.

Ruth ignored her sister; confused and hurt, she refused to engage in an argument with her. As the children reached the bottom of the stairs, Ruth ordered them, as calmly as possible, to say thank you and goodnight to their aunt, and Joe quickly ushered them out of the front door, instructing them to get into the car.

"Dad I don't feel well, I've really got a belly ache," Tyler moaned.

"You've probably eaten and drunk too much, now get in the car."

Ruth walked out of the house, behind the children, without saying a word to her sister or husband, and as she was about to open the car door she noticed Stella catch hold of Joe's arm and whisper to him before she closed the door behind them.

Ruth strapped Lewis into his car seat, and made sure the children had fastened their seat belts properly. She watched Joe get in the car, before she joined him, and without saying a word she started the engine.

The drive home was intolerable. Abbey was over active and talked non-stop, Tyler continued to complain about the pains in his stomach, Lewis, being woken up from his sleep, cried incessantly, and Joe shouted at the children for quiet, while he tried to pacify Lewis. Ruth drove with her head full of questions. Questions that she would insist Joe answer.

As soon as they arrived home, Ruth immediately ordered Tyler and Abbey to bed. As Tyler was still complaining of a stomach ache, Ruth gave him a dose of medication and settled him in bed. She washed and changed Lewis, and settled him in his cot.

Joe said goodnight to the children, and taking four tablets from the packet in his pocket made his way to the lounge where he poured himself a glass of neat vodka, and sat of the sofa.

It was ten minutes later that Ruth entered the lounge. "Well?" she asked.

"Well what?"

"I've had it now Joe. I don't want any more of your bullshit, I want answers. What was all that about tonight? You were running around and agreeing with Stella like a little lackey." She mimicked her sister's voice as she continued. "Pour me a drink Joe, get the nibbles Joe, check on the children Joe, agree with everything I say Joe."

"I don't know what you're talking about. I thought the idea of this evening was supposed to bring us all closer, well I did my bit."

"Joe, you were on edge all night. Every time Stella opened her mouth it was aimed at you. You should've seen your reaction when she mentioned that bloke Andy she knows, the colour completely drained from your face, I thought you were going to pass out. I want to know what's going on."

"Come and sit down."

"No Joe, I want answers. What is going on?" she demanded.

Joe glanced round the room as if searching for answers, and suddenly remembered the untouched bouquet of flowers that lay on the kitchen worktop.

"Don't you accuse me of anything, when you've received flowers this morning from some bloke you've just met."

"Those flowers weren't from him. Stella introduced us and we hardly looked at each other let alone said anything."

"If they weren't from him, who were they from?"

"If I know my sister I wouldn't mind betting she sent them to stir trouble. But why Joe? Tell me, because I have a very strong feeling that there's something going on between you and Stella."

"Don't be ridiculous," he stated indignantly.

Ruth looked at her husband and began to cry. "If the affair you're having is with my sister, or she's got something over you, you had better tell me now Joe, because I really, really have had enough of all this."

Joe immediately stood to comfort his wife, but being wary of her reaction just placed his hands on her shoulders. His sister-in-law had tricked him into having sex; that was not an affair. She was the last person he would ever dream of having a relationship with.

He now studied his wife, and noticed how exhausted she looked. What had he done to her? She had lost her youthful sparkle, and her easy-going disposition. How he longed to divulge all that had happened to him. To confess everything to her now, that would not only take the pressure off him, but together they could formulate a plan to resolve the situation.

He took his wife in his arms and stated. "I'm not having an affair with Stella."

Ruth pulled away from him and stated defiantly. "But something's going on."

The time had come to disclose the truth. Joe could no longer lie and deceive his wife, so he took her by the arm and said. "Come and sit down Ruth."

As she allowed him to escort her to the sofa a piercing scream penetrated the house. Ruth and Joe quickly glanced at each other, and both ran out of the lounge and up the stairs. Joe was the first to reach the top of the landing, and assessing the scream had come from Tyler's bedroom forcefully flung the door open.

As he entered his son's room the repugnant smell of vomit struck him and to his shock, Tyler was writhing around on the floor in excruciating pain. As Joe ran over to him, he heard Ruth shriek in fear behind him.

"Get an ambulance," he shouted to his wife.

"Tyler, Tyler," Ruth screamed, and knelt on the floor to aid her son.

Joe immediately hurried out of the room and down the stairs to call an ambulance, and his parents.

Chapter 29

The paramedics arrived five minutes later, and after administering medication to try to ease Tyler's pain, they calmed him and asked Ruth and Joe numerous questions. To Joe's relief his parents arrived just before the ambulance was about to leave for the hospital, as this enabled him to follow the ambulance in his car.

On arrival at the hospital, packed with Saturday night revellers, Tyler was immediately taken to one of the cubicles. The doctors worked hard and fast on him, as he was still in agonizing pain and being violently sick. They carried out various tests, and admitted him to a children's ward in the early hours of Sunday morning.

The tension between Ruth and Joe was apparent, not only due to the events of the previous evening, which they had not discussed again, but the tedious hours of waiting for the diagnoses on Tyler's condition.

Later that morning, Ruth had suggested that Joe should go home to make sure that Abbey and Lewis were fine and that his parents were coping. He readily agreed, and said that Ruth should call her parents in case his needed to go home.

On his arrival Abbey ran straight into his arms sobbing, and Joe's mother told him that his daughter had been distraught upon learning that her brother was in hospital, and had cried most of the morning. Abbey had pleaded with Joe to allow her go back to the hospital with him, but she understood when Joe explained that she would be more of a help to everyone if she stayed at home to help her grandmother look after Lewis.

Joe returned to the hospital an hour later, and had reassured Ruth that everything was fine at home, and that his parents would stay as long as needed. Ruth had also called her parents who said they would take over from Joe's parents if need be.

As they now sat in silence observing their son drifting in and out of sleep a doctor approached and asked to speak to them in private. He escorted them to a side room and introduced himself.

"My name is Doctor Jefferson, and I'm one of the doctors assessing your son. We have carried out extensive tests on Tyler, and..." He paused before he continued. "Mr and Mrs Cannon, Tyler has been poisoned..."

Ruth and Joe gasped at the same time.

"Poisoned?" Ruth interrupted, "Is he going to be all right?"

"He's going to be fine," assured the doctor. "We have pumped his stomach, and he is now stable."

"But how was he poisoned?" asked Joe.

"That's what we need to ascertain Mr Canon. We believe it was with some kind of household cleaner," Doctor Jefferson said. "Do you have any idea how it could have happened."

"Of course we haven't, don't you think we would have said if we knew he'd drunk something like that," stated Ruth.

"I'm sorry Mrs Cannon, but naturally we have to ask."

"Of course you do, it should be me apologising, I'm sorry," Ruth paused before she continue. "I just can't believe this."

"The police will find out what happened," Doctor Jefferson stated.

"Police!" exclaimed Joe.

"Naturally we've had to call the police, a child has been poisoned, we're also obliged to phone Social Services, and one of the secretaries will attend to that shortly. I know this is very distressing for you, but we have a protocol to follow, and I'm sorry but the police have requested that you stay in here until they interview you." The doctor paused and looked at the distraught couple sitting opposite him. "Let me go and order you some tea, I'm sure you could do with it."

Ruth and Joe nodded their heads in thanks, and watched the doctor leave the room.

"They must have their diagnosis wrong," stated Ruth as she rose from the chair, and began to pace the room. "How could he have possibly been poisoned?"

"I don't know Ruth, but the doctors must know what they're doing."

"No! I won't accept that," she shouted. "There is no way he could have been poisoned," she said emphasising each word.

"Ruth be reasonable, the doctors have completed their tests, so we have to go by their diagnoses. Tyler has been poisoned."

As Ruth began to cry, Joe jumped up from his chair to cuddle her, but Ruth pulled away from him. He had hurt her too much over the last couple of months for her to take comfort in him now.

***

It was now over an hour that Sergeant Wallace and Policewoman Robinson had been questioning Ruth, and to her surprise they were interviewing Joe separately. It shocked and dismayed her to discover that their first line of questioning had been to ascertain if she or Joe could have played a part in poisoning Tyler. They had asked her the same questions, but had worded them differently each time, obviously to try to catch her out.

She had asked several times during the interview if she would be allowed to leave to go and see Tyler, but each time they had refused her request.

When the questions had turned to the possibility of Tyler self-harming, Ruth began to cry. It was unthinkable that Tyler would harm himself, and it was through tears that she had explained that he was due to play a very important football match for the school on Monday afternoon, and he would never do anything to jeopardise that.

They had also questioned her on recent personal events within the household that may have had an effect on Tyler. She felt she had no choice but to explain Joe's unusual behaviour, but had made it clear that the problems were to do with his business, and not the children. The police had asked if Tyler had witnessed any arguments between them, and Ruth had admitted that he may have, and that although Joe had left home for just under a week, they were sure that they had convinced Tyler that Joe had been away on a business trip. Ruth also gave an account of yesterday's events leading up to the call for the ambulance.

"Thank you Mrs Cannon you have been very co-operative," said Sergeant Wallace.

"I just want to get to the bottom of this," stated Ruth.

"As we all do. Now, what I suggest is that you go and see Tyler, but please be back here in half an hour so that we can conclude our interview."

Ruth said her thanks, rose from her chair and left the room. She realised that the police would have been asking Joe all the same questions, and wondered if he had answered them as truthfully as her.

Tyler was sitting up in bed trying to finish a jigsaw puzzle as Ruth entered the ward.

"Mum," he exclaimed when he noticed her. "Where have you been?"

"Sorry darling, I've been talking to the doctor," she lied. "I must say you seem a lot better."

"Yes, I feel better. Can I go home now?"

"That's for the doctors to decide," she said laughing as she ruffled her son's hair. "I've got to go and see him again in a short while so I'll ask him."

"Have they said what's wrong with me yet?" Tyler asked sounding older than his years.

Ruth had dreaded this question, and had decided to keep the truth from him until he had returned home. "No not yet, but the doctor has assured me that you'll be fine."

"I've got my football match tomorrow and I don't want to miss that."

"Don't get your hopes up Tyler, they haven't even said you can go home yet," she laughed.

They spent the next twenty-five minutes completing the puzzle, and Ruth promised Tyler that she would return as soon as she could.

On her return to the office Joe was already seated, as was Sergeant Wallace and a policewoman she hadn't seen before. Ruth learnt, with relief, that the police were satisfied that neither she nor Joe was involved in the poisoning. Although she wasn't happy to discover that the police would now go to the next stage in their investigations and that would involve interviewing Tyler and Abbey.

Ruth had been defiant that she would not allow Abbey to be involved, but the police informed her that it was out of her hands, but had reassured her that they had professionally trained officers that dealt with the questioning of children. Ruth and Joe were also advised that Social Services would probably be contacting them.

Ruth felt as though her world was falling apart. How had so much happened so quickly in such a short frame of time? Joe had acted out of character these past few months, Karen had come back into their lives and Stella was, for some reason, playing a manipulative game with them. Now someone had poisoned her son, and that was the worst of it all, and the hardest to bear.

The police had just finished their interview with Ruth and Joe when Doctor Jefferson knocked on the door and entered the office.

"Tyler has been discharged, so you can take him home."

"Thank you," Ruth sighed. "He has an important football match tomorrow, will he be able to play."

"No. I'm sorry Mrs Cannon he needs at least a couple of days off of school next week. I'll leave it up to you when to send him back."

Ruth nodded her head in agreement, but also realised how disappointed Tyler would be.

Sergeant Wallace advised them that he needed to talk to Tyler and suggested that they carry out the interview later that afternoon at their home. Ruth and Joe readily agreed to this and left to fetch their son.

Once they arrived home they explained to a disappointed Tyler that he would not be allowed to play football tomorrow, but he did cheer up slightly when he found out that he did have a couple of days off school next week.

Joe's parents left at four o' clock and it was around four-fifteen that Sergeant Wallace returned with a specially trained officer, Policewoman Laval, to question the children. Sergeant Wallace explained that Tyler and Abbey would be interviewed separately, although Ruth and Joe would be allowed to attend.

Tyler had been shocked to learn that he had been poisoned, and when the police asked him if he had ever drunk any cleaning fluid, or anything else he shouldn't he became upset. He soon realised in which direction the police questioning was heading, and through tears stated that he hadn't, and that he never would.

When they questioned Abbey she had also stated that she had never seen Tyler drink anything he shouldn't have, and if she had, she would have told her mum or dad because she knew it was wrong.

The police decided to question them both together about the events of Saturday night. They both confirmed that apart from the time they had eaten their meal, they had spent the rest of the evening with Jonathon in his bedroom.

Abbey said that Jonathon had been especially nice, and that he had looked after them all evening. When Policewoman Laval had asked Abbey if this was unusual, Tyler had interrupted saying that normally they would be doing everything for him.

"He was in and out of the bathroom every time we had a drink."

Both the police officers glanced at each other, then at Ruth and Joe. "Why did Jonathon go to the bathroom to get your drinks?" asked Policewoman Laval.

"He said something about getting some water."

"What were you drinking?"

"Not sure, but it was some kind of lemonade."

"So why would he need water for fizzy drinks?" asked Policewoman Laval.

Both Tyler and Abbey shrugged their shoulders. "He said something about washing the glasses," said Abbey.

"Did you keep the same glasses each time?" asked the policewoman.

"Yes," replied Abbey.

"How do you know?"

"Because they were coloured, mine was red, Tyler's was blue and Jonathon's was green," replied Abbey, a bored tone sounding in her voice.

"All right thanks kids, you've been very helpful," said Sergeant Wallace and indicated to Ruth, with a gesture of his head, that the children should leave the room.

Ruth rose from her chair and going over to Tyler and Abbey said. "Who wants to watch a film and have some ice cream in my room?"

"Yes," both children shouted in unison.

"Go on then, go up and chose a film, and I'll be up with your ice cream shortly."

As both children ran out of the room Sergeant Wallace said. "I take it they like doing that."

"Yes, we often do it as a family...but not so much lately," Ruth said as she glanced at Joe.

The subdued look between Ruth and Joe did not go unnoticed by the police officers, especially Sergeant Wallace who remembered that Ruth had mentioned at the interview that Joe was having problems with his business.

"How is the relationship with your family and your sister's?" Sergeant Wallace asked Ruth.

"What do you mean?"

"Well, are you a close family, do the children get on well?"

"Err...well...not that close...I mean me and my sister don't always see eye to eye and the children...well..."

"Her sister is the most vindictive person you could ever wish to meet Sergeant, and her son is a bully right down to his core, exactly like his mother," Joe interrupted having listened for the last twenty minutes in silence to his children being interviewed by the police.

The poisoning of Tyler had brought all Joe's problems into proportion, and they were nothing compared to the possibility of nearly losing his son.

Taken by surprise Sergeant Wallace looked at Ruth and asked. "Is this true?"

Ruth nodded her head and quickly added. "But she would never do anything to hurt Tyler, I'm sure of that."

"I'm sure," Sergeant Wallace agreed, "but it's Jonathon we need to talk about."

"Do you think...?"

"I'm not saying anything at the moment, but I would like more details of the relationship between your son and your nephew."

"Jonathon is jealous of Tyler," Joe again interrupted.

"What do you mean by jealous?" asked Policewoman Laval.

"Maybe jealous is the wrong word," exclaimed Ruth. "Jonathon is a bully, and because Tyler is quite a happy, go along with everyone else, type of lad, I'm sure Jonathon takes advantage of him."

"Jonathon is a bully, it's a known fact. He bullies the kids at school, but the teachers haven't been able to prove it," said Joe.

"Do you think he would be capable of poi...?"

"No!" shouted Ruth, searching Joe's face for assurance. "I know he can be horrible at times, and I'm the first one to say he should be punished more, but to poison Tyler...no, surely not."

"I'm sorry Mrs Cannon," said the sergeant. "But it's something we have to consider, especially when Abbey and Tyler said that he was going into the bathroom to pour their drinks." Sergeant Wallace now glanced at Policewoman Laval and said. "I think a call on Mr and Mrs Sinclair is in order."

***

After they had seen the police officers out of the door, Joe immediately began to put his coat on.

"Where you going?" asked Ruth.

"I'm going round to your sister's to sort that little shit out, I'll show him what it's like to try and kill someone."

"No you're not."

"You still think he has nothing to do with this?"

231

"No Joe, I'm beginning to think he has everything to do with this."

"That little bastard has tried to kill our son and I can't sit around doing nothing."

"Joe calm down, please come and sit in the lounge with me and let's talk about it."

Joe calmed himself slightly and followed his wife into the lounge. "Aren't you bothered about your son being poisoned?"

"How dare you say that!"

Joe had regretted the words as they left his mouth. "I'm sorry, I didn't mean that. I just want to put my hands around the little bastard's neck and throttle him. It frightens me Ruth to think what might have happened if he had drunk anymore."

As the tears began to fall down Joe's face Ruth ran to him and threw her arms around his neck. "I know darling, I keep thinking the same, but let's be rational." She guided him to the sofa where they both sat down. "If it was anyone else I'd be round there before you, but this is Stella's son we're talking about. If you go charging round there and injure Jonathon she will have you arrested by the police, instead of Jonathon being punished for what he's done to Tyler. Anyway, the police are probably on their way round there now." She paused before she added. "Let's do this legal and above board Joe for Tyler's sake."

Joe knew that Ruth was right in all she had said, and made the decision there and then to tell her everything.

"Ruth we need to talk......"

"Of course we do, but let me check on the kids first and take them up their ice cream." Ruth rose from her chair to make her way to the lounge door.

"Ruth."

She turned towards Joe when she heard the urgency in his voice.

"We really do need to talk, I've got something to tell you and it can't wait any longer."

"All right Joe, I'll be back in a minute," she replied suddenly feeling extremely anxious.

Chapter 30

Although not in the least bit concerned, Stella was surprised to learn that Tyler was in hospital with stomach pains. Jonathon had said he wasn't surprised considering the amount of sweets and crisps he had eaten.

Stella had also been surprised, and this time a little concerned when Sergeant Wallace and Policewoman Laval arrived on her doorstep. Sergeant Wallace told her that he was investigating the poisoning of Tyler Cannon and wanted to speak not only to her, but to her son.

After inviting them into the lounge Stella offered a drink.

"No thank you Mrs Sinclair."

"You're saying Tyler has been poisoned?" she asked.

"Yes. It's been confirmed by the hospital."

"What does that have to do with me and my son?"

"I must say Mrs Sinclair you don't seem that concerned that your nephew has been poisoned."

"Of course I am," she stated rather too quickly. "I'm just surprised that you need to speak to us."

"We understand that your sister and her husband, and the children were here last night for dinner."

"I hope you're not suggesting that I poisoned him!"

"No, we are not suggesting that at all."

"We are more interested in the activities of the children, who we believe were upstairs for most of the evening."

"Yes, that's right, they were watching films, playing computer games, and doing whatever children do these days where technology is concerned. They only came downstairs to eat their meal."

"Did they have drinks available whilst upstairs?"

"Yes of course they did."

"What were they drinking?"

Stella shrugged her shoulders as she replied. "Just lemonade, it's rather an expensive one that I buy because it's not as fizzy as some of the cola drinks."

"Did Tyler complain of stomach pains while he was here?"

"No I don't think so, although he may have mentioned it just as they were going home. To be honest I didn't pay much attention."

"Could we speak with your son please Mrs Sinclair?"

"Why do you need to speak with him, he wouldn't know anything about his cousin being poisoned."

"Maybe not, but we have to question him."

"I'm not happy about this, and I'll be putting in a complaint."

"That's your prerogative Mrs Sinclair, now if you could fetch him please."

Stella gave a heavy sigh, and went to call Jonathon from his bedroom.

As Jonathon entered the room Stella immediately said. "Darling, would you please tell the police that you know nothing about Tyler being taken ill."

"If you don't mind Mrs Sinclair, we will deal with this."

"I heard he's been in hospital. Is he all right?" Jonathon said with what appeared as fake concern.

"He is now Jonathon, but he has been very ill. We need to ask you about last night and the drinks that you had. Who poured out the drinks Jonathon?"

"Umm...I think we all had a turn at pouring them."

"Both Tyler and Abbey said that you poured the drinks and went into the bathroom each time, they think, to wash the glasses."

"Goodness gracious Sergeant, you don't believe those two do you, they may look as if butter wouldn't melt, but believe me it does."

"All we know at this stage Mrs Sinclair is that Tyler Cannon was poisoned last night, and we intend to find out who by and how it happened."

"How do you know he was poisoned?" asked Jonathon as the colour slightly drained from his face.

"Because he's had tests done at the hospital, and the doctors found that he had been poisoned with some kind of cleaning fluid. Now Jonathon did you take the glasses into the bathroom for any special reason?"

"Umm...yes to wash them."

"Why would you need to keep washing the glasses?"

"Abbey can be quite a fussy little thing sometimes," interrupted Stella.

"Please Mrs Sinclair I'm asking Jonathon," Sergeant Wallace chastised. "Jonathon?"

"They were sticky, and as mum said Abbey likes everything perfect, so I washed the glasses."

"What did you wash them in?"

"Just water from the tap."

"Where did you pour the drinks?"

"Err...I can't remember."

"Come on Jonathon, you must remember, after all it was only last night."

"Sergeant, my son is not on trial here, if he says he can't remember then he can't remember."

"But I think he does remember, don't you Jonathon?"

"Err...Err...I think I poured them in the bathroom."

"So you took the bottle of lemonade into the bathroom with you?"

"Yes."

"Why would you do that? Wouldn't it have been easier to just wash the glasses and then take them back to the bedroom to pour the drinks?"

"Err...I mean I left the bottle in the bathroom, I didn't take it back into the bedroom." Jonathon began to wipe his eyes with the back of his hand to indicate that he was crying, but Sergeant Wallace noticed there weren't any tears to wipe away.

Stella immediately hurried to her son to comfort him. "I think that's enough Sergeant, my son is becoming very distressed as you can see."

"I'm sorry Mrs Sinclair but a child has been poisoned, and I'm determined to find out what happened last night."

"It was all Tyler's fault," Jonathon blurted out without warning.

"What do you mean?" asked Policewoman Laval.

"Tyler told me to poison Abbey."

"Tyler told you to poison his own sister?" asked the policewoman.

"Yes. They don't get on and he really hates her."

"Why would you carry out such a task?" asked Sergeant Wallace.

"Because he's frightened of Tyler that's why," interrupted Stella.

"Mrs Sinclair, could you please let Jonathon answer the questions."

"Now Jonathon, I don't understand why would you poison Abbey because Tyler asked you to?"

"Because I'm frightened of him, he's a bully and he threatened me if I refused to do it."

"In what way did he threaten you?"

"He...he's the leader of a massive gang in school, and he said he would get them onto me if I didn't do what he said."

"So what did you use as poison?"

"Tyler told me to get some cleaning fluid that is used to clean things, like floors and baths."

"Tyler told you which one to get?"

"Yes I bought it yesterday and he even gave me the money."

"He's very clever and manipulative in that way, only the other day we found items in Jonathon's room that Tyler..." Stella said quickly, but froze after receiving a stern glare from the sergeant.

"Right Jonathon let's get back to the poisoning. You say the poison was meant for Abbey. What glass did you give her?"

"The one I thought had the poison in."

"How did you know which one it was?"

"I...err...gave her the one which was in my left hand, which I thought had the cleaning stuff in."

"Was it the same glass every time?"

"I'm not sure, I don't think so."

"What colour were the glasses?"

"Err...I don't know."

Sergeant Wallace retrieved a notebook from his pocket and turned the pages. "Abbey says that you gave them the same coloured glass every time. Hers was a red one, Tyler's was blue, and yours was green. I think Jonathon that you knew you were giving them the same glasses each time and that you put the poison in the blue one and deliberately gave it to Tyler."

"Sergeant! How dare you accuse my son of poisoning his cousin."

"Mrs Sinclair you fail to grasp that your son has already admitted to poisoning his cousin but according to him just the wrong one."

"But he was bullied into it, you just heard my son tell you that."

"That's something else that we will now have to investigate."

"I do not want you talking to my son anymore until I have contacted my lawyer."

"That's fine Mrs Sinclair."

Both the police officers rose to leave and as they reached the lounge door Sergeant Wallace said to Stella.

"We will be back tomorrow morning, and in the meantime please do not contact your sister or any member of the Cannon family."

Chapter 31

Ruth lunged herself at Joe. Slapping his face and punching every accessible part of his body. "You slept with my fucking slag of a sister!" she screamed at him as another slap stung his face. "You fucking slept with my sister!" she repeated as another blow caught his chest.

"I had no control over it," Joe pleaded as he tried to restrain her arms.

When Ruth had come down stairs, about an hour ago, after tending to the children he had insisted she sat on the sofa next to him. Disclosing the truth to her about his problems was never going to be easy, so he held her hand and decided that the only way to tell his incredible, unbelievable story was from the beginning; but no matter how he told it he knew his marriage was over.

"No control," she screamed. "No fucking control. Of course you had control."

"I think she spiked my drinks."

"Spiked your drinks!" Ruth exclaimed in disbelief as she pulled herself away from him. "What are you saying that she date raped you? Oh, grow up Joe and admit to an affair with my sister."

"You don't know what I've been through these past months."

"How can I when you've shut me out, and now you sit there and have the audacity to tell me that you were caught in a scam, you've been to a loan shark who is now after your blood, and possibly mine and the children's as well, you are practically addicted to prescription drugs, your ex-wife is involved somehow, my sister set the whole thing up, and just to add a little spice to this somewhat boring set of events, you slept with that slag. Have I just about covered it Joe?" she asked with as much sarcasm as she could muster.

"I didn't want to tell you. I thought I could sort it all out without worrying you."

"And how exactly did you intend to sort it out? Wait for your little fairy godmother to show up and throw a little magic dust over you? And please kindly explain to me Joe exactly how your ex-wife is involved in all this?"

"She's not actually involved. I've just seen her a couple of times...and...she...knows all what's gone on...except for the Stella part."

Ruth stared at her husband in disbelief. "What do you mean she knows all what's gone on?"

"I...told...her."

"You told your ex-wife all that was happening to you, and you didn't tell me?"

"I was frightened to tell you. I didn't want to worry you."

"You are unbelievable! Who else knows?"

"What do you mean?"

"It's a simple enough question Joe, who else knows about all this?"

"Ted, but I only told him the other night." Joe paused before he continued. "The one other thing I'll never forgive myself for is in all the years I've known Ted he's always been there for me, but I wasn't there for him when he needed me the most. I wasn't there for him when Heather died, and I don't think he'll ever forgive me for that."

"Do you expect sympathy from me Joe?"

"No, but I want you to understand what I've been through, and try to look at it from my point of view."

"Well I can't," she screamed, as she quickly rose from the sofa and fled from the lounge.

It was at this precise moment that the doorbell rang.

Joe quickly followed her, and placing both hands on the banister he watched as she climbed the stairs. "Ruth please," he begged, but on hearing their bedroom door slam he placed his head on his hands and shook his head.

Suddenly he remembered the ring of the doorbell, so with as much composure that he could muster he made his way to open the front door.

Joe greeted Sergeant Wallace and Policewoman Laval on the doorstep as the sergeant was about to ring the doorbell for the second time.

"Good evening Mr Cannon," said Sergeant Wallace. "Hope this isn't a bad time, but we have an update and we need to talk to you again."

"No, that's fine. Come in," Joe said as he allowed them to enter. They stood in the hallway while Joe closed the door.

"Please come into the lounge," Joe said as he led the way.

"Is Mrs Cannon here?" Policewoman Laval asked as she followed Joe into the empty room.

"Err...yes...she's upstairs having a lay down...it's been quite an ordeal for her." Joe didn't reveal to the police officers that Ruth was up in their bedroom probably cutting his clothes to shreds.

"I understand, but we really do need to speak to you and your wife," Sergeant Wallace said.

"Oh...of course...I'll go and get her."

Joe entered the bedroom and saw Ruth sprawled across the bed still crying.

"Ruth..."

"Get out!"

"The police are here and they've got an update on Tyler, but want to speak to both of us."

On hearing this news Ruth quickly rolled off the bed and hurried into the en-suit to throw some water on her face.

When Ruth accompanied Joe back into the lounge a couple of minutes later both police officers couldn't hide their shock at her appearance.

"Are you all right Mrs Cannon?" Policewoman Laval immediately asked.

"Err... I just don't feel too good."

"It's not surprising, you've had a shock."

Ruth immediately glanced at Joe.

"About Tyler," Joe assured her, hoping she didn't think for one minute that he would divulge their personal problems to the police.

Joe indicated with his hand for the police officers to take a seat, and offered them a drink.

"No thank you," Sergeant Wallace said and Policewoman Laval nodded her agreement. "Jonathon has admitted to putting cleaning fluid in Tyler's drink."

"Yes," Joe shouted as he punched the air. "And let me guess, his mother is defending him saying that it was obviously Tyler's fault in some way."

"Yes...something like that, that's why I wanted to see you in person. I need a few things clarified," said Sergeant Wallace.

"Such as what?" asked Ruth, a bewildered look appearing on her face.

"Can I first ask how Tyler and Abbey get on together?"

"They get on fine," Ruth answered, surprised at the question. "They have their squabbles like any brother and sister, but on the whole I'd say they're quite good ` friends."

"Who would you say is the feistiest out of the two of them?"

"Abbey," Ruth laughed. "Tyler is a much more laid back person, where Abbey is a little more highly strung and energetic."

"They have different personalities then."

"Yes very different. Although Tyler is laid back he's extremely academic, but not always streetwise. Abbey, on the other hand, gets by at school but has such a sensible head on her for her age it's unbelievable. Can I ask why you are asking these questions?"

Sergeant Wallace paused slightly before he answered Ruth. "Jonathon states that he was bullied into poisoning Abbey by Tyler, but he poisoned Tyler by mistake."

"What!" Ruth screamed. "Tyler wanting Abbey poisoned! Tyler a bully! Tyler doesn't have it in him to be a bully."

"I'm sure he doesn't Mrs Cannon, but you must understand that we have to take every accusation seriously, and that's why I must speak with Tyler again."

"By all means, my son has nothing to hide."

Ruth hurried out of the room to the bottom of the stairs and called Tyler down.

Ruth waited for her son to reach her before she explained that the police were here again.

"Why have they come back mum?"

"They just want to ask you a few more questions, but it's nothing to worry about."

"Okay," he replied as he followed his mother into the lounge.

"Hi again Tyler," said Policewoman Laval as Ruth and Tyler entered the room. She knew that she had to tread carefully with her questioning of this boy. She had no doubt in her mind that the only culprit in this whole matter was Jonathon, and that Tyler had been his intended victim.

"Are you feeling better Tyler?"

"Yes thanks."

"What are you up to?"

"Watching a film with Abbey in her room, but mum says I've to go to bed in a while."

The police officer nodded her agreement and said. "Do you like school Tyler?"

"Yes."

"What's your favourite lesson?"

"PE. I love playing football."

"Is that what you'd like to do when you leave school?"

Tyler nodded his answer.

"What other lessons do you like?"

"Most of them really, English, maths, science.

"Do you have many friends at school Tyler?"

"Yes, quite a few."

"What about gangs, are there many of them in your school?"

"Yes a couple, but I stay away from them. I don't always like the boys who belong to them."

"Does Jonathon belong to a gang?"

Tyler glanced at his parents, not sure how to answer.

"Tell Policewoman Laval the truth Tyler," said Ruth.

Nodding his head and looking back at the policewoman he replied. "Yes, he actually leads a gang."

"He leads a gang? How does that affect you? You know, being his cousin."

"Only when he wants me to do something for him and I refuse, he gets a couple of his mates onto me. He always wants me to do his homework, get money for his cigarettes, hide magazines and stuff that he knows he shouldn't have."

"Tyler, why haven't you told me all this before, I knew he was a bully but I thought he left you alone." Ruth was surprised to find out that maybe her son was a little more streetwise than she gave him credit for.

"I can handle it mum. Jonathon doesn't frighten me, I only do for him what I want to. I...also...think...he's jealous of me playing football."

"Why do you say that?" asked Policewoman Laval.

"He sneers at me while I'm practicing or playing a match. He's hid my boots and shin pads before now. He even locked me in the changing room once and told Mr Murray that I'd gone home because I was fed up with football."

Although shocked at hearing this statement, Ruth's immediate thoughts were how like his mother he was.

"What happened?"

"I shouted really loud and a teacher heard me. The following day Jonathon was sent to the headmaster and was punished."

"Did you get any repercussions?"

"Not much. A few pushes and shoves from his gang mates, a couple of my school books went missing, a few threats from Jonathon that he never carried out."

"How do you get on with Abbey?"

"She's my sister," exclaimed Tyler.

"Yes I know," laughed the policewoman. "But that doesn't mean you have to like her."

"Of course I like her, we have a laugh together. I know she's only eight but she always seems older than that."

"You wouldn't want to see her hurt then?"

"Hurt! No. Why would I want to see her hurt, and I'd hurt anyone who hurt her, especially Jonathon."

"Has Jonathon ever tried to hurt her?"

"No. Sometimes I think he's a little scared of her, he never even tries to bully her."

"I think that will do for now Tyler thanks for your help," said Sergeant Wallace.

Ruth smiled at her son. "Good boy Tyler, go back up and watch the rest of the film, and I'll be up in a little while."

Tyler smiled at the police officers, rose from his chair and left the lounge.

Policewoman Laval waited until Tyler had left the room until she spoke. "Mr and Mrs Cannon I have been in this job a long time, especially working with children, and I think I can honestly say that not only is your son one of the nicest boys I've ever had the pleasure to interview, but I can't imagine him ever hurting anyone, let alone his sister."

"Thank you," Ruth sighed.

"We will file our reports and conclude this investigation, and naturally keep you updated. I must ask that you have no contact with your sister or her family until this is all settled."

Ruth glanced at Joe and began to sob. She leapt from the chair and ran from the lounge up to her bedroom.

"I'm sorry," Joe said. "This has been too much for her."

"We fully understand Mr Cannon," said Sergeant Wallace, also rising from his chair in preparation to leave.

"Would you like me to go up and speak to your wife?" asked Policewoman Laval.

"No that's fine, I'll go up to her once you've gone, but thank you."

Both police officers nodded their agreement, said goodbye and left.

Joe did not go up to see Ruth, but made his way back to the lounge for a glass of vodka and his sanity saving tablets.

***

Mortified; there was no other word to describe how Ruth felt when Joe had disclosed the truth that he had hidden from her for the last couple of months. A roller coaster of emotions had invaded her body and soul. She couldn't decide which part of his inconceivable story appalled her the most. The fact that he had borrowed fifty thousand pounds from a loan shark, had been part of a financial scam, was practically addicted to prescription tablets, or had discussed all his problems with his ex-wife of over sixteen years. Although horrified and disgusted by it all, especially as his business and their home were at stake, it was the fact that not only did her sister manipulate the whole event, but Joe had actually slept with her.

Joe had slept with Stella; her sister. A woman Joe couldn't abide and always thought of as evil. He actually cringed if he stood too close to her for any length of time. At least the fiasco of last night had become clear. In Ruth's eyes her husband had humiliated himself, and for that alone she would never forgive him.

It was no secret that the two sisters had never been close. Stella wasn't the kind of sister that Ruth longed for. A sister relationship where they would have shared clothes, shoes, jewellery, nail polish and maybe even a secret now and again. Stella could never share; it wasn't in her nature. Stella used people and manipulated them for her own needs.

Unfortunately, Ruth hadn't realised just how much Stella hated her; to the extent that she had destroyed her life. If this had always been her intention then she had succeeded, and for that Ruth would get revenge.

Ruth did not cry when Joe had first divulged his scandalous secret. Not only was her anger too fierce, but a hatred had emerged from deep within her. The anger was for Joe, but the hatred was for Stella. Ruth had lashed out at Joe to vent her fury. She wanted to hurt him as much as he had hurt her.

Her marriage would not survive this. She could never trust Joe again. Her immediate thought had been to physically march him to the front door and demand he left with nothing. No clothes, no toiletries, no money, nothing. She would have gone through with it if it hadn't been for the ordeal that the children, especially Tyler, had already suffered this weekend. It will be devastating enough for them when their father does eventually leave, but for him to leave now, on top of an already emotional time, would destroy them.

Ruth had felt embarrassed earlier when she had fled the lounge before the police officers had left, but anguish had overcome her. Not only did she have Joe's problems to deal with, but now her nephew had deliberately poisoned her son. The police had stated that they were to have no contact at all with Stella or her family. That was one instruction she intended to ignore, because first thing tomorrow morning she was going straight to her sister to have everything out with her.

When she eventually came down the stairs later that evening, after putting the children to bed, she noticed that Joe was drinking. She told him that he would need to stay at home for at least another ten days for the sake of the children; he would then have to leave. She also demanded that he slept on the sofa and all evidence, such as pillows and blankets, were to be put away every morning out of sight of the children. She also insisted that while the children were around, just until Tyler had got over the shock of what had happened to him, they would act as normal as was humanly possible.

She also informed him that she would be consulting a solicitor with regards to a divorce, and suggested he did the same.

Joe, with a full glass of vodka in his hand, just sat and listened with his head bent. He nodded his agreement when Ruth had finished, and only looked up when he realised that she had left the room. He took his tablets out of his trouser pocket and released six out of the foil container. He put them into his mouth and swallowed them all together with the aid of a full tumbler of vodka.

Chapter 32

Frank had enjoyed his weekend away, and although he enjoyed his rounds of golf, loved the accommodation he was staying at, relished the food and drink, and thoroughly appreciated the company of his friends, his main pleasure was being away from Stella and Jonathon.

Jonathon was becoming more like his mother every day. The lying, cheating, deceitful nature came through as a beacon, warning others to do as he bid or pay the consequences.

While he was away Frank had made a few life changing, belated, new year resolutions, which he had every intention of keeping. The easiest was to leave Stella and file for a divorce, the hardest was to end his relationship with Elaine. He had known from the onset of their affair that they didn't have a future together; but she had been good for him. She had brought him happiness and light, in a dark, dismal world that he shared with Stella. She had also been honest from the beginning where her husband and daughter were concerned, and for this he loved her even more.

He had already telephoned her to arrange a meeting for tomorrow lunchtime, as he knew her daughter was now at school full time. He realised Elaine would be hurt at his news, but also knew that the selflessness part of her would understand, just as he had understood her predicament.

Frank knew Stella had money hidden in all different bank accounts; but so did he. Over the years he had given financial advice to many people for a modest fee and had the good insight to put the money away without Stella's knowledge.

When his thoughts turned to Jonathon it saddened him to realise that he had no love for the boy, and had also decided to demand that a DNA test be carried out to establish if he was his biological father.

He would leave his old life behind, and walk away from everything. He had applied for voluntary redundancy at work about a month ago, and had just received the confirmation letter. He would leave Stella in the house with the mortgage payments, and because the property was mortgaged to the hilt, as Frank had intended, it would not show a return on the equity for many years to come.

He would not be paying any maintenance for Jonathon, whether he was his son or not, and he would leave Stella with all the financial outgoings, knowing full well that she had the money to pay for them.

Frank knew his wife was a prostitute. Not one that stood on street corners, but in his eyes any woman who gave sex in exchange for any service, whether it be jewellery, clothes, horse racing or financial tips, warranted that name. A good friend of his, who he had known for many years, had told him of her activities, and for that he had been grateful; it just confirmed what he already believed of his wife. She was a manipulative, cunning, evil bitch of a woman, and Frank knew that not only was she the devil's daughter, but his prostitute as well.

Frank had decided to disappear, never to show his face again, or more to the point, never to set his eyes on his wife or her son again.

He was sorry his weekend was over, but knew a new life would be his very soon. He had decided to have everything out with Stella as soon as he reached home, but as he was about to turn onto his driveway he noticed a police car pull away. He parked the car, and deciding to leave his bag and golf clubs in the boot, got out of the car and hurried into the house. Stella was in the kitchen

251

pouring a glass of white wine, and didn't notice him enter the room.

"What were the police doing here?" he asked without preamble.

"Hello to you as well," she snapped.

"Stella what were the police doing here? What's he done?"

"Why do you always assume the worse of your son?"

Frank didn't answer he just stared at his wife as she sipped her wine. How was it possible that he had once loved this woman standing before him with a passion? All he felt for her now was hate and disgust.

"The police are accusing Jonathon of poisoning Tyler."

"What!" Frank shouted slapping the palm of his hand on the breakfast bar.

"It was all Tyler's fault," she shouted back. "He bullied Jonathon into poisoning Abbey, and he poisoned Tyler by mistake."

"I've never heard so much rubbish in all my life. Will you, for once, take your head out of the sand and see Jonathon for what he is. I'm sick and tired of all these lies where he is concerned. The one thing I do know is that Tyler is not a bully, but Jonathon is."

"How dare you stick up for that boy, over your own son."

"Is he Stella?"

"Is he what?"

"My son?"

"Of...course...he is."

Ignoring his wife's reply, Frank turned and walked out of the kitchen to fetch his belongings, and as he made his way to the car he made a solemn promise to himself. By the time tonight was over, not only would he have thoroughly searched the internet to discover the procedure for having a DNA test done, but he would have told Stella exactly what he thought of her, and her son.

Chapter 33

The following morning in the Cannon household was like no other normal Monday morning. Joe didn't go into work, Tyler wasn't at school, Ruth decided to let Abbey have the day off due to the stress of the weekend and Lewis was quieter than normal, maybe sensing that all was not right with his family.

At nine-thirty, with Tyler and Abbey still in bed and Lewis amusing himself with his baby gym, Ruth entered the kitchen where Joe was making a pot of coffee. He glanced up and noticed his wife dressed and ready to go out.

"Where are you going?"

"Although it's none of your business, I'm going to have it out with my so-called sister."

"Please don't go and see her today, I need time to think."

Ruth began to laugh. "You need time to think! You've had months to think Joe, and it got you nowhere."

"Please Ruth, and remember the police said no contact with her."

"But the police don't know that not only has she ruined my life, but my husband has slept with her."

"If you go and see her now you could ruin the case, and that could mean Jonathon getting away with poisoning Tyler. You want to see him punished, surely?"

"Don't you dare talk to me like that! You're just thinking of yourself. You make me sick," she screamed, and ran out of the kitchen and back up the stairs.

Although Ruth knew that Joe was right, it didn't make it any easier. She wanted to literally pin her sister up against her 'ever so clean' kitchen wall and tell the evil bitch exactly what she thought of her. She needed to inflict pain on her; she needed to destroy Stella's life as Stella had destroyed hers.

No sooner had she reached the top of the stairs, she ran back down again and fled into the kitchen. "I want you out of the house today."

"What?"

"You heard. I want you out of the house. I'll tell the children you've gone to work, so come home at your usual time. That's around six this evening, not ten tonight," she added sarcastically. "I'll have your dinner ready as normal, well what used to be normal."

"But Ruth I …"

"And we'll have to sit down sometime this week and decide when and how we will tell the children that we are parting. It's not going to be easy but it has to be done." Ruth didn't wait for an answer, but left the kitchen to make her way back up the stairs.

Five minutes later when she heard the front door close, Joe's car engine start and the sound of it leaving the drive, Ruth sat on her bed and sobbed.

Obviously, she had no idea that Joe had driven just around the corner to the nearest lay-by, sat in his car and he too sobbed.

***

Ten minutes later when Joe had regained his composure, he fired the engine and drove to the park that he passed every day on his way to work, but had no idea of its name.

He parked the car in the car park, and noticing a duck pond made his way to it where he found the only empty bench. As he seated himself, he took in the other residence seated around the pond. A young mother with a toddler in a pram, throwing bread to the ducks; two down and outs, with numerous carrier bags, drinking beer from cans; a group of children obviously playing truant from school, and a young couple, wrapped around each other, clearly in the first throws of love.

He sat on the bench for a while with his head bent, when he suddenly glanced out to the water. The toddler had finished feeding the ducks and they had now gathered on the far side of the pond. He watched as they made their way to his side of the bank, and noticed that one duck remained. Why hadn't he followed? Was he an outcast? Had he, like Joe, made mistakes? Was he now paying for them by being banished from his family? Realising that this supposedly tranquil place was making him feel more depressed, he decided to leave.

He also realised that he should go to work, but couldn't face it, so decided to kill some time by strolling around the local market, which he hoped was open this morning.

Once there, and relieved to find it open, Joe found a car parking space, got out of the car, locked it and made his way to the throng of market stalls.

He decided to buy presents for the children; a computer game for Tyler; clothes for Abbey, although he wasn't sure of her size and a toy for Lewis.

Weaving his way through the stalls of various wares, Joe couldn't believe his eyes when he saw the back of him walking through the market. Joe couldn't mistake his straight, taut, structured walk, and because he had no doubt it was him he immediately began to give chase calling his name.

"Andy! Andy Bolan!"

The man who Joe chased didn't stop, but carried on walking, he didn't even turn round, as if he was oblivious of anyone calling him.

As Joe continued his pursuit, he was apologising non-stop as he accidentally pushed, and bumped into people who barred his way. When Joe eventually caught up with the man, he grabbed hold of his arm from behind and pulled him round.

"You bastard, I'm going to fucking kill you," Joe yelled as he lunged towards Andy.

Andy, surprised at the attack on him tried to pull away. It was when he noticed his assailant that he shouted. "Joe? Wow, what on earth is wrong? Joe! Joe!"

As Joe pulled away he noticed a few people watching the fiasco, so said in a quiet, but menacing whisper. "What's wrong, I want my money back that's what's wrong. Stella has told me all about your little scam." He poked Andy in the chest. "So I want my money back now."

"What money?"

"Don't play the fool with me Bolan. My fifty thousand, remember?"

"I haven't got your money Joe. Honest. Stella said she was giving it back to you. She said as soon as you discovered that you'd been had she would return it to you."

"Don't lie to me," Joe said anger overwhelming him. "You're a dirty swindling bastard, and I want my money back."

"Joe, I haven't got your money, you've got to believe me. Look we need to sort this out. There's a pub at the end of the market, let's go and get a drink."

"A drink! You've got fifty thousand pounds of my money and you want to sit and have a drink! Are you for real?"

"Joe, how many times do I have to tell you, I haven't got your money, Stella has. Please Joe, let's get a drink and sort this out."

Joe hesitated slightly, not sure what to do. Stella had told him that although Andy was an investment banker, Joe was a one-off and his fifty thousand had boosted his coffers enough for him to disappear, although Stella did say that she had seen him recently.

"This had better be good Bolan, and believe me when I say that I'm at the bottom of a pit at this precise moment with no way up, so a charge against me for grievous bodily harm, or even murder, would be nothing."

As they made their way to the pub, Joe walked behind Andy where he could see him, and when they entered the premises, Joe did not take in any of the interior or the clientele, but followed Andy to the bar.

"Two pints of lager please," Joe said to the barmaid, and pointing to Andy continued. "And he's paying." He glanced at Andy and said. "Why change habits?"

Joe stayed with Andy while he paid for the drinks, and together they made their way to the back of the pub and a secluded table. Joe waited until Andy placed the drinks on the table, and seated himself in one of the chairs before he took the seat opposite him.

Joe was about to speak but Andy spoke first.

"Right Joe, let's put the record straight, for a start my name is not Andy Bolan, its Max Reeves."

"Max Reeves, the liar and thief, but you won't get away with it. As soon as I leave here I'm definitely going to the police."

"Police. What for?"

"What for? For the theft of fifty thousand pounds. That's what for."

"This is ridiculous Joe, for the last time I haven't got your money, I never did have. Stella's got it. Look, I think we need to get a few facts straight here. Let me tell you what happened, and then we can take it from there."

"This had better be good Andy, Max, whatever your bloody name is." Joe waited for the rebuke from the man sitting across the table from him, but none came, which surprised Joe. He decided to listen to what the man had to say, so waited for him to begin.

"I've known Stella for quite a few years now. We were introduced through a mutual friend and hit it off immediately, and we've had some good times, if you know what I mean," he said raising his eyebrows. "Well, we were having a drink last year, and she was telling me about her family. She hadn't mentioned them much in the past, and to be honest I never really gave it a thought. Anyway, she said she had a sister and brother-in-law, which I now know is you, and that you were all very close. She said that it had become a sort of family tradition to play tricks on each other, and that you had played a corker of a trick on her at the beginning of last year, and she wanted to get her own back. She said that it was all done in good fun and that you often all got together and laughed about past pranks."

Joe sneered. "What are you talking about? This has got to be a joke you've not said one thing that's true yet."

"I'm telling you how it is Joe, and I swear on my life that this is all true. Anyway, she came up with the idea of a financial scam, and asked if I would help her. You see, I owed her a favour. Some years back I got into some heavy financial problems and she helped me out big time. So when she asked me to help her I couldn't refuse. She said that once you found out you had been had, she would give you your money back and you would see the funny side of it."

"Are you actually in the investment game?"

"No, I'm an electrician."

"Electrician! Joe began to laugh. "This has still got to be some joke."

"I'm telling you the truth Joe."

"What about the bet you had with her that I would fall for it? She said she won a couple of hundred pounds from you."

"We didn't have a bet. As I said I owed her a big favour, and that's the only reason I did it. I had no reason to think that she was lying to me."

"She said you'd gone away."

"I've been in Liverpool working on a big construction job, but that's finished now."

"Have you seen her lately?"

Max pondered on this question. "Now I come to think of it, I haven't."

"What about everything you told me about you? How much of that was true?"

"It's true about me being divorced, and having no kids. She said to tell the truth about my personal life, to make it easier for me. She sorted everything else out. The contract, the website, where to meet you, told me what to say, she even gave me the money to buy you meals and drinks."

"I thought it was odd that you never talked about your work."

"How could I? What do I know about investment banking?" he laughed. "I even had a tape recorder on me so that she could hear every conversation we had, and each time before we met, she would coach me on what to say. How much of myself I should reveal to you."

"Didn't you stop to think about the effort going into one joke?"

"Of course I did, but as I said earlier she said that you had pulled such a big one on her, that the jokes were now going to the extreme."

"What about the amount of money I handed over?"

"Stella organised the bank account it went into, and believe me I didn't see a penny of that money. She also assured me that you wouldn't have a problem with finding fifty thousand pounds, and anyway it didn't matter because you would be getting it back."

Joe rubbed his hands through his hair. He didn't know what to think, but his gut feeling was that this man was telling him the truth.

"Do you have any idea what that bitch of a woman has done to me?" Joe waited for a reply, but Max shook his head in answer. "I'm on the verge of bankruptcy, I've got a loan shark waiting to donate my body as part of the cement mix for the next sky scraper about to be built in London, my marriage is about to collapse, my ex-wife of sixteen years is now part of this fiasco, I'm practically reliant on prescription drugs, and if that's not enough your so-called friend thinks she owns my body and soul."

"Joe, I don't know what to say, I wouldn't hurt anyone like that. I know Stella can be a bit of a cow, but I didn't think she'd be capable of doing something that extreme."

"A bit of a cow, that's got to be the understatement of the century," Joe sniggered. "Shall I tell you what that 'bit of a cow' has actually done?"

Max nodded his head and rose from his chair. "But before you start Joe, let me get you another drink. I owe you that much at least."

Joe watched as Max approached the bar, and decided to tell him everything. He had a right to know what Stella was capable of, and how he, although unknowingly, was a part of it.

Joe suddenly took in his surroundings and realised how empty the pub was, but remembered it was only mid-morning. He watched as the staff prepared the tables, obviously for the expected lunchtime rush.

Max returned to the table with drinks and said. "I've got us doubles as I feel I'm going to need it."

"Believe me you are," Joe answered, and began to tell his story.

Max sat and listened in silence as Joe revealed all the details, and when Joe had finished he again said. "Joe...I don't know what to say...I would never have got involved if I had known her true intentions. I wish now I'd contacted her afterwards to ask her how it all went."

"Don't worry mate, she'd have lied to you anyway."

"Is there anything I can do to help?"

"Yes Andy...sorry Max, there is. I think you can safely say that it is now payback time."

***

Later that afternoon, sitting in his car just ten minutes away from Frank's office, Joe phoned his brother-in-law. He didn't chance calling his mobile phone as he wasn't sure if Stella still had it, so dialled the number of his office landline instead.

It was after the third ring that the call was answered. "Frank Sinclair speaking."

"Hi, Frank it's Joe."

"What do you want Joe? I've already told you I'm not lending you any money."

"I don't want your money, in fact I don't want anything from you other than a bit of your time."

Frank suddenly remembered the events of the weekend. "Joe...I'm sorry...if this is about Tyler I just..."

"No Frank, it's not about Tyler...there's something else I need to talk to you about, it concerns Stella."

Frank sighed. "I've told you before Joe I won't get involved with the sister rivalry."

"Please listen to me Frank. This has nothing to do with Ruth it's to do with Stella and me."

"Stella and you?"

"All I'm asking is that you meet me when you finish work this evening and I'll explain everything to you."

Frank sighed again. "I'll give you half an hour Joe, no more. Do you know The Ship and Sail pub round the corner from my office?"

"No, but I'll find it."

"All right, I'll meet you there at five thirty...and Joe..."

"Yes?"

"I'm really sorry about what happened to Tyler, and believe me when I say that whatever punishment the police deal Jonathon, mine will be tenfold."

Joe was about to thank his brother-in-law, but Frank had already ended the call. It was ten seconds later that Joe received a text message from Ruth.

'Jonathon been charged with poisoning Tyler'.

At that precise moment Joe did not understand his own feelings. Did he feel elated now that justice had been done? Did he feel sad that Tyler's own cousin had poisoned him? Was he angry? It was with a roller coaster of emotions that he decided to find a suitable place to park his car, and take a stroll around the City of London before he met the man who was the father of his son's adversary, and the husband of the woman who had caused his demise.

Chapter 34

Considering it was early on a Monday evening The Ship and Sail pub was exceptionally busy, inside and out. City workers flocked there after a hard day's work for alcoholic stimulants before making their way home. It was a cold March evening but every table outside was occupied, as well as groups of smokers taking available space. When Joe arrived at the pub entrance Frank was already waiting for him.

"Thought I'd wait here for you, we'd never find each other in there," Frank joked half-heartedly. "Do you want a sandwich or something? They do a nice basket meal if you want one."

"No thanks Frank just a pint please."

"Shall we stay out here, it's heaving in there."

"Yes, I'll see if I can find somewhere to sit."

Frank had only been gone a couple of minutes when a table became vacant, so Joe quickly took it over. He had called Ruth earlier to explain that he had arranged to meet Frank and would explain everything later. She had curtly replied that she would tell the children he was working late, but told him that they wouldn't miss him because he was never at home for the evening meal with the family anyway. He had felt deflated when she had ended the call without another word.

Ten minutes later he signalled to Frank as he came out of the bar with a tray of drinks.

Frank placed the tray on the table. "Got us a couple of pints I couldn't face going in there again, although I must say its much warmer inside."

Joe retrieved a twenty pound note from his wallet and handed it to Frank, but Frank waved it away and tightened the scarf around his neck for extra warmth.

"What's this all about then Joe?"

Joe was unsure where to begin, but sensing that Frank was not taking this meeting as seriously as he should, Joe decided to go in for the kill. "Stella's had me over for fifty thousand pounds," and added as an afterthought. "Plus interest."

"Fifty thousand plus interest, what the hell are you talking about Joe?"

"I'm talking about how your wife has gone too far this time, and has definitely crossed the line."

An hour later, and after many questions by Frank, Joe sighed with relief in the knowledge that his brother-in-law at last believed him. He had also explained how he had bumped into Max this morning, which prompted him to arrange this meeting.

"That woman is one evil bitch. I can't believe what she's done to you Joe." Frank lowered his head towards the table, as if unable to look Joe in the face. "I know we haven't always got on, but I would never wish anything like this to happen to you. Especially..."

When Frank didn't elaborate any further Joe asked. "What were you going to say?"

Frank sighed. "Especially as the reason we don't get on is because I have always been jealous of you."

Joe stared at Frank in amazement. "Why?"

"Because you have the life I wanted, your own business, a good-natured beautiful wife, children to be proud of, and a home, not a show-house that I have to contend with." Frank took a swig of his beer still unable to look at Joe.

"Well don't worry about that. I haven't got that life anymore either."

"You have my evil bitch of a wife to thank for that. Does Ruth know about it all?"

"She does now. I told her yesterday, so as you can imagine my marriage is now over." Joe paused as Frank lifted his head and eventually looked at him. "To be honest Frank, I expected you to take a swing at me when I told you I had slept with Stella."

"Joe...you're one on a list of many. I gave up caring years ago who my wife sleeps with, and anyway," he chuckled, "it wasn't as if it was through choice." Frank paused before he continued. "The funny thing is I'm more annoyed that she stole my mobile phone than sleeping with you. She blatantly stole it and then helped me look for it. She must have switched it off as soon as she took it because the first thing she did was ring it. It was while I was searching Jonathon's room that I found those disgusting photos and money."

"What photos and money," Joe asked.

Frank began to tell Joe about the incident and when he had finished said. "Stella was only too willing to believe that they were Tyler's, but I knew they weren't and told her so."

"Why have you stayed with her?"

Frank shrugged his shoulders. "Who knows, I definitely don't. Anyway that's all about to change."

"What do you mean?"

"I'd rather not say at the moment, but let's be honest my life can only get better." Frank studied Joe as he suddenly realised that they could have been good friends, and regretted the lost years due to his pathetic jealousy. "What do you intend to do about Stella Joe?"

"I'm not sure. Andy...I mean Max has promised to help me in any way he can. I just need some kind of plan."

"Can you get hold of this Max?"

"Yes, he's given me his mobile number."

"Let's hope it's a genuine one," Frank said sounding concerned.

"Yes, I had the same thought, so I checked it before I left him."

"Well, why don't you call him and make arrangements for the three of us to meet. I'm sure that between us we can come up with something."

"What, you're willing to help me get back at her? After all she's still your wife."

"Joe, nothing would give me greater pleasure than to see that woman get all she deserves."

"Thanks Frank, I'd hoped I could depend on you."

"You're welcome Joe, now if you don't mind I'm going back to that show-house that my wife calls a home before I freeze."

***

When Joe arrived home at seven-thirty, Tyler was in his room watching a film and Abbey was already in bed as she had school tomorrow. Lewis, to Ruth's surprise had gone to bed at six-thirty, and seemed to be getting into a regular routine. Ruth was in the lounge sitting on the sofa reading a newspaper, and made no attempt to greet Joe when he entered the room.

"You'll never believe who I bumped into today," he said without any greeting.

"Elvis," she replied sarcastically.

He ignored this remark. "I bumped into the bloke who did the scam on me."

"That was nice for you."

"Ruth! Please!"

"Please what Joe? You've kept me in the dark all these months, getting yourself deeper and deeper in trouble, and now I have to be the attentive wife when it suits you."

Joe sighed and rubbed his hands through his hair. "Will you give me time to explain what has gone on today? I know what a stupid fool I've been, but now it's payback time for your sister, and I thought you'd like to be involved in that."

Ruth thought for a while before she answered. "Of course I would, but for my sanity Joe, not yours."

Joe nodded his agreement, sat in one of the armchairs and proceeded to explain to Ruth how he had seen Max in the market this morning, their talk and his ignorance of the whole set up. He told her of his meeting with Frank this evening and his response to Stella's antics. He went on to explain that he had contacted Max and all three of them had arranged to meet tomorrow lunchtime.

"I want to be there," she demanded when he had finished.

"I don't think that's a good idea."

"I do. She has ruined my life as well as yours, and I want to be in at the kill."

"What about Tyler and Lewis, we can't take them with us."

She looked at her husband frustrated for stating the obvious. "I'll ask my mum to come over for the afternoon to look after them. I'll tell Tyler I had already made arrangements to meet some old friends and didn't want to cancel. He'll be fine, and I'll tell my mum the same. Anyway, he likes spending time with my mum."

Joe nodded his head in agreement.

Ruth rose from the sofa, put the newspaper on the coffee table, and picked up her book. "I'm going to bed to read. I'll throw your blankets down out of the linen cupboard. Are you going into work in the morning?"

"Yes, I intend to be there by six, I've a lot of work to catch up on. I'll pick you up at twelve o'clock. Is that okay with you?"

"Pick me up in the high street outside the post office."

Ruth left the room without another word.

Chapter 35

The following morning as intended, Joe was in his office at six o' clock. Although he was still taking the tablets he had decided to decrease his dose from six tablets to four, and to also make a determined effort to take them with water and not vodka.

He sat at his desk, and with so much to do he had no idea where to begin. The first job he needed to do was to carry out a complete stock-take. It was also essential to confirm what deliveries were due, and more important to assess all the invoices, incoming and outgoing. He would get Laura on to that task as soon as she arrived. The problem being that he knew that the outgoing invoices were far greater than the incoming.

He sat and put his hands up to his face and brushed away the tears that had formed unwittingly. Composing himself, he pulled a pad of writing paper from his top drawer and momentarily forgetting about his work problems began to write a letter to Abbey and Tyler, which he would give to them after he had left. Although he would tell them face to face how he felt, he wanted to put on paper how sorry he was that he had to leave and that although he would no longer be living at home, he would still be seeing them on a regular basis. He would write and tell them how much he loved them, and would stress that none of what has happened had anything to do with them or their mum, and everything had been his fault entirely.

Tears again filled his eyes as he began to write, and although his brain knew exactly what he wanted to say, it refused to connect with his hand that had to do the deed for him.

Now that his problems were out in the open it had, slightly, lifted some of the stress, but naturally it didn't erase them. He was still in financial ruin, Barry remained after his blood, and his marriage was over. If he was unable to retract the money from Stella then his business, and unfortunately his house would have to go on the market. He wouldn't be able to keep a roof over his children's heads.

At eight thirty, when he heard Laura enter the outer office, he quickly telephoned through to her and asked her to come into his office. After replacing the phone on its holder he immediately heard a gently knock on his door and watched it slowly open.

"Morning Laura," he said as brightly as he could. "Could you get together all the invoices for the last six months please, incoming and outgoing?"

"Of course," she answered.

Just as she was about to leave and close the door behind her, Joe called, "Laura."

"Yes."

"Before you sort out the invoices make us both a coffee and come back in here and drink it with me, there's something I need to tell you."

"Everything all right?"

"Get the coffee first."

Joe had decided to divulge all that had gone on to Laura, but he would stress that she told no one else. He didn't want to panic the rest of his staff. He would let them all know in good time if they needed to search for another job.

Forty minutes, and many questions later Laura sat at Joe's desk with a look of astonishment on her face. "I just can't believe all this. Is there anything I can do?"

"The main thing is not to let on to the rest of the staff. I will only tell them if I need to."

"What a bitch of a woman, and to think its Ruth's sister that's done this to you. It's unbelievable." Laura hesitated before she continued. "Joe, I have about five thousand pounds in savings, if..."

"No Laura," Joe interrupted tears again welling in his eyes. "That's very decent of you but I couldn't take the chance of not being able to pay it back."

Laura nodded her agreement. "Why don't I ring round and try to get some money in off the bad payers?"

Joe laughed. "I don't pay you enough to be my debt collector."

"Joe, I'll do anything to help you keep this business and your house, and don't forget it's my job on the line as well."

"That would be good if you could try. I did try to call a few last week but without much success."

"Well let's see if I can put my womanly charm to good use."

Joe laughed. "All right, but first get me those invoices, and let's see if we can put this business back on track." He watched Laura head back to the reception, and knew he had made the right decision in telling her. He had been as honest as he could with her, and although he had explained Stella's part in his downfall, he omitted to tell her all the sordid details. He also explained about the forthcoming meeting this lunchtime with Frank, Max, Ruth and himself.

Joe left the office at eleven forty-five to meet Ruth, and together they made their way to The Ship and Sail. Ruth did not acknowledge Joe when she got into the car and apart from Joe telling her that he had explained everything to Laura, no other words were exchanged.

The Ship and Sail was relatively empty compared to yesterday evening, and Frank and Max were already at the bar, deep in conversation, when Joe and Ruth arrived.

"You two already know each other?" Joe asked as he approached the bar, warning signs buzzing in his head.

"No Joe," Frank reassured his brother-in-law. "We both arrived at the same time and guessed who each other were."

Joe nodded his answer, realising how paranoid he had become. Ruth approached Frank, who gave her a comforting cuddle saying he could not apologise enough, not only for what Stella had done to Joe, but for the episode with Jonathon and Tyler. He asked how his nephew was, and again stated that she and Joe had a son he'd be proud to call his own.

Joe introduced Ruth to Max and she slightly nodded her head to him in way of a greeting. Joe had tried to assure Ruth that Max was just a pawn in Stella's game, but she wasn't totally convinced.

Frank ordered three pints of beer for Joe, Max and himself, and a dry white wine for Ruth. She never normally drunk mid-day, unless she was on holiday, but she had a feeling that this would be a much needed drink.

Joe noticed a large round empty table over by the window and suggested they sit down. Once settled it was Frank who spoke first.

"I know she's my wife..." and glancing at Ruth added, "And your sister, but she needs to be taught that she can't use people as and when it suits her, and that she's gone too far this time."

"Let's get one thing straight from the very beginning Frank," Ruth said. "She's no longer a sister of mine. For as long as I live I will never speak to her again unless it's to tell her what I think of her. I don't care what you do to her, as the only feeling I have for her is contempt and hate."

The group fell silent for a few minutes before Max asked. "When we talk about payback, we're not talking about physical payback are we? Because as much as I disapprove of what she's done, and now know that she's an evil woman, I'll not be party to a lynching."

"No Max," Joe replied. "But we need to show her that we all know what she's done and that she can't get away with it. I'll be honest with you, my main aim is to get my fifty grand back because without that my business is finished."

He glanced at Ruth, but she would not meet his eyes.

Frank sipped his beer before placing the glass back on the table. "If I get my way Joe, not only will she pay you back your fifty grand, but with a good deal of interest."

"But we need a plan," Joe said, urgency sounding in his voice. The thought of getting his money back raised his spirits slightly. If nothing else, he needed to keep a roof over his children's heads.

When Max suddenly slammed the palm of his hand on the table the other three stared at him. "And I've got the very thing."

When, fifteen minutes later, he had explained his idea to them, they all agreed that it was a brilliant idea and settled down to work out the details.

Chapter 36

Victor Hunter, a short, stocky built, market stall holder, was not only an acquaintance of Stella's, but also of Max. He knew them of equal measure, but the difference being that he immensely disliked Stella.

The only reason he kept in touch with her was because she alone practically kept his jewellery business afloat. Only last week she had ordered a white gold diamond solitaire pendant from him, and as he had decided to finish with jewellery and concentrate more on the fashion industry, he had valued the piece way over the asking price.

***

When Stella received the phone call from Victor informing her that he had her pendant, she squealed with delight. "Wonderful news Victor, I'll meet you tomorrow at the Calyx Wine Bar at twelve-thirty."

"Err... No Stella, I'll meet you at The Steal and Beg."

"The Steal and Beg," Stella screamed. "I'm not going in there."

"Well unfortunately Stella its The Steal and Beg tomorrow or you'll have to wait a couple of weeks for the pendant."

"I don't believe this, we always meet at the Calyx. Why the Steal and Beg?"

"Because I can't make the Calyx, and I've haven't got time to stand here debating where we meet. Are you meeting me tomorrow or not?"

How she detested this grotty little man at the end of her phone line. Not only did he irritate her, but he was the most vulgar man who she had ever had the misfortune to come across. He often tried to paw her, but she had made her feelings towards him known from the beginning.

Scott had promised her faithfully, weeks ago, that he would be able to get the pendant for her, but for some reason he had ignored all her phone calls and texts. So when she had bumped into Victor at the Calyx last week and he'd said he would have no trouble in acquiring the item, she had no choice but to order it from him. The difference being, she wouldn't be offering any of her services for a cheaper price.

Stella had waited so long for this pendant that she didn't think she could wait another couple of weeks; but to enter that den of down and outs? It was a grotesque little pub just off the high street with the given name of The Sailor. The locals had nicknamed it The Steal and Beg many years ago because that was the only way its clientele could pay for their drinks.

"All right Victor, but as soon as we've concluded our business I'm out of there."

"Of course, I'm a very busy man, and have other business besides you."

Stella ended the call after mumbling her goodbyes, and danced around the room at the thought of owning the most beautiful item of jewellery she had ever seen.

Life was good at the moment, even though she still had the charges against Jonathon to contend with. She was absolutely disgusted with Frank who had told her that he had 'washed his hands' of the boy, which meant that she had to deal with the situation on her own. How could any man walk away from his son just because of a little trouble? She would be the first to agree that Jonathon could be a handful at times, but he was a strong-willed, twelve-year-old boy; a son any father would be proud of.

Stella knew her son. She had immediately realised that he was lying when he had told his story to the police. The poisoning of Tyler had nothing to do with Abbey, and Jonathon had, eventually, confided in her that he had put poison in Tyler's drinks on purpose. Stella blamed Tyler. He was as annoying as his mother had been as a child, so Stella could commiserate with her son. Jonathon had explained to her that Tyler had been due to play an important football match for the school, and knew without doubt, that he would score numerous goals. This in turn would acclaim him, as usual, the school hero. She thought back to the times when Ruth, continuously hailed a dancing queen, had been the curse of her life. Why hadn't she thought of poisoning Ruth? It would have solved a lot of her problems.

Even though the police had instructed her not to contact Ruth, she assumed her sister would have phoned or visited her by now. To her delight, Stella realised that Ruth would be absolutely fuming with her, not only about the poisoning of Tyler, but the fiasco of Saturday night where Joe had played right into her hands. He couldn't have acted the part better if she had written a script for him. She now had Joe where she wanted him, and once this trivial incident with Jonathon was resolved she would enjoy her reign over him.

She had received the expected phone call from Barry informing her that Joe had paid fifteen thousand pounds off the loan. Although she had realised the consequences of lending Joe the money, she was slightly disappointed that Barry would have to lay off the pressure until the next payment was overdue. She knew that Joe would have problems with the next instalment, so looked forward to that time immensely.

Yes life was good, and it would improve once she had her long-awaited white gold, diamond pendant in her hands.

***

The following lunchtime, Stella arrived at The Steal and Beg at twelve-twenty, hoping and praying that

Victor was already there. The first thing that hit her as she opened the door was the smell. A combination of body odour, urine and stale beer, caused her to immediately put her hand up to cover her nose and mouth. She entered the pub and thankfully noticing Victor at the far side, tip-toed across the carpet as if afraid to soil the bottom of her shoes.

"You got my pendant?" she asked without preamble, as she joined Victor at his table with her back to the entrance.

"Good day to you as well Stella," he answered with annoyance sounding in his tone.

Even though Victor often made sexual innuendoes to her, Stella knew that he also found her rude and obnoxious, but that was no worry to her. "I'm really busy Victor, and want to be out of this disgusting place as soon as I can."

"You don't want to go and find a hotel room for the afternoon then," he said seductively. "You could try on your pendant with nothing else on."

Stella glared at him.

"Okay, have it your own way," he said with a shrug of his shoulders, as he pulled a large square jewellery box from his coat pocket and placed it on the table, and slid it over to her.

With trembling hands she slowly opened the box to reveal the jewel she had waited so long for. "That is beautiful," she whispered to herself.

"The problem is Stella the price has gone up by fifty quid."

"Fifty pounds!" she exclaimed. "That's outrageous Victor, especially as I know you are already charging me far too much for it in the first place."

"It's your choice babe. Take it, or leave it. Believe me when I say I can walk out of here and sell this beauty within fifteen minutes."

Stella sighed, and decided she would never do business with this little weasel of a man again. She reached for her handbag and retrieved a wad of notes and began counting out the correct money. It was as she passed the money over to him that she heard a familiar voice behind her.

"Stella! Haven't seen you in ages," Max said as he came round to face her, and kissed her lightly on the cheek.

"Max. What are you doing in this dive? I thought you were working away."

"Yes I was, but the job finished so I came home." Max joined Stella and Victor at the table before he continued. "Can I get you a drink?"

"Err...no...I've got to rush, and I wouldn't put my lips on anything that belonged to this place."

"Wow, that's a first you refusing a drink, even for that reason," he laughed. "Oh by the way, you'll never guess who I bumped into the other day, your brother-in-law Joe."

"Joe...did you?" she replied hesitantly.

"Yeah, and I've got to say Stella he's not a happy man."

"Oh, that's a shame."

"He was quite surprised to see me," he continued ignoring her remark. "Kept asking me where his fifty grand was."

"Always the joker that one, that's why I love him."

"Believe me he wasn't laughing, because according to him that wasn't some lighted-hearted prank that you pulled on him. Do you know that he actually is about to lose his business, his house, his family, and probably be buried under a bridge somewhere."

Stella roared with laughter. "He's something else that man. Can't you see what he's doing? He's pulling another joke on you. I'll let him know that you fell for it the next time I see him."

"Tell me now Stella," Joe said from behind her.

Stella watched as Joe came into her vision, a satisfying grin on his face. She glared at all three men at the table and suddenly realised what was happening. Turning her attention to Joe she said. "You seem to forget the hold I have on you..."

"And what hold is that Stella?" Ruth interrupted.

Although her heart was racing, Stella stayed calm. "Why am I not surprised to see you little sister? Tell me, what part of the wood work did you all crawl out of?"

Stella sat and took in the four faces that stared at her. She smiled and nodded her head at each one in turn. "You all think you're so clever, don't you? How long did it take you to work out this little charade? A few weeks? None of you have a decent brain cell between you. I don't know what you think you have achieved, but I know what I have. I've outdone my cocky brother-in-law and smart arse, stuck up sister and all your little schemes in the world won't change that."

"You could go to the police," Victor suggested to no one in particular, and when the group all stared at him he realised maybe it was time for him to leave.

"Oh yes, you want to go to the police don't you Max? They will definitely believe your story that you had no idea it was all for real, especially with fifty thousand pounds missing."

"I want my money back Stella, the whole fifty grand plus interest," Joe demanded.

Stella again gave out an almighty laugh. "I don't think so Joey boy, you can go and sing for it."

Stella had no time to react as Ruth lunged at her without warning, and grabbed hold of her hair. Ruth pulled her sister's head back with such a force that Stella screamed in agony. She immediately held her head to try to take the pressure off and felt relief when seconds later someone abruptly pulled her sister off, before any further damage could be inflicted.

Stella was about to jump up and retaliate, but stopped dead in her tracks. "Frank!" she cried, as he was the last person she expected to see. She quickly recovered from Ruth's surprise attack, and as she noticed that Joe was trying to restrain Ruth from further hostilities, she jumped up from her chair and run into her husband's arms.

"Oh Frank, I'm so glad you're here." She pulled away from him slightly so she could look him in the face. "This lot have schemed up some fabricated story about me, and they are demanding I pay them fifty thousand pounds, and I'm so pleased that you witnessed Ruth's attack on me. Oh Frank I'm so frightened," she whined as she snuggled into him again.

When Frank roughly pushed her away alarm overwhelmed her.

"Shut up Stella, and sit down!"

Shocked at her husband's outburst Stella, reluctantly, picked up her shoulder bag off the floor, threw it over her shoulder and carried out his command. As she did so she glanced around the pub and noticed that the down-and-outs that frequented the place all had their heads buried in their beer glasses, no doubt wondering where their next drink would come from. So it was no surprise that no one had noticed the debacle happening at their table.

Once she had resumed her seat Frank continued. "At this precise moment I could gladly put my hands around your throat and squeeze every last fucking breath out of you to save Ruth the job. But I won't, because I don't intend to spend the rest of my life in prison because of you. Now, I know all that's gone on, so don't give me anymore of your bullshit. You will pay Joe back every penny plus a good deal more, and don't you dare tell me you don't have the money because I know you do."

Defiance now besieged her. "You can't make me."

"Of course I can't, but if you refuse, you can go and get that bastard son of yours and leave, taking nothing with you, but the clothes you stand in."

"You can't force me out of my own home."

""You don't have a home. The deeds for that house are in my name only."

"You liar!"

"Ring the mortgage company Stella, ask them. That is my house."

"Why? Why was the house only put in your name?"

"I was advised to because of tax purposes, but you knew you were onto a good thing when you married me. You didn't even realise that you didn't sign any papers when I bought the house."

"What about Jonathon, our son?"

"No Stella, your son. We both know he's not mine, and if you insist he is then we'll get a DNA check done."

Stella again stood with her body erect, and glared at her husband. "Don't you dare say that about your son in front of all these people, and don't try to come across as whiter than white Frank, especially when you've had a slut of a mistress for years. I'm getting out of here…I'm not listening…"

It was as she tried to leave that the small gathering around the table all stood to block her way.

"Sit down Stella and listen to what I have to say," demanded Frank.

As Stella again grudgingly sat back in her chair, she straightened her clothes, and ran her hands down the strands of her hair.

"As soon as we leave here you and I will be going to the bank to make arrangements to transfer sixty thousand pounds into Joe's bank account."

"Sixty...thousand..."

"And also," Frank interrupted, "you will make arrangements to pay your loan shark, gutter friend off in full."

Stella glanced at Joe, then back to Frank. "Pay him sixty thousand, and pay off Barry as well!" Stella screamed. "You're talking at least ninety thousand pounds."

"Fifty of that is the money you took from Joe anyway. You have a choice Stella. You either do that, or you're homeless. No ifs, no buts, and I'll tell you now I'll burn that house down before you ever live in it again if you don't pay."

"Then I'll get half the insurance money."

"No, you won't Stella, all the insurance on that house is in my name only. I own the house. Remember?"

"I'll drag you through the courts."

"You do that Stella, but if it's the last thing I do I'll never let you live in that house again."

"Transfer the house into my name," she demanded.

"Don't be an idiot, there's no mortgage company that would touch you, you don't have a job remember, and I don't think they accept accountancy books on prostitution."

Stella heard the others snigger, but said nothing. Her mind was whirling. She suddenly remembered her pendant, and noticing that Victor had slipped away, she immediately scanned the table for it, and to her horror realised that the little weasel had taken it with him.

In frustration, Stella banged her head on the table and punched the surface vigorously with one of her fists. She glanced up at the group who were all now staring at her. "You all think you're so clever, don't you?" she snarled.

"No Stella, you thought you were the clever one," Frank answered. "And this is known as pay-back time."

Chapter 37

Ruth and Joe were on their way home from The Steal and Beg, and although driving, Joe talked non-stop. They left the gathering when Frank had finalised all the details and told Stella that he would take her home first to get some identification because of the amount of money she would be transferring from her bank accounts. He also insisted that she call Barry for his bank details, and Joe gave Frank his which his brother-in-law immediately stored into his mobile phone.

As they neared home Ruth didn't notice all the usual landmarks that she passed daily. She wasn't aware of Shaw Park where she often took Lewis to feed the ducks, or the cemetery where her Nan and Granddad were buried which she visited on their birthdays and at Christmas.

Ruth had not said one word since they started their journey home. She was too angry to speak, she was too angry to listen. She was angry with her sister, she was angry with herself, but most of all she was angry with Joe. He continued to talk and waffle on about how he could build the business up again now he had extra money, maybe pay a little extra off the mortgage, and buy the children new bedroom furniture. New bedroom furniture! Her life, as she knew it was finished, destroyed by her own sister, and Joe is talking about bedroom furniture. He also continuously repeated that justice had been done.

How had justice been done? The only punishment that Stella had received was to pay back the money she stole from Joe, plus a little extra, and to pay the moneylender off. She was even allowed to stay in her family home, when Ruth had come so close to losing hers. Not only had Ruth been denied the chance to tell her sister exactly what she thought of her, but she had been deprived of inflicting the much deserved pain on her, and for that she blamed Frank and Joe. She would face her sister before the day was out, this time with no-one else around to dictate the outcome.

Tyler had gone back to school today, and on the pretence that she was helping Joe with a business matter; her mother had again offered to come over to look after Lewis. It was with this in mind that, as they neared home, she said. "Drop me off at Bolton Avenue."

"Why? That's a good five minute walk from home."

"Because I've asked you to that's why."

"I'll drop you home."

"No you won't, you'll drop me at Bolton Avenue."

As they reached Ruth's desired stop, Joe pulled the car into the kerb. "Can we talk later about us?"

Ruth opened the car door and prepared to get out. "No Joe we can't, because there is no us anymore, but I'll tell you what you can do. Once my mum's gone you can come home, pack your bags and leave."

"Ruth!" Joe shouted.

Ruth had already got out of the car and slammed the door. She began to make her way home, and as Joe slowly drove pass her, the tears were channelling down her face.

He did not attempt to stop to try to speak to her again.

Five minutes later, she approached the gates that separated the drive of their house from the pavement. She hoped that her mother was preparing lunch in the kitchen, so would not see her arriving home as she had no intentions of going indoors.

She retrieved her car keys from her handbag and as quietly as she could she opened the driver's door, settled herself in the seat and started the engine. She had one matter to resolve before she could start to plan her life without Joe.

She drove to the tree-lined Gilbert Avenue where Stella lived. An affluent street which was a mixture of two and three storey detached houses. Each front garden was professionally kept, which led to fierce competition between the owners, and Stella, without fail, would yearly proclaim herself the winner.

Ruth drew up to the kerb and parked a couple of doors down from Stella's, but had a good viewing point of her sister's drive and front door. She was prepared to wait for as long as needed for Stella to return home from the bank, and hoped that Frank did not return with her.

She pulled her mobile phone from her coat pocket to call Gill to ask if she would collect Abbey and Tyler from school. She also told her friend that so much had happened over the last couple of days, but because it was too much to divulge over the phone now, she would call her later to bring her up-to-date. She next called her mother and told her that she was still with Joe, and that Gill would collect the children from school and bring them home. Her mother, as Ruth knew she would, replied that she would stay as long as needed and that Lewis was fine and they had just finished their lunch.

Guilt overwhelmed her for lying to her mother, and although her mother and father would eventually have to be told about her marriage failure, Ruth knew that the truth about Stella's actions and involvement in it would destroy them.

It was forty-five minutes later that Ruth heard Stella's car before she actually see it. Stella drove onto her drive as a formula one driver would enter a pit stop in the middle of a race. She watched, and noticed that Stella's body language conveyed temper and frustration as she got out of her car, slammed the door and hurried up the steps to the front door. She watched her sister fumble in her handbag and retrieved a bunch of keys, and as she tried to open the door with shaking hands she dropped the keys twice.

It was when Ruth watched Stella enter her house and slammed the front door behind her that she made her move. The idea was to keep Stella's bad mood on the boil, so she hurried along the pavement to Stella's house where she continuously pressed her finger on the doorbell. From the other side of the door Ruth could hear her sister swearing and shouting for the culprit to stop.

Stella opened the door in a furious rage and Ruth, giving her sister no chance to realise what was happening, pushed her as hard as possible in the chest which sent Stella sprawling across the hall floor on her back with her arms flapping either side of her. It was her left arm that caught the hall table which sent its contents scattering across the floor. Stella, having no way of stopping herself, hit the top of her head on the base of the stair banister which brought her slide to a halt. Stella held her head as she cried out in pain.

Ruth, giving her sister no time to compose herself screamed at her. "Why Stella? Why?"

Stella gradually managed to stand, but held onto the stair banister for support. "You're a fucking mad woman, coming into my house and attacking me like that. I'll have you done for grievous bodily harm."

Ruth ignored this remark and screamed at her sister again with a rage that she had never experienced before. "Tell me why Stella. Why have you ruined my life?"

"Ah, poor little Ruthie," Stella said with a condescending tone. "Poor little princess who had everything she's ever wanted, as a child and now."

Ruth stared at Stella, unable to believe what she was hearing. "You had the same as me. Mum and dad didn't treat us any different."

Stella now pointed her finger in Ruth's chest. "But you got the looks and the figure. You were the one with the dancing ability. You were the one that everyone liked, and the one that the boys chased after."

Ruth continued to stare at her sister, unable to comprehend her reasoning. "So you have destroyed my life because you're jealous of me?"

"No Ruth, I destroyed your life because I hate you."

Ruth stood in front of her sister, knowing that she should, at this point, inflict pain and torture on her, but she was motionless. Her mind refused to oblige and her body would have rejected any orders it may have been given. Was it possible for a woman to hate her own flesh and blood that much?

"Do you know the sad thing about it?" Stella asked.

Ruth just shook her head in answer.

"If Joe had taken up my offer last year, none of this would ever have happened."

"What offer?"

"I offered him a vast amount of money to put into his business, and all he had to do in return was pop in and see me now and again. But do you know what he said? *'I wouldn't touch you with a barge pole. Of course my business means the world to me, but my wife means more, she's my world, not my business'.* Those words have stuck in my head like an old vinyl record stuck on a scratch, so that dear sister, as they say, was the final nail in the coffin for you and him."

Stella's words struck as a thunderbolt. "You wanted to pay my husband to have sex with you! My God, what kind of person are you?"

"Don't you get all high and mighty with me, I've seen the way Frank looks at you."

"What are you talking about? I've never made any advances towards Frank."

"Maybe not, and I really couldn't care, but Joe shouldn't have ignored me."

"So because you didn't get your own way with him, you set up this bizarre prank?"

Stella moved her face close to her sister's as she snarled. "He chose you over me."

"But I'm his wife for crying out loud!"

"Not anymore," she smirked.

Ruth, with anger that she had never felt before, punched her sister so hard in the face that her body just collapsed straight to the floor.

Suddenly the reality hit Ruth; Joe was the victim in this fiasco. If Stella hadn't snared him this time, she would have another. He was doomed as far as Stella was concerned; probably always had been.

Looking at her sister now, crying, trying to sit up as she realised how much blood she was losing through her nose, Ruth fled from the house and back to her car; she had to try to find her husband.

Chapter 38

Although Joe had been surprised when Ruth demanded he drop her off at Bolton Avenue, he hadn't been surprised when she told him to pack his bags; he had expected this command all week.

Once he had dropped Ruth off, he made his way home and parked in a little lay-by, just past their house. From this advantage point, through his wing mirror, he could watch the gate to his house and waited for Ruth to appear. He watched her walk onto the drive and as soon as he heard her car come to life he knew what her intended actions were. His first thought was to follow her to make sure she came to no harm, but instinct told him that this was something she had to sort out with Stella on her own, or she would never rest.

Not having the enthusiasm to immediately return to work he decided to pay a visit to Ted. It was Heather's funeral at the end of the week, and he wanted to see how his friend was coping. He would also bring him up-to-date with his latest developments.

Ted was pleased to see his friend when he opened the door to him, and it was after Ted had made coffee that they discussed the funeral arrangements.

"It's going to be a small affair," sighed Ted. "We both don't have large families or close circles of friends. So it will be just you, and hopefully Ruth, a couple of neighbours, and a few people from the hospital who have known Heather for years."

"What about her parents?"

"They've said they're just come to the service, and leave immediately afterwards. Her mother said she will be too distraught to see the whole thing through. More like an inconvenience if you ask me."

"Are you going to stay in this house?"

"No, it's not practical with all the adaptations. I've already been onto a couple of estate agents, and they've all said I'll have no trouble selling at a good price."

"Where will you go?"

"I've decided to leave the area, and make a new life in Oxford. I've always liked it there."

Joe did not remark on this, but just nodded his head.

"Come on then tell me what's been happening."

Joe proceeded to tell his friend all that had happened over the last couple of days.

"Wow, everyone rallied around you in the end. I'm pleased for you Joe. You did a stupid thing, but you didn't deserve to lose everything. So it looks like all your problems have been solved, apart from Ruth."

Again Joe just nodded his head with a sigh.

"You've got to fight for her Joe, you can't lose her. I've lost Heather, but that was out of my control and I had no choice, but you do. Get her back, because if you don't that will be the biggest mistake of your life."

"I know, and believe me I'm going to do anything it takes."

When Joe finally left it was with tears in their eyes that the friends cuddled and said their goodbyes.

Joe would have preferred to have gone home, but knowing his mother-in-law was there he decided against it, so returned to the warehouse.

It was as he opened the door and entered the warehouse reception that Laura immediately stood up and ran to him.

"I'm so sorry Joe, I tried to tell her that you weren't available, but she insisted on waiting in your office for you. I said..."

"Laura," Joe interrupted. "Who's in my office?"

"She wouldn't give me her name, but I know she's been here before."

Stella! Had she been here before? What did she want? Where was Ruth? Had she hurt Ruth? He hurried to his office door and quickly opened it and shouted. "What do you want...?" He stopped in mid-sentence when he saw who it was waiting for him. "Karen!"

Karen immediately stood up from her seat. "I'm sorry Joe I know I shouldn't..."

"No, sorry Karen, I thought you were someone else," Joe interrupted, relieved to see Karen and not Stella. He awkwardly made his way to his desk, where he sat on the corner facing his ex-wife who had now resumed her seat. "But I suppose I should be asking you the same question. What do you want?"

"I've come to let you know that I'm moving to North Yorkshire. I applied for a job with the County Council's welfare service and have been accepted."

"Wow, that's brilliant news Karen." Joe sighed as the realisation dawned on him that another of his problems was fading into the distance. "Have you had an interview up there?"

"Yes, I drove there last week, and they called me the following day offering me the job. I don't start until the middle of April, but that gives me time to go up and find somewhere to live and get my bearings."

"I'm pleased for you Karen. I know how much you loved your work in the past."

"How are things with you Joe? Did you get everything sorted?"

Joe had no intentions of sitting and discussing further details of his private life with his ex-wife. "Yeah, kind of...let's just say I'm getting there."

"Glad to hear it. Well, I had better go, I've lots to do. Err...Joe...I just wanted to say that my involvement with Ruth's sister was all her doing...I know now that she lied and manipulated me to keep in touch with you. I..."

"I know that Karen. You really don't need to explain, and I think it would be better if it's all left in the past now."

"That's fine by me, I just didn't want you to think I came here to cause trouble for you, because I never. Oh Joe..."

Joe was taken by complete surprise when Karen practically leapt from her chair, wrapped her arms around him and snuggled into his chest.

"I know how much you love Ruth, and I wouldn't jeopardise that for the world, but I just want you to know that leaving you was the biggest mistake of my life. I love you Joe."

It was as Joe was about to push Karen away that he heard his office door open, and as he glanced up it was, to his horror, to see Ruth standing there. He immediately pushed Karen away from him, and hurried after his wife who had turned to run away. He caught up with her just as she was opening the reception door, and grabbed hold of her arm. "It's not what it looked like."

"No?" she screamed. "Then exactly what was it?"

"Karen came to tell me she was leaving..."

"Ruth," Karen shouted as she entered the reception. "Please, listen to Joe, it's the truth. I'm leaving soon to start a new life in Yorkshire. What you saw in there was emotions getting the better of me, and I swear to you that is the truth. Joe had no part in it, and I can tell you for a fact that he loves you much more than he ever loved me, and I think you know that as well."

Karen quickly returned to Joe's office to collect her coat and bag, and as she returned to the reception she took hold of Ruth's hand and said. "Don't let anything that's in your control come between you. I know what it's like to lose the love of your life and believe me, it hurts." She glanced at Joe and then back to Ruth, said goodbye and left.

It was Laura who broke the awkward silence. "Do you want me to make myself scarce?"

"No that's okay Laura, I've got to get home," replied Ruth.

As she was about to leave Joe caught her hand. "Ruth?"

Ruth studied the man who she had loved all her life and knew he loved her as much in return. "Come home for dinner tonight Joe and we'll talk once the children are in bed."

It was with tears in his eyes that he said. "I love you Ruthie."

"I know you do Joe."

30753644R00166